THE KING OF FLAMES

L.B. DIVINE

First paperback edition October 2023

IBSN: *979-8-9873957-2-1*
E-BOOK IBSN: *979-8-9873957-3-8*

Cover by Kelly Carter
Map by Natalia Junqueria
Editing by Poisoned Ink Press LLC
Proofreading by K. Morton Editing Services
Interior Design by Lorna Reid

To anyone who has ever doubted their story.
This is your sign to tell it anyways.

BOOKS BY L.B. DIVINE:

THE PRINCE OF SNOW SERIES

The Prince of Snow

The King of Flames

CONTENT WARNING

This book grapples with grief, suffering, and torture. There is violence, alcohol consumption for of age characters, and some mature language and references. If any of these topics could be harmful toward you, please proceed with care.

NEW
SARRIDOLON
10 KINGDOMS
CLOUD CASTLE
9TH
1ST
THALLGAN
10TH
BRINN
THINKERS
8TH
2ND
7TH
3RD
CASTLE DEAD
4TH
6TH
5TH.

CIAN AND THE CREATURE

MANY YEARS AGO

lames sparked out of the torch that he carried with a crackle, soaring to the white marble floors beneath the feet of the man who had fought destiny and lost. No amount of fire in the Ten Kingdoms could ignite the man that the King of Snow once was. Cian Regavine Saphirrus ignored all the heat that flowed out of his light source and prayed his death would not be painful. He often found his mind wandering to such dark places these days, with little to no desire to awaken each day.

The war was over, yet everything he had fought for was lost. Most days, he could almost be convinced that another war had begun, yet he was the only one to see it brewing.

It was the hardest truth to swallow: no amount of magic could bring her back to life. The King of Snow knew this and forbid the thought to even cross his mind.

Stumbling, he nearly toppled over. Yet, he did not care that the people of the Ten Kingdoms thought him a drunk on this night, unable to handle the circumstances which had befallen him and his beloved not but ten years prior. Nobody would believe him—and he was not sure if he cared—but he had not drank a sip of alcohol tonight. He only carried his golden chalice through the various rooms of the castle so members of his council and kingdom would avoid his stupor.

If they *thought* him to be drunk, maybe they would leave him alone.

Today was the twenty-eighth anniversary of his birth, and he could not find one thing to celebrate. Instead, he staggered to the one voice of reason who would confirm just how shitty he was. For there was one voice in the Ten Kingdoms that called out to him when he was at his lowest, and he sought after such vehement evil only today.

He promised himself that when the night was over, and the moon had crested over into the next year of his life, that he would turn around and lock the door on this source forever.

But he needed to hear it one more time.

His best friend Cyril had been difficult to evade this evening, but Cian took comfort in the idea that he would never find him in the depths of the castle. Cyril would never follow Cian down here—out of fear or prophecy, Cian was unsure. The truth of the matter was that Cian was absolutely and positively alone.

And he could not say he did not mind the silence to the violence.

Cian wound down the staircase quickly, sweat plastering to his back and hairline as he fought to reach the bottom of the steps. It was getting hotter; therefore, it was getting closer.

He was getting closer.

Cian turned the corner at the bottom of the staircase and slowed to a stop. He could hear nothing but the rumbling of chains and the scratching of claws. He closed his eyes, compelling himself to see her as he allowed himself to do on his birthday.

And when he opened his eyes, she was there. More than a distant memory, and very much alive.

***

Talons scraped against the marble floors of the castle with an eerie ode to the King and Queen who once silenced this very castle. Sparks sprouted against the friction, the enamel a force to be reckoned with against the stone foundation. Black lines tainted where the white of the rock once glistened, an eternal stain on the home of the Queen of Fury and the King of Snow.

The creature grumbled, his irritation blatant. Year after year, the sores around his ankles and neck bothered him, yet nobody paid him a visit. He often called out to the men and women above him, attempting to lure them down to see him. Yet, it was to no avail. It had been a decade since his last visitor, and he could only imagine who was standing at his threshold with a broken soul.

He crept forward, his feet rumbling the castle walls with each step. The man that stood before him did not blink, merely meeting his gaze with a blank stare. He was unnerved and perturbed by such a reaction, so stark in contrast to what he had envisioned for this moment.

It was the King, brazen yet crippled by grief. It was the pain of the wound itself which he could not stand, nor could he stand the sight of the beast—the forevermore reminder of the Queen he could never have again. He opened his mouth to blow a puff of smoke into the air, as much a greeting as it was a warning.

With a grumble full of equal devastation and surprise, he hissed, "Hello, Cian."

The King breathed heavily, his crown crooked atop his head in a mockery of all that was and had been.

"You will not speak my name?" the creature asked, his breath smoking before him.

"She never did," Cian whispered.

His blue eyes shone with a darkness that made his talons skid to a halt across the floor. Heat exploded in the air as the marble floors cracked under the pressure of the sharp ends. Cian's head snapped up to meet the gaze of the creature that normally had men fall to their knees as though he were speaking to a child.

"Therefore, I will not permit you the same grace," Cian finished.

The creature laughed, despite its best efforts to remain neutral. "Ah, boy, have you changed in the last decade. Your Queen would be at odds with such a difference."

Cian paused, his exhale long and calculated. "Forgive me, I do not know why I came down here."

"Familiarity, a piece of her which has not been lost to the will of time and the age of men." He almost chuckled to himself, proud of nailing down the essence of Cian so proactively.

The King, despite his best efforts, wore his heart on his sleeve. He always had.

Cian's dark eyebrows raised. "Maybe my wife had some wits about her after all when she said that you were smarter than you looked."

The creature chuckled again, smoke curling out of his mouth with bliss and relief. "She never underestimated anything that came across her path."

Huffing in reply, Cian turned to head up the stairs again.

Chains rattled against the wall as the creature made a move to go with him. "If you're going to leave me here, the least I can do for the company is give you a parting gift."

The King paused, but he did not turn his head to meet

his gaze. It was calculated, and he almost praised Cian for channeling his wife in this moment.

Never give the enemy the upper hand.

"Go on."

As though speaking from text, the dragon hissed, "*The Queen of Fury's battle is not over, for the darkness lies in wait for the ice that has not formed. A great battle looms on the lineage of the greatest King the world has ever seen, a moment to be forged in shadows, fire, and snow. A child will be—*"

"Enough." Cian's voice rang out in finality amongst the chambers.

The creature shirked back, the power and command in the voice shocking to even the largest and oldest of foes. "Very well, but adhere to my warning, my King. There is not necessarily finality in death."

And with that, the King dashed up the stairs, and the dragon was once more alone.

***

Cyril paced back and forth in Cian's chambers so quickly he was sure he left tracks on the marble floors. A hand was perched underneath his chin, scratching out of concern as well as fear.

The King had been gone for an hour, and nobody knew where he went. His wife had kept to the gardens with his daughter, distracting and appearing that all was well to court.

It was so like Cian to disappear, or at least, it *had* been like him. In another life, Cian would have evaded Cyril at every turn, some old game they would play together.

Typically, Ciara had deliberately disobeyed the order of things, but Cian had learned from her when to push and when to pull.

Cyril paused with a deep breath, one which rattled his

lungs and nearly left him breathless. He would never get used to her being gone, though he had to stop comparing what was.

Running a hand through his light brown hair, only to be interrupted by the sound of the chamber doors flying open. A cool breeze rang through the air; ice crept and frost permeated on the walls of his majesty's chambers instantly.

"Where have you been?" Cyril asked, the worry in his voice clear, though it did not stop him from being direct.

Cian was his responsibility, and he had failed him this night. He had failed at being a Thinker—a protector.

Cian's dark blue eyes thundered with warning and grief. "You know what day this is. How dare you ask such things of *me*? Am I not free to wander the grounds as she did? Am I not able to grieve for the life I have lived and lost? Am I supposed to sit here and accept that I am to live another year on this continent without half of my heart?"

He sagged onto the floor, his back resting upon the foot of his bed. Breathing in a sob, his head collapsed into his arms.

Cyril coughed to hide a sob of his own. It had been a decade, yet it was as if no time had passed. He had prayed for his King over and over, dreaming of salvation and a solution to the never-ending turmoil.

Yet, no reprieve had ever come for Cian Saphirrus. It seemed as though the Gods had truly abandoned him, a refusal of the gifts he harbored as much as the woman he had loved.

The woman he had burned down the world for.

I

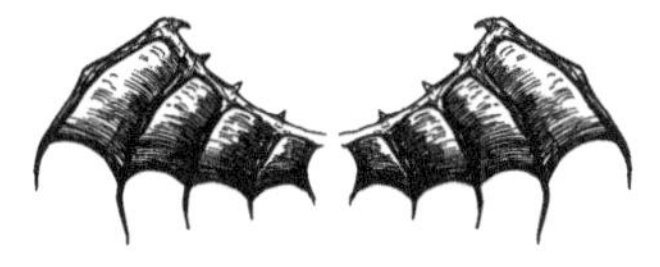

THE DESCENDANT OF THE SNOW KING

ONE

MANY YEARS LATER

alton Saphirrus danced in politics as though he were in a ballroom. He moved gracefully with his body, jousting with glances and nods that left the members of the privy council battling one another for another opportunity to please his majesty. In just three months, he also had learned to dance with his tongue, though Cyril knew as well as anyone who knew the King that he had mastered that skill before ascending to the crown.

Raising a monarch had been hard in Cyril's first lifetime, so much so that he had worked with Cian relentlessly to develop himself into the man he wanted to be. In this lifetime, at the age of one hundred and seventeen, Cyril could not contain as much as an eyebrow raise from Dalton. This monarch was an uncapped turbulence of raw power and unidentified emotion. Dalton never spoke to Cyril like Cian had, confessing all that laid within his head and heart alike.

Instead, he operated on a scale of pure chaos. It was as maddening as it was beautiful for Cyril to endure, as his key advisor and fatherly figure.

"So, tell me Lord Peach, why is it that when I lift my left wrist, you flinch?"

Dalton moved his left wrist, and on cue, Lord Peach flinched.

Cyril put his fist to the crest of his forehead and tried to ignore the continent-shattering irritation that had built within him in the last hour.

To no one's surprise, Dalton could be utterly ridiculous. As a monarch, however, he could be humored, even captivated and serious. Dalton had only one demand of Cyril and this chaotic court, one which he was adamant about. He had gained his crown upon the death of his father, and he did not run from the destiny which had haunted him the past twenty years. He did not like it, but he did not shy away from responsibility.

He wanted to wait to be coronated three months after the death of his father, the day following the funeral service. Dalton wanted to ensure a smooth, not fast, transition of power. He never admitted it to Cyril, but Cyril assumed he wanted time to help others heal. He would never say otherwise, but Dalton needed to heal too. Even losing parents one detested still meant losing family. Begrudgingly, Cyril had accepted this as Dalton's only term. As far as rising monarchs went, this was a rather easy wish to fulfill. Despite not wearing the crown, Dalton was still expected to participate in courtly politics.

"I am sorry, your Majesty."

"Lord Peach, I just want you to answer me." Cyril could hear the eye roll in his tone.

The Saphirrus line had long been ruled by those with iron fists, and today, Dalton would have to decide who he wanted to become. And once he chose, there would be no going back. Cyril had warned Dalton that he would have to play his cards right.

Was he going to be like his great-great-grandfather Cian or the Queen of Fury, Ciara?

"Did you flinch at my father's disposition, Lord Peach?" Dalton hissed as Lord Peach declined answering him.

Dalton's irritation was blatant, but it was humorous for Cyril alone.

"No, your Majesty. I did not mean to insult." Lord Peach shook so much he was doomed to fall out of his council chair.

Dalton stood up without warning, his gold throne falling backward with the force of movement. "Then why in the Ten Kingdoms do you continue to shrink when I do so much as breathe?"

Cyril stifled a laugh. Lord Peach looked like he was about to shit his pants.

"You are very powerful, your Majesty." Lord Peach breathed out, his voice wavering.

Cyril quirked an eyebrow at the peculiar response, unsure about the methodology of Lord Peach's appeal to Dalton. If he wanted the King to like him, it was obvious what had to be done.

Cyril thought this privy council was lucky for more than one reason. First, Dalton had elected to keep six members of the council as permanent seats, while he allowed for others to come and go as they needed their complaints or issues to be solved within the Kingdom. The monarchs of the First Kingdom were able to set their own parameters for their privy council. Dalton had done well demonstrating tolerance with an even number of members. Second, Dalton was not hard to please. It was plain as day that he valued one thing and one thing alone: tolerance.

Dalton looked around the room, a fading dark eyebrow raised in mischief.

Cyril loved every moment of this disaster of a council meeting. It was not to Dalton's avail; the Lords of the First

Kingdom would give any new monarch hell. But it was the way Dalton was handling it—handling them—that had pride swarming within Cyril's soul. It threatened to explode all over this room. He nearly wanted to go over and kiss the boy. Dalton would never admit it, not even to Cyril, but he was born for this.

Now, if only I could get him to embrace it.

"Does anyone else feel uncomfortable by my presence? I thought we were getting along swimmingly. I hate it when I'm at a party where I am the guest of honor, yet I'm unwelcome. Lord Peach, do you care to explain?" His eyes darted to the man again, who shrank back in his seat at being targeted as such among the council members.

Cyril put his fist to his mouth and bit on it, containing every budding laugh that was threatening to spill from him. Dalton was utterly relentless.

Dalton turned around and picked up his chair loudly. He threw it back into place and sat in it as if he were the Beloved King in Thallgan. Leaning back, he put his leather boots on the table as casually as one would if they were singing with a bard, an ale in hand. His golden and sapphire crown was placed erratically atop his head. His white hair had been cropped, less wild than normal, so Cyril figured this was his latest way to defame his own position of power. The crooked crown was symbolic of all he had lost and how he now had nothing to lose.

Cyril loved every minute of this unbridled catastrophe. The Lords were horrified.

It made Cyril love it more.

"Lord Marsh, why do you think Lord Peach does not want to play with me?" Dalton had the audacity to purse his lips, his dark blue eyes baiting like a dog with a bone.

Lord Marsh was the biggest prick in the Kingdom and

had been the largest kiss up to King Ronan amongst the privy council members. It was long standing tradition in Ronan's court that Marsh would appease anything he wanted, whether it was out of fear or desperation to be thanked by a King, it did not matter. It was exquisitely frustrating, and Cyril never had any respect for the man. Cyril had not told Dalton any of that, but the fact that Dalton knew without his council was impressive enough.

Taking the bait, Lord Marsh stood up, his green gaze blazing with wrath. "I think Lord Peach is hesitant to accept such a lovely, charismatic, and handsome young King—"

Dalton waved a hand, cutting him off suddenly. "Lord Peach, I am promoting you. You will be getting fifty percent of Lord Marsh's lands. You can claim up to twenty-five percent of his crops, as long as we are not in famine or having a period of bad crops in the First Kingdom."

Lord Peach fainted.

But Dalton was not done.

"Lord Marsh, you are being punished for not doing what I wanted. I *wanted* you to tell me why Lord Peach does not want to play with me. You told me what I wanted to hear, not what I needed to hear. And as King, I will not be lied to. I do not want you to kiss my rear-end like you kissed my father's. If anything, I would prefer it if you told me how you think I am an ugly, rat bastard, who is far too young to lead the Kingdom from this wretched throne."

Dalton stood and snow fell from the ceiling. The other Lords looked up in wonder, while Lord Smith's mouth hung open in complete shock.

Cyril snorted.

"I am exactly who my father thought I was going to be, but I am also so much more. I do not want you to tell me what in the name of the Ten Kingdoms to think and do. I want you to tell me what *you* think. We can only be leaders if we lead. Do not inflate my ego and expect to be rewarded."

Lord Marsh opened his mouth to protest. As he did so, Dalton flicked a finger in his direction. Lord Marsh's lips were suddenly covered in frost, stuck together.

Cyril burst out laughing.

"Do not speak while I am speaking."

One by one, the Lords of the privy council bowed their heads in unison. They murmured their prayers to the King, keeping their faces down as Dalton strolled out of the room without a care in the world. He would leave them like they were, debating over things that would need his royal signature anyway. He was done entertaining them, and with this display, he had put himself in an irrefutable position of power.

They would not cross him again. Especially when they realized that this behavior was him being nice.

His tunic was in disarray from fumbling with it for the past hour. His boots were untied, and his crown was still crooked on his head as he made his way toward the light of the castle once more.

"Dalton!" Cyril chided, following him out into the hallway.

"Yes, my precious?" Dalton said with a smirk.

"You were beautiful in there."

Pride flashed in Dalton's eyes at the admittance, but there was only sadness as he spoke. "Thank you, Cyril."

"What is wrong, boy? You did wonderfully. They all bowed, and you iced out the most annoying Lord in the Kingdom."

"Doing wonderful and feeling wonderful are two different things."

Cyril nearly stopped in his tracks. "Who are you going

to be? Are you going to rule with an iron fist like Ciara? Are you going to put the law and respect above all else? Or are you going to rule like Cian? With your heart—"

"I am going to rule like Dalton."

Cyril stood, mouth agape. "They're looking to you—"

Dalton nearly lunged for him. "I know! They are looking for my power, looking *at* my power, rather, and I understand, Cyril. I do."

Cyril moved to say something comforting, anything, but nothing would come to the surface of his lips.

"I know who I represent, what this power means to these lands, people, and court," Dalton said softly. "But I cannot be who they want me to be. I did not know him. I did not know her."

"I could teach you," Cyril said sadly, wishing he could take the burden from his friends off of this boy.

Dalton smiled sadly. "I cannot do them justice. I think it is best to be me, and let the snow fall as it may."

He spun to walk down the hallway, his shoes clicking incessantly with each step.

Cyril sighed, his eyes falling to the floor as he nearly toppled over with the pain of his own recognitions.

"They are looking to you to save us all," he said to none but the dark walls around him.

TWO

or not the first time, Randolph Eniar walked amongst men like a King.

Thundering past the living quarters of the castle-dwellers, servants skirted to the side of the hallway to avoid contact with the anguish that blackened his heart. His irritation and frustration bled into his veins, toxic and irritable beyond fixing. Vexation seized within him, his skin hot to the touch. He snarled at anyone who stepped even an inch into his path, feral to all in his way.

He straightened his tunic, wiped his hands on his leather pants, and knocked on her chamber doors. He had arrived. He crunched his knuckles against the palm of his opposite hand, the sensation a release, yet agonizing. It was the last place he wanted to be, yet it was the only place he needed to be.

He had not uttered a word to her in seven days, and he was inexplicably guilty.

He had been waiting for the right words to come to him, for the moment where he felt like he could be reaccepted. Ten Kingdoms, he had been waiting until he felt like he could be forgiven. But even when all was lost, he had still been a better friend than this. He knew he had nothing to apologize for; she had told him as such over a thousand times now.

He was the one who had told her that her brother was dead.

He knew the pain which infected her heart now because he had been destroyed by it once before too. Death was a disease which one could not rid itself of. It was all consuming and took every piece of soul away from the body. It was the uncontrollable which wanted to be controlled, that piece of the universe which was darkness reincarnated. Evil at large.

He stood now facing her chambers, pain pulsating through him like an electric current. Fire built in the pit of his stomach, and he could barely contain the smoke that left his mouth on the exhale. His power seemed to have accelerated the more he felt. The pain of what he had done, the weight of who he was, and the agony that his mere presence inflicted upon others; it had been a magnifying glass on what he had been suppressing for so long.

As if he did not have anything else to deal with, now he was one meltdown away from becoming a full-blown dragon.

He took his right thumb and touched the scabs which had formed on the innermost corner of his wrist. He touched the vines which he had inked there seven days prior, a permanent reminder of the fire soul of James Grimes. Even if he was not responsible for the death of Charmaine's brother, he felt like he was, and feeling was all that mattered anymore.

For someone who used to pride themselves on a lack of feeling, he really was becoming unrecognizable.

He breathed in once through his nose and out through his mouth. On the exhale, he shoved his hands onto the doors of her chambers and pushed. The wood groaned with the effort, and the cool breeze of lavender wafted toward him as he stepped through the threshold. He kept his head down as he stood before her, his eyes not leveling up until he heard the *click* of the door behind him.

Lifting his eyes, he met the familiar violet stare of the girl he once thought he was worthy of befriending—even courting—all fear of redemption crackled like embers in a fire beneath him. Her once smooth and sleek curls in her hair fell flat. The midnight hue that had driven her dark hair was now muted, no longer that of the night sky. Her eyes were the only piece of her face that was familiar, but they too looked like they were broken.

He stifled a sob, instead falling to his knee. He was not sure what he was looking for or what his purpose was. However, he knew he wanted to be here. He wanted to do *something*. He opened his mouth, but nothing came out. Not even a puff of air or the breath he had taken fully before he opened the door.

Instead, she spoke, her voice clear as day despite the change in her inner light, "Randolph."

A word. A name. *His name.*

He lifted his head and stood. He knew there were tears in his eyes before he even stepped toward her. But here they were, two broken souls who needed to be put back together. They connected in a hug, embracing fiercely with a love he did not know he could receive.

"Where have you been?" she asked, her frail hands tracing the familiar lines of his tattoos.

He breathed deeply in response, her familiar scent intermixing with his own as he tried to separate the two. This was what he had wanted. He was always so comfortable around her, able to drop the veil he had covered his soul with.

This friendship and bond that connected them was beyond anything Randolph had ever experienced. He could not remember the last time he had a friend, and a true one at that. Yes, he had Lawton, but Lawton had secrets Randolph was not yet ready to explore. Randolph's secrets were his own, and he intended to keep them that way for as long as possible.

"I have missed you so. It has been a week since you visited me last." Her voice was so quiet. She sounded as tired as she looked.

"I did not mean to abandon you," he said, not quite knowing why.

The past three months had been grueling for all who were on King Ronan's quest to salvage the country. Since then, it had been a whirlwind of power struggles, political alliances, strife, instability, and grief all intertwined in the courtly atmosphere of the First Kingdom. Randolph knew Charmaine had never been alone, not for a second, but he still felt terrible he had not been able to comfort his friend the past week like he wished. Any moment she had been forced to reckon with her pain without a friend to lean on wrecked another part of him.

His position kept him too busy, and frankly, if he could alleviate some of the King's meager duties, then he would. He would never admit it to Dalton, but Charmaine needed him. They had formed a deep friendship in the last three months, bonded together by grief and anger. There were other elements at work too, elements Cyril was working tirelessly to define. However, it was not as simple as a mere attraction between the two of them, and Cyril had yet to come up with an answer.

She pulled back. "You could never abandon me."

He lifted his hand slightly and gestured for her to look at the new ink which had begun to settle into his tanned skin. "For him. I meant to show you when I had it done, after we were together last week, but the King's guard took me off of castle grounds. Every night, I got back, and I wanted to come here to show you and to talk, but I did not want to disturb you . . . It was so late," Randolph rambled like an imbecile.

Clearly, he cared, because he was never at a loss for words like this.

She covered her mouth with her hand, her eyes closing for a second as if imprinting this moment into her memory forever. "I am not upset with you." She touched the mark on his hand, the mark of her brother's memory. "It is beautiful."

It is another one of my sins. He brought her in again for another hug, wrapping his muscular arms around her small frame. It was clear she had lost weight in the last three months, the grief taking hold of more than just her mind. In the past few weeks, however, she seemed to be taking life in stride again. She was still far from the girl she was when she arrived, but she was speaking now and showing signs of her old self.

"How is he?" Randolph found himself asking as he pulled away, his eyes reverently searching hers for any concerns.

All morning, he had tried to build up the courage to ask Charmaine about the now-to-be King, but he had not had the guts. Dalton had been under wraps the last three months for security measures. However, it was no secret amongst the folk of the castle that the young King was visiting the chambers of the Grimes girl, instead of his own wife. Randolph did not care what those visits entailed; he could only imagine that they did not mean what the dwellers *thought* it meant. Dalton, after all, had been there for Charmaine more than he had. However, now Dalton was skirting his duties as a monarch in waiting, running amuck around the castle land avoiding all decision making until Charmaine's brother and the King were in the ground.

What Dalton did not understand was that the act of being King did not start when you put the last King in the ground, it started when the prior monarch's heart stopped beating, and they took their final breath. Sure, Randolph had spoken to Dalton. He had even been in numerous council meetings with him, but he was not close enough with him to ask him a question. Especially *how are you?* Dalton would not survive such a question. Randolph was sure he would laugh so hard that he would drop dead. A large part of that was their own fault; two men at different ends of the same spectrum.

As of tomorrow, three months had passed without a crown on the head of the First Kingdom's monarch.

And things were going to shit.

He had briefly thought of going to Elena Leclair, but the Princess of the Fourth Kingdom and Queen of the First in-waiting, were grieving as well. He did not dare come between that girl and James Grimes. He had seen their electricity together and had been moved by it, even when he did not understand it.

And to be frank, despite his murderous history, Elena Leclair terrified him.

So, instead, he had decided to check in on his friend and ask about the whereabouts of the King-in-waiting, to find out what in the Ten Kingdoms he was doing.

"Avoiding," Charmaine said frankly, sitting down on the edge of her bed.

He nearly jumped out of his boots to hug her. Her casual sarcasm he loved so much had returned for a moment.

Cian, help me. I really am turning into a soft bastard.

As her fingers interlaced around his arm, he was hit with the sweet scent of her power, one which he could now recognize. His training had come back in waves, but this, he could not shake. Charmaine was more powerful than she realized, grief aside.

"Me or the crown?" Randolph asked, sitting beside her and taking her hand.

"I suppose both," she said with a half-smile. "He stands by his refusal to not be crowned until everyone is laid to rest. I understand it, I really do, but I do not want everyone to feel like they are tiptoeing around me because they are scared to let me go."

Randolph looked at her half expecting tears, based upon how she had been so grief-stricken the past few months. The girl before him seemed as though she were dried up; no tears were left to bring her any sort of emotional comfort and allow her to work through it. She was in emotional limbo, the sadness taking over her body now as it had her soul after the battle.

The mercenaries would pay for what they did to James; he swore it.

"I am glad to see you. I am sorry to ask about the King. I do respect his choice to wait," Randolph said, trying to avoid the subject again.

He was so pissed off by the whole avoidance—maybe it was selfish of him—perhaps a tad hypocritical. A small part of him admired Dalton for it, though. It was customary in the Ten Kingdoms to wait a few months for a proper burial, since members from all the Kingdoms were invited, and travel could take weeks. Randolph knew it was a political move as well because everyone in attendance to the funeral would bear witness to him taking the crown.

It took everything in him not to kick his own backside. He was so conflicted these days he was surprised he even remembered his own name.

Taking her hand, he looked into her violet eyes. "And I don't think anyone is scared to let you go, I think they're scared you're going to lose yourself without a helping hand."

She smiled with half of her mouth in return, a little bit of life returning to her eyes as she touched the blue sapphire ring on her finger. She twisted it methodically, and Randolph's stomach sank, for he could only guess where she got such a regal piece.

"You won't know until you try to let me fly, Randolph." She sighed. "He will have to put the crown on at the ceremony, and not just for a moment."

"Do you think he will let Cyril put it atop his head? Or do you think he will dodge it and snatch it like a dog, only to run around the throne room until someone stops him?"

She barked a laugh, covering her hand with her mouth before hitting Randolph lightly on the shoulder. "That is your King you are talking about, Sir Randolph."

"I think it will be the latter."

"Let us hope you lace your boots tight then, Rand. He is fast."

THREE

TEN YEARS AGO

harmaine stood at the threshold of her father's bedroom and waited to say goodbye.

Sobs ricocheted off the wooden walls of their home, lingering longer than they would if her house was made of stone. Shock splintered through her tiny hands, gripping her doll for dear life as she thought about what she would say to her father. James was in there now, speaking so low she could not get an idea of what they were talking about. Her mother had been with him all night and had gone out for water not too long ago, from the well in the center of Brinn. She had kept much of father's sickness a secret over the past year, but even at seven years old, Charmaine knew when things were turning bad.

Her father had stopped working and attending the privy council months ago, too weak to walk from the confines of their household to the chambers where they met in the town square. People had visited more, then people had visited less. Tommy Cheshire, James' best friend, had been over more than the average person. He had spent weeks asking James to come and play, and Charmaine overheard her mother thank

Tommy for the distraction. In a way, Tommy had done this for Charmaine as well. She had friends—girls in Brinn who she played with—but it was hard sometimes for the Grimes children to let people in fully. They cared too much, were too open, and they had their walls up with other children, due to the circumstances of their family.

Despite their best efforts to not let it affect them, the circumstances of Charmaine's gifts were rather isolating.

Her mother did not want to see her children experience death, not like this. Not so young.

Charmaine wondered if her mother had seen this in any of her visions. She was not sure why she was not allowed to talk about it outside of the home, the fact that her mother could see things that had not yet happened. But she followed the rules—she always did. She could not imagine what it would be like to know you were going to die, so she hoped her mother never said anything to her father.

Charmaine had heard about grief in nursery rhymes and read about it in novels. She knew children in the village who had lost a parent, a brother, or a friend. She knew the legends of King Cian, who had almost laid waste to their kingdom with his Queen at his side. But it had never hit home for her before. She knew about dying from stories, though she did not understand what it meant to truly be in pain.

The agony, the misunderstanding, and the anger that blitzed through the Grimes' household was too much for a child to bear.

Following the creak of her father's bedroom door, James stepped out. His face was red, his eyes redder. He tried to smile at his sister—that familiar warm embrace of James' love that people would die for. But it was to no avail. It did not meet his eyes, and Charmaine did not believe he was happy.

"Go ahead, Char. He is ready to talk to you."

Charmaine nodded, squeezing her doll a little harder as she strode into the room, closing the wooden door behind her with a creak.

"My darling girl," her father whispered, his blue lips barely moving.

She silently walked over, fear overtaking her.

What if I said the wrong thing? How do I make this right?

He took her hand, his own cold at the touch. "I have to tell you something, my child." His violet eyes shone with the agony of death. "And you cannot tell your mother I did so."

Her eyes widened, and she nodded, encouraging him to go on.

"You have to promise me, Charmaine Elizabeth Grimes. Promise me that you will keep this secret from your mother, as well as Jamie."

"I promise I will keep this secret from mother, as well as Jamie."

He smiled softly, his hands still wrapped in hers. He looked up to the ceiling briefly, as if seeing something that was not there. "Good, you always were such a good girl."

"What is it, Father?" she asked, unable to focus on anything but the task of listening at hand.

"Long ago, I met a man. He had blue eyes and the kindest of hearts. He did not tell me his name, but he worked at the castle. He serves the King now, as he had served many Kings before. He told me something once which I have carried with me every day, a prophecy which he said I can only tell my daughter when I am about to leave this world."

Charmaine gripped her doll against her chest, willing it to comfort her.

"You must remember this, Charmaine. It will help you when you need it the most, when times are dark. And I know the dark times are coming, especially for you and Jamie. And I am sorry I will not be there to help you."

A single tear dripped down Charmaine's cheek, hot and fast. "It's okay, Father. I understand."

He leaned closer, his blue eyes blazing with all the fires of the world. "The man told me to tell my daughter to embrace all that she is, and the world will embrace her back."

She nearly gasped, unsure of the meaning of her father's deranged words. He was so ill, and he had been for many months. How could she know he was telling the truth, and this was something to be taken seriously, rather than the words of a dying man lost to the sickness?

"I will try," she said, her lips quivering.

"No!" he shouted, the breath leaving him more with every strangled motion.

This was his dying wish, his last act. Whether she believed it had any significance or not, Charmaine could not deny this was important to him. So, she would remember, or at least she would try to.

"You *must*."

"Okay," she whispered, stroking his forehead with her free arm. "I will."

"Good. You always were such a kind girl."

Her father died at sunrise.

FOUR

alton once laughed in the face of his destiny, coddled in a room all by himself as his father had tried to shield the world from his raw power. The Prince was stronger than the King; it was ironic. Dalton wondered if his father had died as terrified as he was in life.

It haunted him more than he cared to admit—that *something* clearly had haunted his father. Ronan had been terrified that there was a threat to his throne. It was the only viable explanation for why he had treated his only son like vermin.

Dalton sat in his chambers now, sprawled on the white marble floors around him. A plethora of opened books laid on display at his feet. The past few hours, he had studied, learning all there was to know about the Lord's financial books and the families that funded the First Kingdom by proxy. There was much to learn as King and even more to memorize. It was daunting, but Dalton loved reading and welcomed the challenge.

His display the other day in the council chambers with Lord Peach and Lord Marsh was pure strategy. He had picked it up from these books, the records and book-keeping that his father's financial advisors had recorded over the years. Ronan had even kept clear notes on each member of the council. He wrote down every detail, journaling his correspondences and interactions with the Lords who served him yet ruled him too. Dalton had been shocked to find such meticulous records, especially due to how wicked his father had become toward the end of his reign and life.

Interestingly enough, the records ceased six years ago. *Hmph, maybe Carinthya's death plagued my father more than I thought.*

Enraged by the memory of the man who wore this crown before, he tried not to ponder all that flew through his mind. King Ronan had done his job for so many years, and honestly, by the books, he did it well. Dalton could not remember a time where his father really feared magic—up until Carinthya was not found. If only Ronan had just accepted what laid before him, instead of trying to change the course of fate, maybe his end would have been different. Maybe he would still be alive to this day. Ronan had tried to capitalize on the good people of the Kingdom with the horrors of two individuals who only had one another.

And it had led to the death of James Grimes.

Despite everything these books made him feel about his father, he could not move past the fact that his last five years on the continent were monstrous. They could not be forgiven. No matter how sad it was.

Dalton was so immersed in his readings that he did not hear Cyril come into his chambers. He had thought of this moment hundreds of thousands of times, even though he never wanted it to come. He never pictured he would gain his crown on the remains of a world fragmented and polished to look like it was good.

"Your Majesty." Cyril put a hand on his shoulder.

If this were the coronation day he had imagined as a

boy—before all the shit—he would have embraced him, a smile erupting for both of them in a celebration of freedom at last. They would have laughed and drank all the wine, paving a way to a world they wanted to see. Instead, Dalton sat on the floor of his chambers, defeated by the mental games of trauma, refusing to acknowledge the crown he was to put atop his head.

As if the bastard read his mind, Cyril said calmly, "You won't lose her by putting it on, you know."

Dalton scoffed, his eyes practically rolling out of his head and onto the floor. "Cyril… you know it will change things. The minute I touch that disgusting relic that sits down the hall, I will be different, whether my mind reminds me of the same, or whether I am changed by its weight. There is a reason I never wanted the blasted thing!"

His shoulders sagged at the thought of having it atop his head. The same crown that had been worn for generations of Kings, this one not worn since King Cian's coronation. The Thinkers believed he was fit to wear this crown, and prophecy said so. Not the crown that the prior Kings had worn, like his father. They had been deemed unworthy, for they did not share in Cian's gifts as members of the Saphirrus bloodline. Dalton almost chuckled at the thought, wondering if his father knew he had been given a crown reserved for the lesser of Kings.

What a joke.

Gods damn him and Gods bless him, Cyril had once again interrupted his thoughts. He reached into the leather bag that Dalton realized was slung over his shoulder. Cyril took a deep breath, lifting the crown from the sack carefully.

Instinctually, Dalton extended his fingers toward the crown in a desperate attempt to reach it. His eyes widened as he took in its white jewels, cloudy as if they were filled with the icy power. The rim was covered in tiny diamonds that spiked across the top in an almond cut, dripping from the top to where it would rest on his head. That was, if he ever decided to put the damn thing on.

"Gods," Cyril said, as if he was drinking. Dalton was sure there was some beauty in watching him touch the crown that had made his best friend a King. "Dalton, you cannot shirk this."

"This?" Dalton asked, irritated that Cyril had seemingly fallen into the gawking that everyone seemed to do around him these days. "Gods, Cyril, not you too, with the King shit. You can call me your Majesty, but for the sake of the Gods, please do not bow to me in private . . ."

Cyril took both hands to his shoulders, turning him to face him. His eyes were wild, and his wrinkles made him look older than usual. "Dalton, this is your *destiny*. I know the circumstances of your life thus far have not been what you dreamed of as Prince of the Kingdom, and your father has ill-prepared and frankly, neglected to raise you into the man you need to be at this very moment."

If it was anyone but Cyril, Dalton would have hit him.

Cyril smirked, indicating he knew he was royally pissing Dalton off, but continued. "But you *are* the right man for this. You are strong and have overcome all the trials the Gods set before you because you are the rightful King. I knew when you were born that you were special. The Thinkers did not lightly tell Ronan that you would have insurmountable power. They would not have told him and changed your entire trajectory of your upbringing along with it if they thought any different."

Dalton blinked, not rattled by Cyril's testimony, but by the look in his eyes. There was a certainty he had not seen before, a love that ran so deep he could feel himself pushing back down his power. The last thing he needed was to freeze Cyril right here.

"Cyril," Dalton said, for once in his life rendered speechless.

He waved as if to shut Dalton up. He was not finished. "And Charmaine . . . I know we must not speak of her if you do not wish to, but I could feel her power before I knew who she was. Her mother was a Cipher, Dalton. It is something I have learned as of late. A woman, who by right of power, should be a Thinker, but whose gender prevented such a possibility from coming to fruition. One that aligned circles with the most powerful of the Kingdoms during the time of her life, particularly when she was younger. I did not realize until the preparations for James' funeral that her lineage was so . . . *precarious*."

Dalton's jaw dropped, shocked by the information presented to him about Charmaine, and the fact that Cyril was speaking of her at all. Especially given all the moments these past moons where he had nearly lost it on him in her name. Cyril had been sympathetic to Dalton in the name of romantic dalliances, but something, some emotion, had awoken within him at the realization that Charmaine was more than a young adult fascination.

"I would keep this information private, Dalton. Do not share anything that might . . . inhibit your relationship." He smirked. "I cannot share all the details with you, for it is not my story to tell. It might not be her story to tell either, if she is not willing. Gods, she might not even know. Not all of it, anyway. All her nervous movements, the attachment to her brother and Randolph . . . The girl was terrified of your father's resistance and bigotry. Give her time."

With this, Cyril took his hands off Dalton's shoulder before embracing him in a fierce display of affection. Dalton snorted on instinct, unsure of how to handle himself. It was all so damn overwhelming. Talking about women with Cyril was not on Dalton's bucket list.

Also, he was not a hugger.

He sat with her in her chambers, wrapped in one another's arms as though he was her husband, and she was his wife. He combed his hands through her hair with great care, careful not to touch her bare skin with his own. They wore their night dressings, the robes floor-length and long-sleeved. Dalton wanted nothing more than to kiss her, to have his hands run down her soft jawline and trace her lips with his tongue.

However, he knew the draw would demand more. Even in this position, he was compromised. His power thrummed through his veins, icy and filled with rage. He was mad at everything and anyone who interacted with him.

Cyril for not finding out how to dim the power of the draw, nor understand it.

Randolph for being able to touch her, hold her hand, and comfort her when she cried out, without threatening to shroud the world in a winter wonderland.

Elena for being taken by her own numbness, when he felt everything that touched him and those he loved.

James Grimes for dying. It was a stupid outlet of emotion, but he felt it all the same.

His father for dying too. Dalton did not want the throne, and he never did.

Carinthya for leaving him, being taken, and murdered. He missed her more than anyone else could know.

Cian and Ciara, for curing the world of darkness, only to let more in.

"Are you okay, Dalton?" Charmaine sniffled, her voice raw. "You seem very far away."

He moved his hands from her hair and slid his body out

from under hers. The physical breaking of the connection between them knocked the wind out of him, the draw becoming more painful every time he left her in this state. It was as if it had a soul, this connection between them, and demanded to be fed by their time together.

"I will send for Randolph; he will sit with you," he whispered, barely drawing a breath. Even her scent was intoxicating as it was sickening, the power of the draw agonizingly beautiful, just as she was.

"Dalton, you seem very far away," Cyril whispered suddenly, just as she had, bringing Dalton back to the present.

He blinked, that prior irritation still flaring like a dimly lit candle within him.

Sadness bubbled within him at the realization that Charmaine was still keeping secrets from him, despite all they had admitted to one another over the last few months. He figured there was nothing more to reveal between them, not *big* moments, anyway. Dalton could never quite bring himself to describe what he felt when they were alone. It was impossible to share every facet of who you were, who you had been, and who you would become, with someone you had only known for less than half of a year.

However, it hurt him to know there was still so much left undiscovered between them.

Why was she hiding it? Did she not trust him completely, as he did her?

Despite the fact that he too kept things from her. He did trust her. He just did not trust himself not to break her, out of duty to the Kingdom and the Gods-damned prophecy which inadvertently ruled him.

With a deep breath, he tried to shut his mind temporarily off. Kings were no good if they were in a spiral, one which he felt was fast approaching.

"So, you dump this on me, and expect me to walk out of this room and become King? Are you bloody serious, Cyril?"

"You are ready, boy. Now stop hiding in the shadows, and claim what has been gifted to you by the Gods."

Cyril stood, taking the crown and placing it back in the leather sack with care. "How did you get that out of the Chamber of Jewels? Isn't it under lock and key?"

Cyril smirked, his eyes blazing with mischief that reminded Dalton very much of himself. *Well, that is not terrifying.* "I am the lock and key, boy. You will do well to remember it."

Dalton snorted and looked up at his friend who stood before him. "That was kind of you to say."

"I meant every word, boy."

"You need to stop calling me that. I am a King. Remember?"

Cyril smiled, carefully placing the leather bag over his shoulder once more. "You are a King when you want to be a King. I will stop calling you boy when you are a King all the time, a force to be reckoned with, when you embrace your destiny."

"That is a big list of things I need to do to earn your respect."

"You earned it years ago, Dalton, but now you need to command it."

Dalton raised an eyebrow, exhaustion seeping into every crevice of his body. He was depleted: mind, body, and soul. "I cannot believe I have to bury them tomorrow."

Cyril crouched down again, meeting Dalton's gaze head on. "And you will have to bury many more in your lifetime, my boy. I am so sorry to be the one to tell you. Being a King is a burden that many want until they feel the weight of the title."

"Uplifting as always, Cyril."

Cyril huffed a laugh. "My advice for tomorrow is to be present. Yes, you will have eyes on you. But they do not matter until the coronation. Be there for Elena, and be there for Charmaine." He paused, scratching his chin. "I would also be wary. There will be many Kings and Queens in attendance tomorrow. Even if they do not directly interact with you, they will be watching. You have not been at court with all members of the continent since your birth, and even with some missing, there will be a weight that has not been there before."

At the mention of Elena, Dalton put his hands to his forehead. "I do not know how to help Elena."

"I think the biggest help for Elena will be time. She has always been hesitant to help, that fierce friend that tends to self-sabotage any happiness. If you are there for her, as she has always been for you, it will mean more to her than you think."

"I assigned her a personal guard, one of our best behind Randolph. It was his recommendation."

"Greyson Althan?" Cyril knew the name as well as the rest of the guard did.

Dalton nodded. With key members of the First Kingdom's knighthood still out on a mercenary detection mission across the kingdom, they were rather pressed for good men. They had strong men and women left, but none to the caliber of Randolph and Greyson.

"And did she appreciate Greyson being assigned to her?"

"She threw a candelabra at my head."

"So, it went swimmingly." Cyril chuckled.

"I told her that she is my best friend, and I will do anything to keep her safe. But I also told her that she is my wife, and as my consort, I need to keep her safe. Hence the guard."

"Smart," Cyril agreed.

"Even though I do not think she needs protecting, the people do not yet know that she has powers, and I will not unveil that she has two, unless she commands as such."

"On her terms, Dalton, you are a good man."

The corner of Dalton's mouth quirked up. "I will not take any risks with the people I love, not until we understand more about what in the Ten Kingdoms is going on."

"We will figure it out. I am sure of it."

"I am glad you think so, Cyril. So, enlighten me, who is not going to be in attendance to my dearest father's funeral? Or my lovely coronation." Dalton asked, his voice dripping in sarcasm.

"The Seventh, which is not a surprise, given your choice in comrades. Princess Reine has not been active in politics since she assumed regent rights."

Dalton scoffed. He wondered if Randolph was privy to this information, but he found himself too exhausted to inquire further. He had enough going on and did not need to drag the Seventh Kingdom's drama into his own. "Anyone else?"

As if reading his mind in stride with his question, Cyril said, "I will speak with Randolph. And to answer you, the Fourth Kingdom will not be represented other than by your wife. It seems that Queen Maria has no desire to attend a funeral, nor a coronation that is not her own daughter's."

Dalton rolled his eyes, and his hands rubbed his temples. "I have to speak with her about that soon, the fact that she is my wife."

Cyril laughed, pure and filled with love. "She is healing. You can give her time before you bring it forth to the council."

"The longer we wait, though, the harder it will be. Especially with more public appearances coming."

Cyril nodded. "You will figure it out. Both of you. Together. I am sure of it."

"Do not tell me this is another prophecy of yours. I do not think I can handle more information than is already circulating in my vicinity." He gestured to the books open before him.

Cyril chuckled. "No, it is not a prophecy. But I am still working on figuring it out. Clearly, we are already in the thick of it, as the death of your father has passed."

"He will rise from the death of his father," Dalton chided sarcastically. "I hate that blasted prophecy."

"The next line is that the Ten Kingdoms will fall." Cyril was serious; his expression stoic and eyes fearful.

"Let's hope it waits to pass until the day after tomorrow."

Cyril smiled sadly. "Yes, I hope it waits."

FIVE

andolph swung his sword in the training yard, aware of every onlooker. The castle had been bustling the past few days. The preparations for Dalton's coronation and the funeral procession had attracted individuals from all over the Ten Kingdoms. A group of women stood off to the side of the courtyard, fanning themselves with parcels and attempting to sway their dresses nonchalantly.

It took all within Randolph not to roll his eyes at their feeble attempts to gain his eye. He had no romantic inclinations, not recently, anyway. Months prior, there had been a moment when he was with Charmaine, who James had told him personally to try to court, but it had been short-lived when Dalton had nearly frozen the First Kingdom over at the sight of them speaking.

Charmaine was beautiful, precariously charming, and had a heart worthy of all the thrones in the Ten Kingdoms. When she laughed, he was lighter. When she checked in with him, he found himself relaxing naturally. She made him want to tell her the stories of his past, for he knew she would do nothing but understand. Or at least, try to. But he could not subject her to more pain.

And if there was one thing Charmaine did, it was to bear the burdens of others.

He lifted the hilt of his sword, the blade gleaming in the daylight, despite the chill in the air. It was bright today, the sun glaring amongst the clouds. The warm seasons had gone and passed, and winter would be upon them soon.

He breathed in and out as hot breath turned to smoke. He focused his energy on the movements of battle, movements he had curated for what seemed like centuries. He swung the blade with precision, slicing his invisible enemy straight through. Dodging a fake offensive hit, he blazed with speed to the side. Lifting his sword again, he slashed sideways, dealing the killing blow to the air.

He turned, stopping to center the sword along the bridge of his long nose. Smirking, he looked at the women who stood to the side of the courtyard. As his amber gaze met theirs, they blushed and squealed. He was not sure what kingdom they were from, but it was not his own. He wondered if—

"Ah! Sir Randolph, just the knight I wanted to see!" Cyril's voice boomed from the other side of the courtyard.

Randolph huffed a breath, his sweat cold on the back of his neck. "Yes, Cyril? Is everything all right with his Majesty?"

This was their greeting as of late, always inquiring about the King in one way or another. The King, it seemed, was everything. Even though Randolph knew that, he wished he was rather nothing at all.

Cyril snorted. "Fortunately, for us, yes. However, I do not know how long his Majesty will be sedated in joy, so I must be brief."

Randolph smiled softly, sheathing his sword to walk with Cyril from the courtyard, away from the ladies.

"A crowd it seems, your Majesty?" Cyril inquired, an eyebrow raised inconspicuously.

"It would seem so." Randolph was in no mood for light conversation.

"Cian used to get crowds as well," Cyril said softly. "It used to drive Ciara mad, though she never would have admitted such a thing."

Randolph chuckled against his own inhibitions to be cold. He was always interested in learning about the man who he had been named after. "It seems as though Ciara and I had a lot in common then."

Cyril pondered this for a moment before replying, "No, no, Randolph. You are much more like Cian than you realize."

Randolph blinked, trying to take in the meaning of Cyril's words as they turned the corner of the castle and entered a long stretch of hallway. He opened his mouth to speak, and Cyril put a finger to his mouth in a motion of silence.

"Into my chambers. We need to speak privately."

Randolph's heart nearly plummeted out of his chest. "Is everything all right?"

The door closed behind him with a deafening *click*. "Yes, in part. No, in other parts."

Quirking an eyebrow, Randolph nearly lit aflame with the impatience that seethed from him. "By all means, Cyril, waste my day."

Cyril's mouth turned into a side smile, as if Randolph's irritated behavior was natural to him. "I am trying not to. I too have other people I would love to be with right now, and I cannot say you are at the top of my list."

"Then why have you dragged me here amidst my productive training session, oh wise, Cyril?" Randolph sat down on the chair in the corner of Cyril's chambers, as if to emphasize his irritation to the situation. He was ungodly and unprofessional.

He did not care.

"The Seventh Kingdom representative is not coming to the coronation, nor the funeral. I wanted to tell you before the ceremonies started, so you are not looking for her."

Randolph's mouth went dry. Clenching his hands, he nearly bled on his palms from the pressure. Fingertips threatened to cut open the palm of his hand, the intensity so devastating he hoped he would draw blood just to feel something. He managed to get one word out, despite the beats his heart was skipping. "Why?"

Cyril hesitated, and Randolph shot up. The tattooed fingers of his right hand grasped the cusp of Cyril's shirt, while his left hand sprouted a flame from each finger. Anyone else in the Ten Kingdoms would have screamed at such a frightening and sudden display of power, yet Cyril only beamed with pride.

"Atta boy."

But Randolph would not accept this at face value. "Why isn't she coming?" His usual casual tone came out strangled, as though someone were standing on his windpipe.

"Put out your fire, and put me down," Cyril commanded.

Consciously, Randolph put down the old man and shook out his hand. "I'm sorry—"

"No, you are not," Cyril said, "and that is fine too. I do not know why she is not coming. The Seventh Kingdom has always laid more by themselves than with the other kingdoms, and frankly, I have never blamed them. Even in the days when we referenced the ten kingdoms by the continents title, Sarridolon—the Seventh—had always been at odds with others."

"Sarridolon?" Randolph whispered the name like an old friend, one which he had not heard since childhood.

"Ah, so your father did teach you of it. He was a cruel

man, but not a stupid one. He was very much like King Ronan in that retrospect, yet your customs tended to be crueler than that of the First." Cyril paused, pondering. "We have never had much of a chance to speak of your education. It always seemed as though Ronan had another plan for you, a job which he could not complete himself. You learned much in your studying in the Seventh's reformation, am I correct?"

Randolph did not dignify that with a response, though it did darken the corners of his mind. Instead, he whispered, "Do you know if she is—"

Cyril raised a hand in warning. "Do not ask questions you do not want the answers to."

Randolph closed his eyes and breathed in through his nose. Heat exploded from his nostrils, and he could taste the smoke in his mouth. "Is she okay?"

"I will not lie to you, Randolph. It has been sometime since the First Kingdom has received correspondence from the Seventh."

"How long?" Randolph growled.

"Three months since we have heard but a whisper from the council. As for—"

"The Queen."

"The *reigning monarch*," Cyril corrected with fury. "We have not heard from her directly since you joined our ranks, three years ago."

Randolph sat down in response, a tattooed hand rubbing his brow line viciously. "Three years?"

"I told you not to ask if you did not want to know."

Randolph closed his eyes, breathing in the heat that built in his chest. He knew this emotion; he was not fond of it. *Heartbreak.*

"I wanted to know. Thank you for telling me."

"Not all is lost," Cyril said, sitting down next to him

slowly. "The world does not know it was you who drove the blade into your father's chest."

Randolph scoffed. "And you think they would forgive me if they knew what I have done? Who I am? How could I face them? How could I face those who I have come to call my friends, my family?"

"Ah," Cyril whispered, his blue eyes not breaking contact with Randolph. "Therein lies the commonality between you and Dalton. I am afraid you are more similar than you care to admit."

Randolph rolled his eyes and rubbed his hands together to escape the friction that built at his fingertips. He knew he would have to go to the dungeons sooner rather than later, or risk explosion. "I think you have the wrong man. There is no possible way I am like Dalton Saphirrus."

Cyril chuckled, a hand coming to Randolph's shoulder. "Destiny is a funny thing; it does not ask permission before taking hold of you, nor does it let you in on all of the keen details."

"So, our destinies are linked?"

Cyril pondered this for a moment. "Both you and Dalton are inheritors of some part of Cian. Dalton is in the physical sense, the power which controlled the lands and reunited the world in harmony. You, my boy, are like Cian in a more literal sense. You see the world like he did, broken and dissolved, despite its holistic appearance. You do not want to accept yourself because you do not want to assume the responsibility to which you already think you have failed. So, yes, you and Dalton are more similar than you care to admit."

"How long have you been pondering this, Cyril?"

"I am afraid well before my own time, Randolph. You see, I have a gift that is but a curse too. I can touch destiny. I can see it in my hands, but I cannot speak it until the Gods tell me as such." His eyes were very far away.

"We have not heard from the Gods in a long time," Randolph muttered softly, thinking back to when he had prayed to them not three months ago for the first time in years.

"I believe it is time I begin to teach of them again. Ten Kingdoms, we will need their strength again before the year is out."

Randolph and Cyril were quiet for a moment, yet not in awkward silence. It was as if two souls were in unison, which they had not been for many years before.

Randolph broke the silence and thoughts between them, asking genuinely, "What do you think Cian would say of my destiny?"

Cyril tipped his head back and laughed, pure and obstinate all in one. "I would give anything in the Ten Kingdoms for you, Dalton, and Cian to be in a room together."

Randolph threw Cyril a crooked smile. "It would be that bad?"

"I can envision it perfectly, but one thing would remain true," he whispered, suddenly serious. "He would tell both of you to stop pretending, stop running, and put on your crowns."

"I cannot say I would heed his advice then." Randolph sighed, leaning back on the couch.

"I would not expect you to at first, but Cian had a way of breaking people down and bringing them into the light."

"I am sorry for grabbing your shirt."

Cyril snorted. "I have had much worse done to me, boy, do not worry. Dalton once froze me to a wall, rat bastard King."

Now it was Randolph's turn to tip his head back and laugh.

SIX

er brother was dead.

Charmaine Grimes shook violently as she took to the front of the funeral procession. Randolph was on her arm, his tattooed hands a steady weight against the thrum of the First Kingdom's massive gathering. Charmaine felt nothing but the pounding headache and the hot tears running down her cheeks to her chin. She had no desire to wipe them, nor to erase this pain from her physicality.

Her black lace gown draped behind her; the six-foot train delicately lapping at the white marble floor on their journey to the burial site on the castle grounds. James would be buried amongst Kings and Queens, an honor that neither of her parents received. She would be able to visit him as long as she remained at the castle. Dalton had promised her incessantly over the last three months that no matter what happened in the future, she would never be denied entrance to seeing her brother.

She had asked if he implied he would not take the crown, to which he answered with a straight face, "Monarchs do not live forever, darling."

She had pondered the comment but left it be, too drained to probe him the way she so naturally had when she had arrived at the castle. Her spirit had been broken by this—shattered. Not even the darkness of her black gown could describe what went on in her heart.

There had been moments of the last few weeks where she felt like she was coming back to herself. She would laugh, find the urge to read books again, want to stroll around the castle, and even find herself waiting at her chamber doors to see if she could catch someone passing by to converse with. But then there were moments where it was all darkness again, all hatred and sadness. It was up and down, the worst grief she had ever experienced. But she knew, despite the pain and agony, she could get through it. She always did. She was a survivor and would not give up.

"Steady, Charmaine," Randolph whispered in her ear, his normally stoic gestures also overcome with emotion.

"Don't let go of me," she whispered in a gasp of air. She leaned her head onto his shoulder, holding herself together.

They walked together through the burned remains of the rose garden, destroyed by a mercenary attack on the castle. Nonetheless, they pushed on. The roses which were not destroyed still fought the smell of smoke as they lay to rot on the ground. They descended beyond the rose garden to the winding staircase, which took them a level below. Charmaine had not realized until after the battle in Brinn that this was the location of the First Kingdom graveyard at the castle. She had always been distracted by pretty things, or at least, she had put her focus there unintentionally.

Charmaine could see Dalton walking up ahead with his *wife*. He and Elena proceeded on opposite sides of the caskets laid amongst the tombstones. They were untouchable, standing apart from the masses that gathered to pay respects like the royal monarchs they were. Elena's gown was just as dramatic as Charmaine's, except with it, a veil shrouded her face from view. Charmaine knew Elena had requested this, unwilling to let the people of the visiting Kingdoms see her weep over another man.

Charmaine had once told Dalton there was no linear way to escape the clutches of grief, and she believed it still. When her father had died, she had wept, and life had slowly begun to pass her by as it returned to the way it was. When her mother had died, James had guided her away from despair with love and acceptance.

And she would survive this, she knew it at her core. James would never let her live it down in the afterlife if she did anything but.

She leaned on Randolph a little harder, the weight of acceptance dragging her down with each step she took toward the caskets amongst the graveyard.

"I have you," he whispered to her. "I will always have you."

"And I will always have you, my knight."

She glanced at him and was shocked to see his brown gaze full of emotion. So much so, she noticed for the first time his eyes carried harmonious flecks of green, so complementary in the light. Randolph, of all people, did not seem possessed by the fear of death. He had been the one to tell her the truth, that her brother had not survived the attack. He had not been harsh, but he had done what he knew was right. Randolph Eniar was not afraid of what must be done.

She hated that Randolph hated himself—for what reasoning, she was unsure. She had admired him from the moment she met him, so intrigued by the intricacies of his inked hands and arms, but plagued by the trouble in his beautiful amber eyes. She wanted him to reveal his truths to her, as Dalton had begun to do so more easily. The Prince of the First was more likely to lay bare than the Legion Head of the First. It was an interesting dichotomy.

She moved an inch closer to him, that undeniable tug to go to Dalton building within her chest. But she knew she could not seek his comfort, not here and not now, with so many prying eyes. Dalton was the King of the First Kingdom, and following the laying to rest of those who had fallen three months ago, he would take the crown for himself without delay.

Tomorrow, he would be officially crowned.

A part of her was terrified of the prospect, but not because she was fearful of what he would do as King. If anything, he would be an incredible King. He took initiative, possessed forward thinking, and he laced every word with an undeniable fervor for life. She was possessive of the boy that had brought her back to life these months, and he had not even done anything drastic. He had simply been there.

And being there was more than she had before. It was more than enough.

She grabbed Randolph's arm for support as they stepped forward to pay their respects. Hundreds of eyes glanced in their direction. Charmaine heard her name whispered amongst the lips of those in the royal court.

Dalton and Elena bowed at King Ronan and Queen Aine's closed caskets; they did not touch them, though, as it was ceremonial. A smile tugged at the corner of Charmaine's mouth as pride swarmed within her at Dalton not giving his parents one last look at dignity. They had done nothing to earn the respect of the King of Snow.

Randolph walked slowly as they rounded toward a violet casket which sat in the corner of the throne room.

"Are you ready for this?" he whispered, his eyes nearly bloodshot from the tears he had clearly shed before this.

Charmaine lifted her thumb and ran it over the single tear that dripped down his cheek. "Why are you crying?" she asked, afraid he would push her away.

He had opened up to her more and more these past three months, an anchor for her when Dalton had been whisked away. She knew he still had secrets—and dark ones—but he had shown her his true personality. He was honest, kind, and a fierce friend. She cherished him, and even though she could not find the words to tell him as such in this moment, she hoped he knew.

"You do not deserve the hurt you have taken on. The weight of it is so heavy. I cannot imagine having to bear that type of pain alone."

She smiled, bringing her mouth to kiss the tip of his nose. "I am not alone. I have you to help me up when I fall down, remember?"

"I remember." Another tear fell down his tanned skin.

"Come, let us say goodbye," she said, strength guiding her every step.

They approached James Grimes' casket with hesitation. Their strides matched in synchrony, as did their breathing. She held Randolph's hand tightly, her thumb running over his tattoo for James with rhythmic precision.

Standing before it was different than it had been looking at a distance. The casket was beautiful, a true tribute to the man her brother had been. It was violet and covered in golden swords. A mark of honor, even in death.

With a thin hand on the casket, she used her free one to wipe the tears free falling from her eyes. She leaned forward, pressing her lips and then her forehead to her brother's casket. She silently prayed to the Gods to watch out for him, give him guidance and strength wherever he went. She and James had never been privy to stories of the afterlife; they had always been so focused on the present. She hoped, though, that if there was an afterlife, that James had found it.

She stood, with Randolph holding her tightly around her waist as she breathed through the sobs that wracked her body.

"I'm going to say goodbye," he murmured in her ear. He was asking permission to let go, just for a moment.

She nodded, wrapping her arms around her chest in an embrace. He did the same as she had, his powerful hands touching the casket as he prayed to the Gods. She did not know what he was saying, or if he was saying anything at all, but she was grateful he was here regardless.

He stepped back after a moment of silence and reached his hand to extend to hers. As she grabbed it, a chill was sent through her spine. She knew Dalton was behind her without even turning, the draw altering her to his closeness.

She kept her gaze focused on the casket as the King of Snow came into view. He did not look at her as he approached James, his focus set and his brows furrowed. His eyes were clear of tears, despite being clouded by fury and despair. He leaned down, his white hair spilling wildly over his crown. It was decorated with silver leaves, diamonds intricately placed on the steel that bound it together. He closed his eyes, and the mere sight of him bowing before her brother knocked the wind out of her lungs.

A King was bowing to a commoner.

She could barely hear the whispers around her, but she knew they were there. Kings never approached the knights' caskets at funerals. Randolph had warned her as such. He was trying to protect her, keep her from additional sorrow if Dalton did not acknowledge her. It was not that Dalton owed her anything, not publicly, anyway. But this act, this testament of friendship and love, it meant the world to her.

Dalton stood up slowly after he finished his prayer to the

Gods, his eyes closed as he breathed out slowly. Only Randolph and Charmaine were close enough to see the white smoke that came out of his nostrils. He was releasing power; clearly, he was fighting something internal today.

He turned his back to extend his long fingers, and Elena emerged from the masses to grab them. Her face was veiled in darkness, but Charmaine could see the anguish on her face. She took Dalton's hand with precision and grace—the interaction of a King and Queen. The draw thrummed through Charmaine's veins so intensely that she held on tighter to Randolph, afraid that if he let go, she would collapse.

"I have you. Do not worry, I have you," Randolph whispered in her ear so low that only she could hear it.

Elena stepped forward toward James and placed a hand on his casket just as Dalton had. Instead of removing her veil to kiss it and pray, she beckoned Dalton closer. They stood together, two best friends who were forced together in the name of a madman's agenda, and they bowed as one.

Charmaine gasped as another sob took her, but she refused to bury her face in Randolph. She needed to watch. She needed to see.

They lifted their heads as one, the masses that had gathered behind them completely silent. Elena removed her hands from the casket and turned to face her husband. Dalton smirked at his wife, his eyes blazing with that familiar damning mischief that made him so intoxicating. He bowed his head to his wife, and Elena simultaneously plucked the thin crown off the King's head.

The crowd gasped, as did Charmaine and Randolph, while Elena turned to face James' casket again and placed the crown on top of it.

They turned, without a word or a glance at anyone but each other, and grabbed one another's hands. It was a signifying moment, a stand against the world his father had built. It was a defamation of tradition and the forging moment of a new world they were going to build.

And with that, they walked from James' casket, signifying the funeral procession was over.

53

SEVEN

atching her during the funeral procession broke something within Randolph that he did not know existed—a piece of him that he thought was lost forever and healed again with his tattoos. Randolph refused to touch Charmaine once they made it back up to the courtyard, afraid of what he would do to her frail frame as she shook violently walking toward the South Wing.

His fire had been completely out of control, and his emotions so heightened, he did not trust himself not to slip up.

He had practically shoved her onto Lawton when they saw him, for he too was wrecked by the display of the new King and Queen of the First Kingdom. Randolph had been in awe of Elena and Dalton plucking the crown off his head and giving it to James. It had been an unbelievable message, a moment that would be discussed for centuries to come across all Ten Kingdoms.

It was not easy to hold bitterness in one's heart when the world had just witnessed such grace. The King and Queen wanted a fair world. They wanted a just world. And those who were fair and just, as James had been, would be rewarded like Gods. Randolph did not believe in much anymore, and what he did believe in he questioned, but he knew that much was true.

Holding her in his arms had been too much for his heart. He had not been needed like that—by anyone—for years. It was as wondrous as it had been punishing.

He had to remind himself throughout the funeral that he was the one who told her James was dead. His memory and guilt were his punishment for it. He hoped it was the final punishment for his life of sin. He was terrified of losing her; he could feel it with each step he took behind her. Every glance he stole at her seemed to take her further away, that fear of happiness being stolen from him thundering against the back of his mind constantly. She was withering, and his friendship with her by association caused him to wither too.

He sat with her as much as she requested, holding her in silence if that was what she needed. He would never be the cause of her pain again.

He vowed it.

She was stronger than she looked, despite being broken within. And he begged the Gods silently for her peace. He could almost see the sun rising on her face again when she spoke, her familiarities coming back little by little. She was recognizable now, even if she still bore the ramifications of such a loss.

He spotted Dalton's white hair from afar, on the outskirts of the funeral dwellers as he strode toward Charmaine. Randolph noted that his eyebrows had a white hue to them today, for they were normally a raven black.

That is odd.

His King was slipping, an icy wind blitzing through the air as he approached her. He laid a hand gently on her arm, touching her finger with one of his as he drew the girl away from Lawton.

Jealousy stirred within Randolph as Dalton pressed his lips to her ear to murmur something he could not make out. As much as he had come to care for the Prince, there was an innate distaste for their obvious affection for one another. He wanted that type of connection for himself; it had been so long since he had someone to lean on like that.

She nodded softly and closed her eyes as she took his hands and walked with him. She was broken, and this was her missing piece. The human that would glue her back together.

Randolph could not deny that part of him wished this was him; he played the role that Dalton got. Randolph accepted the truth that he knew—it could never be him. He did not deserve redemption. He did not believe he deserved her friendship, but here he was. He stuffed his hands in the pockets of his leathers indignantly, pushing away the temptation to reach out to her and beg for the forgiveness that she had already given him.

And he did not want her like that, he simply wanted her.

It was hard to accept what you knew was true, when you were certain to crumble all that you touched.

"She will be fine," Lawton said, appearing next to him without warning.

"I do not know if I will be," Randolph said indignantly, silently cursing Lawton for appearing without much care.

Dalton had not outwardly admitted that magic was allowed yet, though he had demonstrated and insisted on tolerance. Until it was adamantly safe to do so, Randolph would not exhibit his powers unless he was alone. It was too risky, and the people of the First would not be able to change overnight.

Lawton scoffed, tapping Randolph on his shoulder with his hand. "We can survive more than we think we are capable of."

"Survival can be relative. What is existing if you are not living?"

Lawton snickered, "So philosophical and pensive tonight, are we?"

Randolph's eyes blitzed to Charmaine and Dalton, who silently walked from the crowd together. They did not draw an eye, for they seemed to blend into the masses seamlessly. That was their energy together; natural yet stifled. There was something between them that was bigger than they both realized, a wall of some sorts which Randolph knew they were both trying to climb.

"I am afraid I have been pensive for a long time. Philosophical has never been who I am."

"I fear prophecy guides us all, whether we like it or not."

Randolph nearly snorted at the change in Lawton. Recently, he had been more focused, his energy less chaotic. Although his language and jokes were wildly unpredictable at best, he had not been up to his usual shenanigans. "Have you grown up in these last few months? I barely recognize the cocky young man I used to know."

Lawton's full lips grew wide in a grin. "I fear that times are upon us, and dark ones at that."

"You can feel it too then?"

"I cannot shake the feeling that I need to be centered and practice my gifts."

Randolph sighed, his shoulders sagging with the effort of Lawton's truth. They did need to practice, and soon. Randolph had tried to get at the sword more, but he needed to exert more of his power. Whether he liked to admit it or not, there was a time fast approaching where he might need them. Especially if the King opened up the world to the realm of magic.

"So, we train then."

"And so, we train."

EIGHT

Dalton thrust the door open to his chambers with a menacing smile, enjoying every second of the thrill of being improper. He cast a quick flurry of snow as they opened the door, so nobody would make out who was going inside.

He was getting damn good at managing his powers, controlling the primal urges to lash out. Cyril had told him that Cian had taken years to achieve the type of precision he was able to execute. It gave Dalton a sense of sick satisfaction that he was a faster learner than the famous King Cian, but it also terrified him. What would the expectation from the world be when they learned he was more powerful than the most famous King of all time?

He shook his head slightly, pushing it out of his mind as he led Charmaine toward the loveseat in his chambers. Finally, they could get some peace away from the crowds. He had the full intention of returning her to the funeral—they could not be long—but he had to talk to her.

And he could not do it after such a display of power with Elena.

She threw her arms around him, shaking with sobs as she whispered *Thank you* over and over in his ear.

Holding her tight, his lean arms wrapped around her frail frame. He needed to make sure she took care of herself today, that she remembered to take care of herself tonight and tomorrow. Getting to this point—the funeral—had been challenging. But the real difficulty settled in tomorrow, when he wore the crown, and the focus turned away from those who died.

He would never let the memory of James cease to be a mere sentence in one of the Thinker's books. *A casualty of the battle of Brinn*, they would try to call him. No. Dalton would not allow it.

"You gave your crown to him." She pulled back, sitting down abruptly on the velvet white loveseat with a *thump*. The train of her gown spilled around her wildly, swallowing her up with darkness.

"It was the least I could do for him," Dalton said softly, crouching down to meet her gaze.

He could not fit on the velvet couch next to her while she wore that gown. And he figured it was best if he did not touch her right now. The draw was still so ambiguous between them, and he had not touched her since she had turned invisible.

Well, he had touched her, but not like *that*.

And today was not the day for that, despite them being alone.

"I will be thanking you for the rest of my life."

"He did not deserve what happened to him, Charmaine. You know I will do all within my power to keep him alive for all of us."

"You immortalized him by doing that." It was an admittance, an understanding.

"It was Elena's idea to go up together, but it was my idea

to give him my crown. I am sure I will hear about it from Cyril later."

She huffed a laugh, but it did not meet her gaze. "You will be King tomorrow. How are you feeling?"

He nearly fell over.

Ten Kingdoms, this girl. She just said goodbye to her brother at his funeral, and here she is asking if I am okay?

"Charmaine, I am fine."

"You do not look fine." Her brows were furrowed, the dark circles under her reddened eyes enhanced with the expression.

"Thanks, darling, that is very nice of you."

"That is not what I meant. Your eyebrows . . . they look lighter." She reached out to touch him, and he moved backward.

He would not touch her. Not today, especially.

"Shit."

He stood up quickly, striding over to the mirror on his desk. He picked it up, and Gods-be-damned, she was right. Clear as day, there were gray hairs that blurred with his usual black eyebrows.

When had this started? What did it mean?

"It does not look bad." She stood and smoothed her dramatic skirts.

He noticed her hands were shaking slightly.

Was she nervous?

Her fingers slowly picked at the pieces of her gown that needed to be flattened. It was odd to see her so meticulous now, especially in front of him.

He laughed, tipping his head back and letting the sound fill the room, pushing away any clouding thoughts. "I could care less about it adding to my good looks, Char. I am more concerned about why it is turning the color of my hair."

He breathed in, and on the exhale, he released a small blast of cold air. It fogged in front of him, smoking and dissipating into the air quickly.

This is not the focus of today. We need to get back to the party. People are going to notice we are gone, and I will not have any more whispers about her. Not today. Not ever.

"Do you feel . . . in control?"

He paused, rather surprised by the forwardness of her question for a moment before remembering who he was talking to. "Yes, I have been getting more comfortable."

"If the shoe fits," she whispered with a smile.

He returned it. "What a funny expression. I guess that Cian's shoe does fit . . ."

"You wear his shoes well."

"They are mighty large to fill." Dalton inhaled a breath before changing the subject, willing himself to relax. "Do you want to return to the party? Or would you like me to cause a scene and take you back to your chambers to tuck in for the evening?"

Charmaine's violet eyes twinkled in the candlelight, and despite the dark circles that sat beneath them, she looked more awake than she had since James died. "Since when did you become such a gentleman?"

Faking chest pains, Dalton stuttered with a laugh, his voice rising in volume. "Charmaine, I have always been a gentleman when it comes to you."

Now it was her turn to laugh. "I suppose you have. I simply mean that you do not have to keep treating me like I am broken glass. I will be fine. I am no stranger to this type of pain."

Furrowing his brows, he began to reach to take her hand, and then paused. She looked at it, noticing he stopped the movement. Dalton cleared his voice. The hand he had retracted lightly smacked the apex of his chest in exaggeration. "Just because you're familiar with pain does not mean it should be considered something natural."

"I think we both think of it that way, whether we want to or not."

"Whatever do you mean?"

"I have not forgotten that . . . that your father hit you, Dalton. You were beaten." Her voice was stern, sadness draping through every word as it shone through her violet gaze.

Dalton sighed. "But I survived."

"But you cannot tell me the wounds are fully healed. Yet, physically, they may be." Using her pointer fingers, she pointed to opposite temples on the side of her head. "It is in here. I know it is."

"You know, royals like my father and noblemen like ghastly Lord Peach would argue that commoners of the Ten Kingdoms are simple folk."

She raised a dark eyebrow in irritation with the comment.

Continuing, he pushed on with a smirk. "But I would argue that royals and rich men are the simple folk, for thinking the world is black and white. You see all the colors of the world, do you not, Charmaine? And you embrace it."

"I think you see the same colors, Dalton."

"You do not have to be afraid," he whispered for what felt like the millionth time, but he knew he had to say it regardless. "Your power . . . I will never hurt you for it. Those days are over—"

Her cheeks heated, flushing quickly against the porcelain of her skin. "I know . . . I just do not feel ready."

Dalton extended a hand to her, as a flower bloomed out of snow he had generated with his palm. Before she had the chance to reach out and grab it, he threw his hand up in the air, and the snow fell around them calmly.

"I used to be scared of my ability, particularly when I was first let out. I could not quite control it, for it seemed to feed off of my emotions."

"Does it not still?"

"It does." He smiled to himself at some of the blizzards he had created. The awesomeness of the power was overwhelming at times, yet he refrained from telling her that. He wanted to encourage her, not scare her with how intense it could be—if he let it. "But I have found that with practice, especially now that I am not contained, I am able to keep it at bay."

"It is not that I do not want to. I always thought it was something to hate myself over."

He nearly took a step forward to embrace her, but he shoved the thrum of the draw away so she could continue.

"I never thought it would be something to celebrate. My power is not as expressive or beautiful as yours."

He was rather taken aback by the comment. "You think my power is beautiful?"

"I think it can be, as you wield it for goodness."

"I think you should consider practicing, embracing it. There is no rush, though. I can go with you to any sessions as you would like." Feeling confident, he decided to venture. "You told me when James and yourself escaped Brinn, he suggested you go to a castle so you could be trained."

She smiled at the memory. "Yes, he was rather insistent that it was a good idea, despite the fact that he had no basis for that statement whatsoever."

Dalton chuckled quietly. "Well, it is a new age. I think we could make that happen, if you desired."

"You would do that? For me?"

"Power should be embraced, never shamed."

"Dalton—" she started, her eyes pleading for something Dalton knew he could not explore further.

He cleared his throat and extended his bent arm, gesturing for her to take it. "We need to get back."

She grabbed his jacket, and as she did, a current pulsed between them. Her lips parted in surprise, a soft gasp escaping her throat. The draw was alive and full of warmth, sending a jolt down each of their arms. They spread apart quickly, looking at one another in a mix of wonder and horror.

Dalton cleared his throat, feeling uncharacteristically uncomfortable. His heart thundered in his chest irregularly, his breath hard to catch as if he were running.

"I told myself I would not touch you, Char, but I figured you could at least grab onto my jacket."

"You told yourself you would not what?" she asked, horrified.

He strode toward his chamber doors as he propped it open for her. "After you, my lady."

She walked ahead of him, her dark gown reflecting its hue onto the white walls. He was two steps behind her. Watching her casually walk through the halls filled his heart with pride. She turned around, catching him smiling, and raised a dark eyebrow.

"Is something funny, your Majesty?" she asked.

He nearly choked. *Was she flirting with him?* It was as if she had drunk the root of the lily again, her eyes hazy and her lips pulled back into a smirk that he only knew on his own face.

"I did not know you could smirk, Miss Grimes," he said. "I was admiring the confidence as you walked down the hallway. You are admirable." He could have sworn she flushed, but it was hard to tell with the candles lighting the hallway.

She paused, turning to face him, and curtsied. "Thank you. Your admirations are received."

He stepped forward, resisting the urge to move her curls out of her face. "But are they accepted?"

She smiled softly, her hands folded in front of her waist. "I will always accept compliments from you."

It took everything in him not to grin like an idiot.

She made another step forward, her violet gaze deeper in the darkness. She had no shadows under her eyes tonight, as if she had evaporated her demons, despite all she had gone through. Her strength propelled him forward, inspiring him. He was moved by her breaking points as well. She had been embarrassed the first few times she had lost her composure to her grief. But there was nothing to be ashamed of in expressing feelings, and she had reminded Dalton of that importance.

Being true to oneself was everything, and if honesty was not reality, one might as well be nothing.

Pointing a long finger, he gestured down the hallway. "We should get back," he whispered. "Before someone thinks we are up to no good."

She leaned closer. It took everything in him not to meet her halfway. "You are always up to no good."

He huffed a laugh, avoiding eye contact. The draw was strong tonight. He had felt her amongst the crowd without even laying eyes on her. If he had been blind, he would have found her. If she had been elsewhere, he would have known.

Cian save me. Why is being King so Gods-damned complicated?

"You are right."

Unannounced, he began to walk down the hallway, praying to Ciara that she would follow. If they stayed, he would do something stupid. And he did not have time for mistakes, not this night.

A moment passed, and he heard her heels clicking on the floor behind him. She followed him slowly, cautiously. Whatever had just transpired between them—a moment of flirtation, he supposed—he had to put a stop to it. Insecurity flushed through him, his mind somersaulting and spiraling. He hoped she did not take offense to him not entertaining the prospect.

He wanted to kiss her, but now was not the time. It was wrong to lead her on like that, to give her hope that he could provide her what she deserved when he had nothing to offer. Especially after she had said her final goodbye to her brother. He would not play with her emotions like that, stringing her along when he was clearly fumbling through this new life. Dalton would not disrespect Charmaine, nor stand for anyone taking advantage of her, subjecting her to foul treatment from those at the castle that lived life arbitrarily. Even if she wanted to kiss him like he wanted to kiss her.

She leaned in, after all, or did I merely imagine it?

They exited the hallway, this time Dalton ahead of Charmaine. He paused, looking around the room for on-lookers. By the work of the Gods themselves, nobody had realized he had returned to the party yet. He bowed before her, hoping his eyes conveyed all that he could not say. Leaning forward, he kissed her on the hand lightly. Her violet eyes widened, and he supposed she felt exactly what he did.

His chest constricted, the tug of the draw almost unbearable. It was a constant ache, but now, it was not ignorable. It took everything within his power to stand up straight, forcing a relaxed expression all over his body. He was suddenly grateful for the years of playing the role as the prince locked away, for shielding his emotions was second-nature to him. The perfect practice for being King.

"Your Majesty," she said with clenched teeth, as if she

was rigid with pain. "Congratulations once again on your crown. I will see you tomorrow."

He forced a toothless smile, knowing that if he opened his mouth, the draw would overwhelm him. He deemed in that moment that he was the biggest idiot in the Ten Kingdoms, especially when it came to this girl. Sense went out the window whenever he was alone with her, yet being with her was like being doused with a bucket of cold water. It was a stark reminder of how vastly different they were, yet he welcomed it every single time. She was a shock to his system. He prayed for the strength to not keep coming back to it, for it could never be as he wished.

She lifted her gaze, accepting with a twinge of sadness in her eyes that he would not dignify her with a response. Bowing her head one more time, she strode toward the party, leaving Dalton frozen and cursing himself for all that he could not have.

***

Elena Leclair might as well have been dancing in darkness. Her ballgown had been hand-selected and designed by herself. It was a commemoration of James Grimes' life, beautiful and as black as the thick eyelashes that used to veil his violet gaze.

She knew she was beautiful, though her heart was so heavy she was not sure she felt anything at all.

Gazing at Lord Ambrose, stoic as always with a black beard and dark skin, Elena tried to wipe away any emotion that may reveal how broken she truly was. As a Queen, it was her political obligation to put on a brave face in the name of adversity.

"Are you preparing for your ascension soon, Queen Elena?" Lord Ambrose asked, his voice filled with inquisition.

Rapidly cleansing herself of all irritation that built within her at the question, she opened her mouth to reply, when all she saw out of the corner of her eye was the darkest of flower tattoos. Her eyes darted from the handsome face of the Lord and landed upon the amber gaze of the King of the Seventh Kingdom.

She would never tell Randolph to his face that his title was how she thought of him, even though it was not something he had obtained recently. Being royal was like being a part of a cult, which one either relished in the opportunity to be a part of, or felt like it was a prison cell. Most of the time, she felt like the latter. She guessed Randolph felt the same. Trapped. Boxed in. She would never make anyone feel that way.

"May I cut in, Lord Ambrose?" Randolph said quietly, exuding so much charm that Elena thought she must be dreaming.

Turns out he did have a political face, and now she was seeing it. And she could not say she hated what she was seeing.

She made a mental note never to admit that to him.

"Of course, Sir Randolph."

"No need for formalities, Lord Ambrose," he said softly, taking Elena's arm in one swoop.

Elena could not help herself, suddenly feeling lighter in his grasp than she had all night.

As they began to dance to the rhythm of the slow string's music, she asked, "Did you want to dance with me, *sir*, or do you have something to say?"

"Can I not dance with the Queen of the First Kingdom?"

She swore she saw a twinkle in his eye.

"Have you been drinking?" she asked, suddenly concerned for Randolph's wellbeing.

"Immensely."

"Ah," she whispered, now smelling the wine on his breath. "You know, it is okay not to be okay."

"I do not need a therapy session right now, Elena."

She stopped; her feet were stuck in the same place by the tone in his voice. It reminded her of something, but she could not place it. She knew it was not a memory—for this moment had never happened before—yet it was the equivalent of déjà vu.

Randolph paused with her, his hands coming onto her forearms as he took a deep inhale and exhale. "I am sorry. I am quite . . . tense this evening. I am not quite—"

"Yourself," she finished for him.

"Yes," he said with a sad smile, his gaze suddenly heavy with whatever weighed on him. "Enough about me, I actually . . . I wanted to check-in on you."

"Check-in?" she said as they resumed dancing in one another's arms, slowly rocking and twirling to the beat of the music.

They were in perfect harmony with one another, their bodies curled together, fitting like the white marble stones that were cut to build the castle walls.

"Your mother is not here."

"Thank the Gods."

"It must be hard to be without family in a place that is not your home."

Raising an eyebrow she quipped, "Are you speaking of yourself, or of me?"

The side of his mouth quirked up. "I suppose both. I am . . . struggling this evening, Elena. I figured you above all would understand."

"I do not think we are exclusive to struggling."

Leaning closer, Elena was consumed with the smell of wine and ash. "But, you know what it is to be lost. You know what it is to be controlled and shoved into a service you did not ask for, though you are solely responsible for getting yourself to your current destination."

"Randolph Eniar, are you suggesting I am just as broken as you?"

"I am suggesting we may have more in common than you think."

She huffed a laugh. "You know, I thought when you came over here to interrupt, you were going to give me some type of damning intelligence on my husband."

Randolph barked a laugh, and Elena nearly jumped. She had never seen him so relaxed.

How much wine did he drink?

"I do not have anything damning at the moment. He has somehow been on his best behavior."

Now it was Elena's turn to lean forward, her lips nearly an inch from his mouth as she whispered into his ear, "He is *never* on his best behavior."

"Your Majesty, it is time to retire to your chambers," a voice rang out behind her.

Pulling her head away from Randolph, she met the gaze of Greyson Althan. "Greyson," she said without any adoration in her voice.

She could feel Randolph chuckling softly as they twirled one final time, before they paused. Lifting a tattooed hand, he bowed slightly to Elena in a dignified manner. So proper, it almost made Elena sick with shock.

Almost.

Kings did not bow to Queens; it was just the order of things.

"Go with Greyson," he urged. "The party shall be winding down any moment, and Dalton will want you to be safe."

Lifting the dark corners of her dress's skirt, she curtsied. By the time she lifted her gaze to meet his again, he was already striding away, a glass of wine in hand.

NINE

he grief was so heavy sometimes that it was suffocating.

Elena Leclair breathed in deeply, trying to shake it off for not the first time this day. She closed her eyes as she tried to wash it away. She made her mind play images of joy: the first time she met Dalton, playing in the courtyard with Meredith when she had been years younger, her mother giving her a crown fit for her coming of age ball . . . There was so much good in Elena's life, yet the bad as of late seemed to overtake it.

She dipped her head as she exhaled, letting all the ugliness within her go as she tried to reframe her mindset with the good. Sorrow escaped her when she was not breathing, the stillness of the wind grounding her. She could see everything, but she was removed—an outsider looking in on the world as it passed her by.

But when she lifted her head, her auburn hair spilling around her and flowing down the tops of her shoulders, sorrow broke through once again. And she could not bear the weight of this pain for more than a few moments before lashing out with her powers.

Coughing behind her, she shot a gaze full of pure death

at Greyson Althan. The young man did not look at her, nor did he impede on her methodology for coping. He simply sat in the corner, his hands on his leathers, watching the ground until she stood. There was no way he was oblivious to what she was doing, but he never said anything about it. He was professional, and he was merely assigned to keep her safe.

Elena was not bothered to continue questioning why Dalton, her husband, had sent a man to her balcony to take care of her, but she knew nonetheless. Greyson was a force to be reckoned with on the battlefield. He was lethal, a legend amongst the young members. He was not as talented as Randolph Eniar, but he was a commoner, and that was a feat to be acknowledged. Randolph had many secrets that kept an edge on his persona and rank, despite what he would have his men and women believe.

Elena was grateful for the protection, for Greyson never made her feel uncomfortable as a woman.

As a Queen.

Though she would not give Dalton the satisfaction of being grateful for the protection and company. At first, she had been wildly offended, then he had told her his reasoning. There were too many uncertainties, and he was not about to lose anyone else he loved. She was safe, even though she did not deserve to be.

James was dead, and she was alone with the memory of her visions.

Dalton and Elena had mutually agreed to dismiss her chambermaid Meredith after they returned from Brinn. She needed the protection of someone with skill, someone to give Dalton peace of mind. Elena understood the sentiment, and if he was not so heavily guarded himself as the King of Snow, she would have requested that he hire a personal bodyguard as well.

In the past three months, she had berated Cyril with questions that received no answers. She demanded to know why James had left her, what prophecy was in store for her, and if there was anything she could do to get him back.

Cyril had told her in many more words that he did not know, he had no prophecy, and she could never get him back.

Elena had lifted her fist to hit him, completely unjustified in her nature, and Dalton had whisked her back to her chambers before she could strike. She had screamed—blood-curdling and devastated. She had nothing if not her power, and even that would not bring back the things she wanted.

Her inner peace and James Grimes.

"We cannot have the Queen of the First Kingdom attacking the King's only friend," he had whispered.

Elena had wanted to punch him then too, that ridiculous humor he wore like armor as a shield to the rest of the world. It was so irritatingly charming that she hated it as much as it brought her comfort.

Feeling more composed than she had been when she left the ballroom at the end of the festivities, Elena turned to face Greyson with her usual stoic face. She crossed her arms and lifted her head high, refusing to show Greyson she had been affected by her emotions in such a way.

She stepped toward him slowly, the gown she wore dancing behind her.

"Greyson," she said, her voice hoarse.

His eyes roamed up to her face in hesitation, blinking twice, his full lips parting slightly. Elena realized this was the first time she had spoken to him without giving a command. She noted his green eyes flashed with understanding, his lips tightening across his mouth as he took in all that she was. A Queen, married, but deserted like a widow.

He moved a piece of his long black hair out of his face and tucked it behind his ear. It had fallen loose from his ponytail which was neatly tucked behind the nape of his neck. He bowed his head, his emerald gaze never leaving her own.

"My Queen," he whispered.

"I wish to go for a walk."

She was not sure why she was asking, despite not posing the phrase like a question, other than the solitude of the moment prior had pushed her to the brink of losing it once again. She had completely removed herself from most people. These moments alone under the water were the only time she felt truly herself.

She had given up on practicing her powers in the last few months, leaving her constantly aching for something more. There was no way Greyson could know the depths of who she truly was: someone who carried three gifts from the Gods. She was ready to begin her ascent back to the light, even if she would never admit that to anyone. She had found enjoyment in the numbness of grief, its pleasure sufficient and its capabilities vast.

Elena knew she was not ready to take on such responsibility, such as the crown she wore atop her head like Dalton, so soon after the chaos which had ensued. He was stronger than her. He was better than her. And for the first time in her life, she had no issue admitting that.

Tomorrow would be different. Today had been the funeral, the final moment to lay to rest all that had happened.

Did she feel better? Did she feel complete? Did she have closure? No.

If anything, the wound in her heart had opened and closed, then reopened again a thousand times during the procession. But seeing she was not alone made the depths of her grief nearly unbearable. The numbness faded with each step, a fragmentation of herself coming back with every waking moment.

She turned to stride toward the grand white doors of her chambers—the Queen's chambers—when Greyson stepped before her. His pale skin glistened in the candlelight, and his emerald eyes deepened with worry.

"You are blocking your Queen," Elena said vehemently. "Do I need to ask you to bow? To remember who it is you are talking to?"

"My Queen, with all respect, it is late." His eyes danced dangerously, his voice cool in tone.

Elena looked down, a laugh escaping her mouth for the first time in a long time.

Ten Kingdoms. She was losing her mind.

"Is it not proper for a Queen to walk whenever she wants? What do we have to fear, Greyson?" She smirked, that familiar fire returning to her dark features.

Greyson gulped, and she knew it was not fair to prey on her personal guard. But she was so broken, and she had nothing. Greyson could be her everything if she let him in.

"I am afraid the King would have my head if I were to let you walk the grounds this late, your Majesty," he said softly. His hands were interlaced behind his back, unwilling to touch her if she made a move forward.

Elena smiled sweetly; all the sarcasm she could bring forth doted on her tongue. She leaned forward, so close to his ear that she could hear her own breath beating against his skin. "The King does not put a leash on his wife. Now out of my way." She paused, feeling dangerously relaxed and daring with the knowledge she had. "The King is not even here. He ditched his guards hours ago. Did you know that?"

"Ten Kingdoms," he hissed through his teeth, standing in front of her to block the door.

Elena's soul ignited with her familiar persona. She found herself raising an eyebrow at the young knight, despite her best efforts to remain neutral. Instantaneously, his expression changed, clearly reading her own and finding surprise in it.

"Please," he whispered again, gesturing toward her dressing cabinet. "At least put on a coat."

Without another glance in his direction, she found herself gliding over obediently. She did not have it in her to fight back, to bring forth that fire within her fully. But the eyebrow raise had been a start, and for the first time in three months, she felt as though she were putting on an old glove that fit perfectly.

"Fine," she grumbled, picking out a soft, yellow, tulle gown from the cabinet. She dropped her robe without warning, ensuing a plethora of soft curse words from Greyson, then slid into the fur overcoat without further delay.

Spinning around she uttered, "I am ready for my walk."

***

They walked together almost in complete silence, as they did every evening that Elena requested to do so. The quiet was an unspoken rule, and they never did it with intent.

Elena did not know much about Greyson beyond what he had told her on the surface; he was a talented knight, and he was hand-selected to protect her from harm.

Scoffing, she rolled her eyes at the memory. As if she needed protecting from anyone.

"Is something the matter, your Majesty?"

Wiping the smirk off her face, she replied casually, "Just thinking about how I am to embrace the doings of my husband and run from you."

Greyson turned a sickly pale, and it brought Elena joy. There was no way he was not picturing some type of frozen repercussion from the King, even though they were not married out of love. Or that Dalton had ever hurt someone out of punishment. She had half a mind to request Randolph as her personal guard over Greyson. At least she knew he would not talk to her—despite their dance this evening. At least he would respect her space.

"I am kidding, Greyson. It is okay to make jokes and laugh."

"Your Majesty, I am just trying to do my job."

His eyes shone with pure honesty. She could not fault him for that.

"You are doing a fine job," she said in earnest. Lifting her wrists and hands, she showed him, "See? My hands are attached. No scars. No bruises. I am as healthy as a horse."

Now it was his turn to scoff.

Rounding the corridor once again, out of prying eyes from the general public of the court, they kept walking in tandem. Their silence that had momentarily been broken by a good-natured jest resumed once more.

And as they departed for the evening and Greyson returned her to her chambers for sleep, Elena somehow felt like the pain of the last few months was beginning to wash away with the friendship she was not ready to fully embrace.

TEN

Dalton tried to stay away. He really did.

Yet, here he was like it was three months before, in the middle of the night, frolicking to Charmaine's chamber most improperly. He guessed it was well past midnight by now, but it was a day for celebration—being his coronation and all—so it was not peculiar to him that people were still bustling throughout the castle at this damning hour.

He had returned to his chambers as a reformed king, someone who despite the distance between them could respect that their stations were now formidably inadequate for one another. Yet, he still stood at the precipice of his bed and could not stop his mind from spiraling. Despite everything—politics, social status, hierarchy, and the millions of reasons why he could never have her—he still did.

Grunting, he paced back and forth for a minute. He even created ice caps on his fingertips in order to find release, to get rid of the pent-up energy that continued to ravage his mind away from duty.

With a snarl to nobody in particular, Dalton said, "Am I really going to do this?"

Yes. Yes, he was.

***

Dalton was now the King of the First Kingdom, yet he still let the whims of shenanigans overtake him with little to no convincing.

Throwing a black cloak with a large sweeping hood over himself and changing into the clothes that he believed made him look normal, Dalton grabbed the arm of the girl who had lost everything and made his way into the town of Thallgan.

He had approached her door sheepishly—though he had never been shy before in his life—and rather commanded to her that they were to have fun this evening. She had lit up, to Dalton's surprise, at his chaotic suggestion that they escape. And without another glance behind her, they were off.

As they descended the winding road to the village below, Dalton found himself making light chatter, though he was not saying anything of substance. Charmaine was passive in conversation, clearly letting her walls down, yet Dalton knew the implications of being alone together.

With The Beloved King in sight, Dalton found he had a lightness to his steps. Despite the horrid memories of what had happened here before, there was comfort in knowing his father was dead and could not hurt him again.

Holding the door, he ushered Charmaine inside. She wore a large, black, velvet cloak in a feeble attempt to make Dalton look like no one. The celebrations of the coronation were still underway, so Dalton did not feel as though he were in danger. Though he knew Cyril would lose it if he were to be discovered missing.

Oh, well, it would not be the first time.

With his face nearly completely covered by the hood, he lifted only a finger to gesture for two pints of ale. With steady hands, he lifted the drinks and brought them to the table where Charmaine sat. She removed her hood slowly, the wisps of her hair sticking out wildly. It was utterly adorable, yet Dalton knew he could not touch them, despite the fact that he wanted to push them back.

"Are you OK?" Charmaine asked, her violet eyes dancing with the light of the adventure he had instigated this night.

"I suppose so," he said softly. "I apologize for this . . . wall that has been between us as of late, Char."

She sat back in her chair, as though she were not expecting such a statement from him. "There is nothing to apologize about. You are the—"

"King," he finished for her with a sip of his ale, low enough that nobody would hear around them. "But I cannot help but feel as of late that you and I are not who we were three months ago—"

"We lost—"

"It's not about loss," Dalton said, cutting her off matter-of-factly. "There is distance between us. I did not want to acknowledge it prior because it was not natural in conversation, but—"

"And it is natural in conversation now? Why did you ask me here tonight, only to remind me of things which are damaging?" she asked, her voice raising an octave.

"The dust has settled a bit from the evening. I am merely thinking out loud at this point." He took another sip of his ale before continuing, "Rather rambling at this point."

"We are not normal, Dalton. Neither of us are."

Looking around the tavern, Dalton imagined what it was like to live among the townsfolk. Surely, he was at the tavern, but he was cloaked. His destiny had been written before he was even born. He carried the venom of a tragic power in his veins. He had gotten better at controlling it, but sometimes, it felt as though it were controlling him.

He supposed she was right, though the truth stung.

He was anything but normal.

Smiling softly, he leaned toward her, somehow able to drink in the smell of lavender that always followed her. "I do not want there to be this space between us."

Now it was her turn to drink a sip of her ale. "I do not think there is a way around it, Dalton."

Sitting back in his chair—pulling away—he picked up his chalice with both hands. "Distance will only grow if we let it."

"You have saved me more than you will ever know, and I am eternally grateful—"

"You have saved me too," he interrupted her, his mind wandering to the kiss in Brinn that had brought both of them back from invisibility.

"Let me finish," she said. "I am eternally grateful. You brought me back in more ways than you will ever know, but we have this distance between us because it is the way of things. I have been doing some thinking, Dalton—a lot of thinking—and I do not want to bring you down—"

"You do not want to bring me what?!" he shouted, before realizing he was supposed to be, by all accounts, discreet.

"I am a commoner, Dalton. A commoner with power, yes, power I am learning to embrace in a world where you are forging a better path for people like me . . ." She paused, taking a deep breath. "But there is a wall between us because I am putting it there just as much as you are putting it there. We are *different*. We are different in every way people can be different. I am so blessed and thankful to the Gods that our paths collided the way they have. But I cannot have you be what I think you need to be for me."

"That does not make sense." Dalton sneered, still holding his ale with two hands. "You have a beautiful life, Charmaine. A hard one, yes, but you have been reborn from the ashes more times than you give yourself credit for."

"Dalton—"

"Now, you let me finish, Charmaine. I have a wall up too, for I refuse to cause you more pain than you have already endured. I keep you at arm's length because without it, I do not know if I would ever let you go an arm's length away from me."

Flexing his free hand which did not touch his ale, he dreamt of reaching out and grabbing her hand for such a declaration. But he did not. Her cheeks flushed against the candlelight of the tavern, but he kept going, power building within him as he spoke the words he had been wanting to say for months but did not have the strength to say.

Taking a deep breath in, he continued, "I am sorry for bringing you here tonight. Your insinuations are correct that it is inappropriate. I merely—I merely care for our friendship, above all else that is between us. I do not want me being King to change that."

"It has, Dalton."

Before he had a chance to respond, she reached for him with the utmost care in the world.

And he snapped.

Without warning, the chalice he had been holding froze within a second and then cracked as though it were made of glass. Shards of ice tumbled to the cobblestone floors, as the ale it had contained fell with it.

Charmaine was speechless and pulled back her hand slowly.

"Your soul should not be tainted further by the darkness that enriches my veins."

"Whatever do you mean?"

Shaking his hands to rid himself of the ale that had spilled, he replied darkly, "I can feel the ice that resides within me. It burns sometimes, demanding to be released. There is so much built within me . . . I cannot explain what it is to have a power that is so full of life, but also full of harm."

He whispered so low that it was almost impossible to hear his own question, "Do you feel your power, Char? Do you feel it like I feel mine?"

***

Dalton walked back to his chambers as the sun rose, with his head hanging low and his cloak billowing behind him. Exhaustion danced through every muscle in his legs, every bone in his bone, and in every vessel of his brain.

He had walked Charmaine home in silence, afraid of what he might say if engaged once again in conversation with her.

What in the name of the Ten Kingdoms was wrong with me? How stupid was I for thinking we could go on a jaunt together without any implications? Yes, we were not discovered by anyone, but it was stupid nonetheless.

As he shoved open the doors to his chambers with a groan, it was none other than Cyril who sat on the bed.

"Where have you been, my liege?" There was no humor in his voice.

"Out."

"What in the name of the Gods do you mean *out*?" he shouted, and his hands balled into fists at his side. "You are the *King*! Do you not remember earlier when they placed the crown on your head? We assumed you were paying attention, but—"

Sitting down slowly against the wall, Dalton sank as Cyril's chiding subsided.

"What is it, Dalton?" Cyril said, concern filling his voice.

"I am afraid she and I are never going to climb the wall together."

And then he did something he had not done in many years.

He wept.

ELEVEN

alton dreamt of running through the castle walls without a crown on his head.

Much to his own dismay, he awoke with a crown at the foot of his bed, awaiting him, along with the rest of his dressings for the day.

"Cian save me," he muttered to himself impatiently, flopping over onto the other side of his bed.

Without noticing he was doing so, he grabbed a white curl that laid lazily in front of his eyes and began to twist it. Ignoring the duties of his kingship, he found himself rotating his shoulders and burying himself deeper under the comfort of his bedding. The chill that overcame him was torturous and slow, as if it were intentional. Dalton was unsure what made him think such a thing, though he thought it outwardly nonetheless.

"Ten Kingdoms, what is happening?" he cursed, flipping again, as his teeth began to chatter incessantly.

He nearly cried out for Cyril, not out of necessity, but out of comfort, when the faintest whisper of the wind danced over his upward facing ear.

"*Dalttonnnnn . . .*" the voice sang, drawing out the latter part of his name.

He froze, though the temperature of his body continued to drop. He opened his mouth to cry out again for the only person he had ever depended on, when the voice sounded again, more urgently.

"Daltonnnnnnnnnn . . ."

"Yes?" Dalton asked softly, his own voice matching the energy and design of the one that called out to him.

Despite his best efforts, he felt like he knew this voice from somewhere before. It seemed familiar, as if it were an old friend. Though he could not place it.

Standing up, his vision blacked out. With a fumbling hand, he grabbed the edge of his nightstand, barely holding onto any sense of reality as he fought to be upright.

"What the fu—"

The voice sounded again, the deep hiss scratching against his eardrums. With his free hand, he reached to hold his ears, as if that would do anything to stop the pounding and throbbing sensation of the cruel voice.

Dalton's vision flashed—he saw white scales and amber eyes against the darkness of his own mind. Claws scraped against the marble of the ground, sparking the floor of his bedroom with the most disturbing of noises. His shoulders rose instinctively as he found himself hissing in displeasure, the sensation of the collision of claw and stone unbearable to his ears.

He fought to open his eyes again, blinking rapidly until his vision came back to him in spurts. Sight toggled between fire and reality; the cold that had awoken him was now a burning that he could not put an end to. He tried to call out, incessantly trying to find reality again, but nothing came.

He swore he could hear a woman speaking in a language he did not understand, yet one he swore he had heard before. Growling and rumbling replied, though the woman's voice expressed pleasure at whatever had been communicated. Red hair draped down the woman's back—a fiery wave—and the cold chill of death enveloped him from within.

A part of him wanted to call out for Elena, though the woman that stood with her back to him had skin paler than the moonlight. She was also shapeless, her body elongated in ethereal perfection, so stoic she did not appear to be real. She did not have the muscles that Elena had, and none of the same fire that blazed within his wife. Instead, she oozed dark power. And cold.

She did not look real, though Dalton knew she had been.

With a gasp, his vision returned, no longer flashing strange images.

"Ten Kingdoms," Dalton whispered again, catching his breath as if he had been running. "What in the name of Cian was that?"

"*You must find me,*" the hissing drawled, as if it were lazy and patient.

Dalton flew onto his bed, momentarily disarmed by the intensity of the voice he had figured had gone with the imagery.

"And who might you be?" he asked softly, careful to keep his usual sarcastic tendencies out of his voice.

"*You must find me and speak my name,*" the voice repeated. "*You must do what she could not, and you must bring me forth to teach the will of the Gods.*"

"Where do I look?" Dalton asked the voice.

He prayed no servants, except Cyril, would enter the door. Surely, the whole kingdom would be privy to his own madness if they saw him speaking to himself on the morning of his own coronation.

"*You must go under the castle, and speak the language of my brethren.*"

Dalton almost tipped his head back and laughed, his body nearly entering shock with the heat that still burned within him.

As if in answer, the voice hissed once again, *"Read the diary of the Queen of Fury, and you shall find all you are looking for. Read the diary of the Queen of Fury, and you shall be prepared for the evils to come. Read the diary of the Queen of Fury, and better understand the fury of snow and the fury of fire. Read the diary, and all shall come to pass as it should."*

Dalton opened his mouth to reply—to what, he was unsure—but the voice and the heat left him at once. His familiar cold sensation exploded within him, coating every inch of his skin in the comforting embrace of winter's blessing. He wiggled his toes uncomfortably, his power coming back to him as if he were trying on an old shoe.

Sitting up, he ran an unconfident hand through his white hair, then got up to explore anywhere the castle could have a relic from the Queen of Fury.

TWELVE

thelred popped into Charmaine's chambers without a knock. She nearly screamed when he entered, his face wide with a peculiar grin. At her horror, she collected herself quickly, running her hands through her hair and thanking the Gods that she was not indecent. She somehow found herself apologizing, even though nothing was her fault. She made a note to tell Randolph later, so he could have another talk with him about knocking. If she told Dalton, she knew he would be sacked immediately.

"I have a gown for you, my lady, from the King." He looked nervous again, that weirdness wiped away.

Charmaine was determined to be patient with him, for he had been nothing but helpful for the past three months. He had even sat with Elena during that final battle in Brinn when the world had turned upside down.

But he was no Gwendolyn.

She stifled a gasp as she looked at the gown which he laid on her silk bed. It was a rich violet color, with long sleeves ordained by a number of encrusted diamonds that were meant to have her stand out amongst all of those in attendance for Dalton's coronation.

Athelred had turned around when she slid it up her grief-stricken body, but he helped her tie the corset on tightly. It was anything but uncustomary that a man be helping a woman tie her corset in this kingdom, yet times were changing, and Charmaine's kindness was all but traditional. She did not think it odd as some did. A person was a person, and Athelred was the person who was helping her.

"Come look, my lady. The King did a wonderful job. You look beautiful."

This gown, in its beauty and shine, felt like it was wearing her. No longer was she the young woman that wanted to shine against the crowned jewels of the kingdom. She wanted to hide among the shadows, praying one more person would not tell her what they thought she wanted to hear.

Sadly, she looked in the mirror as she touched her curls, once bountiful and now dreary. She blinked at the memory of Dalton's thin hands stroking her hair blindly, as if any touch in the world would not mend her heart but would remind her that he was there. Her heart lurched at the sight of him on a normal day, for he was the only man that brought her comfort like James did. Their friendship had grown exponentially since her arrival to the castle. James had been hiding secrets from her, and Randolph was sworn to duty. Dalton had been able to reign free for the first time in five years. And they had time to attach to one another, to figure out what was going on between them with the draw. Even three months later, they still did not have answers, but Cyril was working on it.

Dalton and Charmaine were connected forever by the moment they had both been thrust toward their destiny. Dalton had lost his parents; therefore, the role of King had been bestowed upon him. And she had lost her brother, her only family wiped from the continent. They had been able to find one another in their grief, for they had experienced it as one. Charmaine had held him when she should have found James and saved him. She did not realize before that she could take people with her, turn them invisible with contact and sheer will.

She thought of him, standing there frozen as he asked what he already knew. His eyes had blazed dark blue as he understood what she could do and who she really was. She had never thought of telling him before, but now that he knew, the draw between them was less urgent. It was a constant pulse, strengthening.

She was slowly coming to terms with the fact that she had taken him with her in her change because she was scared to death of losing him, and if the mercenaries could not take her, they would not be allowed to take him either.

But they took her brother. They took him from her in a finality she did not believe she would ever understand or comprehend.

Shuddering, she broke herself away from the nightmares of three months past. Athelred murmured something she failed to hear completely. She assumed by her looking back to admire her work at putting her back together, it meant that he had told her she was done.

That she was ready.

She was ready to watch Dalton become the man he was born to be.

The King of Snow.

She did not bother saying thank you, an immature comeuppance for him scaring her invisible earlier.

She tried to hide the shock on her expression as she looked at herself— really looked at herself. The dress that probably would have fit her before they arrived, hung around her waist as if it were the ghost of her former life. Her hair was dull, her skin gray, rather than its usual porcelain. Her violet eyes seemed dimmer somehow, as if the light behind them had not returned.

Ten Kingdoms.

Grief was a total body experience.

"My lady, are you ready?" Athelred asked, his voice wavering slightly, watching her analyze her new imperfections.

Charmaine prayed silently to the Gods that people would see her tonight and not offer her anything other than a glass of wine.

"As I will ever be," she said, trying to reassure her as Athelred saw the worry flash across her big eyes. She took a deep breath, putting her hands in front of her bodice and interlacing them.

She had not gone invisible since James died. But she knew if it came for her again, she would not fight it.

Dalton was King, and the world would become a better place.

She left her chambers, the doors closing behind her as she pushed herself to the throne room. She could see the masses of people beginning to enter, the door not capable of holding them all at once. She stood there, her head high, her eyes never leaving the head of the person behind her.

She could feel the stares, their eyes shifting toward her, then looking away.

Dalton coming to her chambers had been no secret—nothing with the King was—but she did not know it would cause such a stir. He had been adamant that it was none of the their business, but just because he said it did not deem it so.

"I will not live like my father made me. Sneaking around and hiding away, hiding those I love from my presence because it is improper or bolstering it because it is. This world is too messed up for me to bend to the will of random men and women who just want to gossip. Let them. My wife permits it."

He had paced reverently around the room, as he did every time he came to her, and she began to crave his presence. Unlike Randolph, he did not fear stepping too far, pushing her until she broke. He already knew she was broken, shattered with grief. Slowly, he had been putting the pieces back together the whole time by treating her like *her*. She came back, the memories of the last few months flashing before her. Entering the throne room, a long white velvet carpet draped the way to the throne.

She took a deep breath as a hand interlaced with hers seamlessly.

"Look who came out of her frozen dungeon," Lawton said with a smirk.

Charmaine snorted, rolling her eyes as she locked her gaze with him, letting him take the lead of their stride as they walked toward the front of the room.

Lawton had been a tether for her these past few weeks. He pushed her, yelled at her even.

"You need to get the hell out of this room. James would not want you to sit here like a sob story. He would want you to move on, do good in his memory, make your mark on this place. Instead, you sit here and waste away, shove everyone away from you that wants to baby you."

She had launched herself at him, punching and screaming, relentless because he was right. Looking at him now, it was hard not to be overtaken with emotion. He was harsh with her and rough, but he reminded her that she was real and that pain is realer.

It was natural to be blinded by rage and pain. But it did not have to cripple. When it did, the mercenaries won.

She thought of her mother promising her that the Gods would bow to her. Now she bowed before them. She was about to bow before the new God.

The King of Snow was back on the throne, and long may he reign.

"Stand here, darling. Let's get this show started." He winked as he grabbed two glasses of red wine from the waiter passing, handing it to her gently. "You need it, love. This is going to be a long night."

She rolled her eyes again and begrudgingly took a deep sip from the glass. She felt lighter already, the grief momentarily parted by the drink. She had not drunk anything since the dinner party where she had consumed the lily root with Dalton. Her cheeks deepened red at the memory of them, even last night. She had awoken almost ashamed of how she had been with him; it was most improper. But there was something about the two of them since they had experienced so much together . . . Charmaine could not put it to words, but the comfort and symphony that her heart felt when she was near him was enough to bring her to ruin.

Charmaine tried to ignore that he had that effect on her.

But it was nearly impossible.

Here she was with a friend, and she would not let it become a method to cope with loss. She squeezed Lawton's hand gently, reassuring him that she was okay. He could be harsh, but he was here. She needed him to know that whatever piece of her was still here, was here for him as well.

Suddenly, the trumpets began to sound at the back of the throne room. People stopped coming in at once, as if they were completely frozen by the God that walked amongst them.

Charmaine found herself frozen as well.

This was the man who promised himself to be whatever he needed to be for her, who stayed day and night in her chambers upon her request in order to ensure she would make it through the night, and the man that was her best friend.

She had never admitted it to him out loud. She had known for a while now, but never found the right moment. She had said it to him once, under the influence of wine and potions.

Somehow, she thought she had meant it then.

She looked at him, his pale features sparkling against the divinity of the decorum in the throne room. As he passed, his citizens could sense his power rumbling behind him. The wind sent an icy chill down their spines as they all collapsed into a bow. His dark blue eyes were focused, all remembrance of the nights past erased from under his eyes. His lips were flushed, as if he had been biting them on his way down to the throne room from his chambers. Charmaine blushed, knowing these little nuances about Dalton.

Dalton looked like the man he was born to be. The man he was about to become.

She tried to avoid making eye contact with him, for their conversation last night was still a fresh wound. This was his moment, one she knew he was not taking lightly.

She struggled—and was still struggling deeply—with the loss of James. Dalton did not struggle with the loss of his father or even his mother—he struggled with the change in his power. The weight of who he was crashing upon him before he had time to learn what it meant to be Dalton. His parents were nothing to him, but his power was everything, whether he accepted that or not. It was what kept him company, while the world passed by for all those years. It was the familiar hum and tug that made him feel grounded.

Charmaine knew it too well. And it had cost her.

He would never admit it to her, but she knew he had scars from the last five years. Being so isolated had without a doubt been the root of some of his antics, though she knew they were good-natured. He enjoyed being disrespectful, to play in moments where others would deem it inappropriate.

He relished in making people uncomfortable, enjoying every smirk and sarcastic remark that he could throw into even the most casual conversation.

She tried to avoid making eye contact with him as she rose softly with the crowd of his citizens. However, her violet gaze found his discreetly, for only a second. Her gaze would always find its way to him.

Her heart was brushed by a gust of icy wind. It was not angry, nor was it sad. It was grateful; somehow, she knew that. It cherished that she was here, standing with him as he took the oath of the Kings of Old. He let his power ravage around the room and welcomed the whispers of rumor that Ronan had tried to silence for so long.

She blinked, tears clouding her eyes.

He is really doing this.

Cyril stepped forward from behind the throne, appearing with a scepter and the Book of Old in his hands.

She stifled a gasp and heard Lawton do the same. The Book of Old was nothing but a legend amongst the common folk. The tool utilized to swear in a King of Old, imprinted with the legends of all the prior Kings and their knowledge.

"If you were to speak with a King of Old, that is how it would be done." She could hear her mother saying, those many teachings and moments she had repressed now flooding back to her with force, and James scoffing at her abilities. Her vision continued to cloud at the memory of James—what he would have given to see this, a chance at a better world. A chance with a good person on the throne. A chance to grow old.

Charmaine blinked rapidly as Dalton reached to grab the scepter and kneel before Cyril. He was probably internalizing the motion, threatening Cyril in his head over and over that this would be the last time that he did a public event like this. Not even his own wedding had been so public.

Cyril smiled. "Now you repeat after me, your Majesty. *I do solemnly swear upon my life and the gifts given to me by the Gods, that I, King Dalton of the Snow Kingdom, First of His Name, will abide by the past lives of the Kings of Old, and will put my Kingdom and its people above all else.*"

Dalton spoke, clear and unabashed for all in the Kingdom to bear witness. "*I do solemnly swear upon my life and the gifts given to me by the Gods, that I, King Dalton of the Snow Kingdom, First of His Name, will abide by the past lives of the Kings of Old, and will put my Kingdom and the one I love above all else.*"

Cyril gasped, as did the crowd behind them.

"Holy shit," Lawton said.

Dalton placed his hand over the Book of Old, and the room began to swirl with a beautiful snow, as if the Kings of Old themselves were blessing the union of Dalton, his crown, and their legacy.

"Long Live the King!" they shouted, as the room became a winter wonderland of joy and shadows.

***

Dalton was the King of the First Kingdom.

It had been about an hour since the ceremony had commenced, and he had not seen one person since that he cared about deeply. He had been swept up in conversation with the Kings and Queens of the Kingdoms in attendance.

When Dalton was a boy, he had never imagined his coronation. He knew it was imminent, as his sister would not take the crown before him. But he had always envisioned that he would be surrounded by the people he loved—whether that was his wife, Cyril, and anyone else who made up his family. It was never like this in his head—pulled in different directions, people bidding for his attention, whispering about the power he had just claimed for all to see.

If there were one person he could invite to this coronation, it would be King Cian. Only he would be able to navigate such an event. And he needed guidance, not from Cyril, and not from those he loved. It helped to have people who cared so deeply, but what Dalton needed was someone who implicitly understood what he was going through.

And that only person had died long before his own time.

He turned around, amidst the chaos of the throne room, to a delicate hand touching his elbow. He spun, grateful for the distraction from the women gawking over him and asking if he could make them a snowball.

Ten Kingdoms, how did Cian survive life like this?

As he turned, he saw a flash of pink hair. It was vibrant, like that of cherry blossoms. A crown was hidden amongst the tumbleweeds of long hair that spilled down his pink jacket. The crown looked like it was made of tree branches, if trees were made of gold that was. Raindrop shaped pink jewels sparkled all around its perimeter, seemingly placed without reason. His bright blue eyes were full of laughter, and his straight nose was crinkled as if he were constantly amused. He wrapped his thin arms around Dalton, the gesture fierce in friendship.

"Dalton Saphirrus, I never thought I would see the day that you wear that blasted snow king crown."

"Titan Ashdown, I never thought I would see you with such long hair." Dalton embraced the King of the Sixth Kingdom with a squeeze. "Thank you for saving me. They were trying to convince me to make a snowball."

Titan laughed, the beautiful sound whimsical against Dalton's ear. "Becomes King of the First Kingdom to make snowballs for pretty women. What a life you live, Dal."

Dalton clapped a hand on Titan's shoulder,

overwhelmed with the joy of seeing a familiar face amongst the chaos of the day. "Was your coronation anything like this? Sorry, I missed it, all locked up and everything."

Titan had been crowned two years prior, following the death of his mother. Dalton had been devastated that he was not able to go and support his friend. They had not met many times over the years, but most of the royal children had met before. Pride swarmed within him that Titan had made a name for himself amongst the Ten Kingdoms since he was crowned. He was renowned, a brilliant mind and an excellent King.

Titan's blue eyes glistened, clearly taking in the greater meaning of Dalton's words. "Dalton, the first rule of being King is to not apologize for things that are out of your control."

Dalton snorted, blowing a piece of hair out of his face as they walked. "Is it time already for the meeting?"

After every coronation, all the attending Kings and Queens met in the council chambers of the royal who was to be crowned. They would discuss strategy, provide updates on their kingdoms, and share whatever they wanted to share. It was also the perfect opportunity for the older Kings and Queens to rile the younger, especially the one who had just taken the crown.

Dalton cursed Cyril for his absence, not sure where he had run off to. He prayed he would meet him in the council chambers, to provide any solace of comfort while he was berated by the rulers of the continent.

He could hear Cyril's voice in his head now. *"Who are you going to be, Cian or Ciara?"* Dalton figured that the Kings and Queens of the Ten Kingdoms would be thinking the same thing.

Unfortunately for everyone in that council room, it was time for Dalton to make that decision.

***

King Titan of the Sixth Kingdom entered the dark council chambers seconds before Dalton. Elena sat next to Dalton's seat with her hands crossed in her lap, ensuring direct eye contact with all the other Kings and Queens of the continent. Cyril had come to get her moments before to let her know the Kings and Queens were gathering, and it was imperative that either she or Dalton was there before the majority arrived. It was customary, and frankly rude, that a ruler of the home kingdom would not be there to receive the others.

Elena relished in the opportunity to best the other Kingdoms, especially now that she informally belonged to two of them. Her mother had strategically avoided the invitation to Dalton's crowning, so she was therefore the representative monarch of the Fourth Kingdom, in addition to being married to the King of the First.

It made her the most powerful monarch in the Ten Kingdoms, and no amount of sorrow could take that away from her.

She was like her old self sitting before the Kings and Queens as Dalton took his seat beside her. Her sapphire lace gown was regal, covering from her wrists to her jawline. She wore no extraneous jewelry, instead letting her flame-colored curls naturally lay along her back. Her crown was covered in rubies, an homage to her usual persona. Dalton had been insistent that she wore whatever crown she wanted, for it was in the First Kingdom where everyone would have the right to choose.

Dalton had often reminded Elena that no part of her was guilty for being more distant from him over the last three months. But here in these chambers, with these people? It was absolutely electric, and she would not waste one moment.

She stood up as Dalton sat down, bowing her head. The

other leaders of their continent followed in suit, congratulating and paying respects to the newest member of the aristocracy.

It took everything in her not to smirk, for she was the one in control.

"Thank you all for coming to my party," Dalton said with a calm voice.

King Titan laughed, his smart features brightening.

Queen Vanellope of the Ninth Kingdom stood, her ethereal coloring a beacon against the black chamber walls. Her dark, hooded eyes were warm, as was the friendly smile that encroached on her thin lips. She lifted a delicate hand and combed it through the bottom of her straight, white, shoulder-length hair as she spoke, addressing Dalton directly. "Your Majesty, thank you for welcoming us into your home. Your crowning was a magical sight to behold. I am so grateful you extended your invitation to the Ninth Kingdom to witness such a historical moment." Her beige skin flushed below the candles that hung from the black diamond chandeliers above.

Elena had heard she was one of the more soft-spoken monarchs on the continent.

Dalton smiled softly in return, bobbing his head in thanks. "Queen Vanellope, you and your people are always welcome in the First Kingdom."

A booming voice sounded from down the table, and Elena nearly lashed out her water at the stark transition in volume.

"Yes, that is lovely for the Ninth Kingdom and the First Kingdom, but will the First Kingdom go back to welcoming all who do not worship in the powers of the Gods? It has been so long that we have all nearly forgotten their names."

It was King Blarquenza of the Second Kingdom. Smoke nearly huffed out of Elena's nostrils at the sight of the most pompous ruler on the continent. Where Queen Vanellope was all kindness, he was all wretched testosterone. Elena had never been formally introduced, but it took a lot to piss off her mother, and Queen Maria had complained about Blarquenza's attitude on numerous occasions.

"So lovely of you to join us, Blarquenza," Elena said, purposefully leaving out the Kingly title. "Where is your wife, Queen Elliana?"

Blarquenza's flame red hair lit up amongst the candelabra that sat directly above his head. Elena suddenly dreamed of having the ability to control fire over water; that would truly make this a council meeting to remember. His brown eyes flashed, his pale skin not flushing in the slightest.

He did not miss a beat as he replied, "She is enjoying the party. I did not think it appropriate for a woman to be amongst leaders tonight."

"But she is your Queen, Blarquenza. Or should we just call her Elliana?" Titan said, humor lacing every word. He leaned on the table like a child, the side of his head propped up by his fist.

"You may refer to her and me as King and Queen."

"Interesting," King Loe of the Fifth Kingdom chimed in. His curly black hair sat atop his head in a perfect knot, his white teeth shining as he smiled cruelly.

"To answer your question, *King* Blarquenza, the First Kingdom is no longer under the control of my bigoted father. I am not sure why you would even question the ability to let people live as they were born to do so. My father might not have worshiped and respected the Gods, but I never stopped." Dalton's voice was lethal.

Elena patted the top of his thigh under the table, letting him know that she was here to defend him by whatever means necessary.

Blarquenza sat back, his thick shoulders wide against the structure of the chair. He did not dignify the straightforward reply with a retort.

King Amethyst stood next, gesturing to the table. His violet eyes nearly took Elena's breath away, and she caught herself unable to break eye contact with them. They looked just like James's eyes; it was disconcerting. She closed her jaw, which had momentarily fallen open, then leaned forward. King Amethyst and Queen Elinoah of the Third Kingdom had been married for years, a dynamic duo who fostered their lands on trading and transporting horses across the continent. As a kingdom of mostly forests, the Third Kingdom needed the horsepower in order to move about the land. Queen Elinoah stood before them a heartbeat later, rising after her husband, her golden eyes shining with interest and genuine kindness.

"Now we should get to the real business of this meeting, so we can return to the lovely festivities the First Kingdom has to offer. I believe we should start with updates on our Kingdoms." Amethyst looked to Blarquenza. "That is, if you are willing to share the truth with us."

Dalton huffed a laugh, then gestured for the King and Queen of the Third Kingdom to speak accordingly.

Slowly, all the monarchs spoke around the table. They recounted their current matters of state, hardships, and any recent activity they considered to be important. All in all, none of the reigning monarchs had much to say. However, Elena could not shake the aching in her chest that they were waiting for something. Some darkness was looming over them, holding out to be unleashed.

Dalton's turn came at last, and he stood.

Extending his hand to Elena, she took it, rising with her husband. They were locked hand in hand, and Dalton recited what Elena was sure Cyril had prepped him on earlier. He mentioned the aftermath of the attacks they had undergone. Elena noted the other monarchs sat up straighter in their seats when he spoke of the mercenaries. It was no shock to her; there was not a chance in this world that they had not heard of such direct attacks. But Elena found it odd that none of the other Kingdoms spoke of attacks. Unless they were lying, which was plausible.

Dalton sat down when he was finished speaking, but he did not let go of Elena's hand. He was shaking slightly. Elena unleashed a spout of her healing magic in the hope that it calmed him. He did not look over at her, but instead, he squeezed her hand ever so gently.

She smiled to herself at his way of thanking her.

To no one's surprise, Blarquenza spoke, "So, the mercenaries have attacked the First Kingdom mercilessly?" He barked a laugh as if his pun was original and fantastic.

Pig, Titan mouthed at Elena.

She nearly spit out her wine.

"So, who is to say that we are not next? Who is controlling this threat, and where are the answers, your Majesty?"

Dalton leaned back casually in his seat. "We have been dealing with it, and we have not seen an attack for three months."

"They could attack at any moment, and you have not caught them yet? I am sorry, your Majesty, but I find this to be a ludicrous waste. Aren't you the Gods-forsaken King of Snow, the inheritor of King Cian's power? Where the fuck is your lineage, boy? Your old King never would have stood for this!"

Fast as lightning, Dalton stood. Snow whipped through the council chambers savagely, ice coating the black marble table as spikes protruded from its sides.

"How dare you enter my Kingdom and threaten me with your heartless attitude, Blarquenza. Innocent members of my court, my Kingdom, and my own family have been taken by this invisible enemy for too long. How *dare* you insinuate that I sit here with my power and do nothing while the people of my Kingdom suffer." He strode toward Blarquenza, the snow relentless as his voice carried above it. "How dare you speak of my great grandfather as if he did not give up all he held dear in this world to make it better. How dare you think I do not give a damn about this. I told you I am handling it, and I will do so without your input."

He paused, an inch from Blarquenza's pained face. Blarquenza's red eyebrows were covered in frost, his lips chattering. Dalton, on the other hand, looked unaffected, as did everyone else in the room. Queen Vanellope stared upon Dalton with wonder, her thin lips spread wide in a smile. Elena looked around to the rest of the monarchs and found the same reaction. She forced a stoic expression, but pride swarmed within her. That was her best friend. That was her husband.

That was her Dalton.

"I am the King of Snow. If you do not respect me in my own kingdom, Blarquenza, Gods help me, I will freeze your crops. I will shackle your knees to the marble floors of my throne room and force you to bow with a frozen spine. I do not give a fuck about many things, but you will not disrespect the memory of those I love."

Elena froze in her seat, not at the dropping temperature, but the word she had never heard out of Dalton's mouth. *Love.*

Dalton waved his hand, and the snow ceased to fall.

He turned to the Kings and Queens of the throne room, his sapphire eyes blazing in agony. He looked at each of them, nodding in their direction one by one. "The King or Queen of the Kingdom which has been crowned is able to dissolve the meeting as they see fit. I deem this meeting over." He extended his long fingers toward the other side of the table, "Loe, Amethyst, Elinoah, Titan, Vanellope." He paused on Elena, smiling genuinely. "My lovely wife, Elena. Thank you all for coming. Please, take your time following the rest of tonight's festivities and enjoy the celebrations. I much appreciate all you have shared tonight, and all the restraint you have shown, despite your burning questions about our current state of the world."

He turned to Blarquenza, all affection dissipating from his face instantly. "You are hereby banished from the First Kingdom, until I see fit to declare otherwise. Your subjects shall remain, for I have nothing against them."

He strode out of the throne room abruptly, leaving all but Blarquenza smiling. Elena knew in that moment he had decided who he was to become.

He was Cian.

THIRTEEN

It was like stepping back in time for Charmaine and Randolph. They moved about with one another with less awkwardness than they had the last time they were in the ballroom dancing. Randolph had his hand on the bodice of Charmaine's violet gown, graceful and respectable as always. She held his muscular arm tightly as they spun in synchrony.

With Randolph and Charmaine, things were not the same as between Charmaine and Dalton. Their friendship was different. When she was with Randolph, she was centered. Steady. When she was with Dalton, she was alive. Electric.

She needed both of them—that much was certain.

"I remember when we danced like this for the first time," Charmaine reminisced.

Randolph smiled. "Ah, yes. And then our charming King whisked you away. I was livid."

"Were you really?" she asked, unable to hide the laugh in her voice.

"I was trying to figure you out, and he robbed me of the opportunity."

"Why didn't you stop him?" Genuine curiosity plagued her question. "If you wanted to talk to me, I am sure you could have persuaded him with little to no effort. A diversion, perhaps?"

Randolph raised a dark eyebrow. "Have you ever been able to dissuade Dalton from anything?"

She pursued her lips in defeat. "All right, I give in."

"I remember trying to figure out what you were hiding."

She paused. "Was it that obvious? I could practically smell it on you."

"Those who are familiar with secrets are able to catch such curiosities." Now she was the one to quirk up an eyebrow at his comment. "I have not seen Dalton and Elena in a while."

He was clearly changing the subject, but Charmaine did not want to press him. That was another difference between her two best friends. With Dalton, she could push. He *needed* to be challenged, for he always rose to the occasion. With Randolph, she could do no such thing. If she did, then she risked closing all the walls that had been built before. And it was not a risk she was willing to take.

She would not lose anyone else.

In stride with the conversational switch, he replied, "They are probably meeting with the other Kings and Queens of the Ten Kingdoms, who have arrived for the coronation and funeral. It is ceremonial, but necessary."

She blinked, responding with a laugh. "And how do you know so much about the traditions of the Kings and Queens of the Ten Kingdoms?"

His cheeks flushed red, his brown eyes diverting anywhere but Charmaine's face.

Was he uncomfortable?

She was not sure she had ever seen him so momentarily disarmed. "I do not. Just picked up a few things from Ronan over the years, I suppose."

"Interesting," she said, not believing that for a second.

They spun again, regaining their footwork with the death of conversation. Without warning, they turned and Charmaine's shoulder collided with someone else. She stumbled, spinning, and profusely apologized before laying eyes on the most divine woman she had ever seen.

The woman looked to be young, maybe a bit older than Dalton. She had straight white hair that hit her shoulders and thin black eyebrows that were raised in amusement. She wore a white silk gown, thin straps holding it together and offsetting her beige skin beautifully against the candlelight of the ballroom. Charmaine admired how much the woman glowed in the moonlight, for she was clearly the most ethereal woman in the room. She smiled, dazzling and forgiving. A thin crown of leaves sat atop her head, almost a headband it was so subtle.

This was a queen.

Charmaine bowed her head, curtsying with her violet skirts outstretched. "I am so sorry, your Majesty."

The woman continued to smile, her dark eyes shining with mirth. "No need to apologize. It is I who should not have been walking throughout the dance floor." She nodded in Randolph's direction, an acknowledgement of his presence.

Charmaine swore the queen's features tightened at the sight of him, as if she were disturbed and shocked. But it was gone so quickly she was sure she had imagined it.

"Queen Vanellope, it is an honor to bump into you this evening," Randolph said, bowing. "May I introduce Miss Charmaine Grimes of Brinn, a member of King Dalton's court."

Queen Vanellope is the Queen of the Ninth Kingdom. Cian help me, she traveled all this way for me to run into her with Randolph!

"Ah, the girl from Brinn. I have heard much of you, Charmaine."

"You have?" Charmaine asked, concern flooding throughout her blood.

"Your eyes are very interesting," Vanellope commented, stepping closer. "Violet eyes are quite rare amongst the Ten Kingdoms."

Charmaine froze, unsure what to make of such a comment. Nobody ever seemed to say anything about the coloring of her eyes, and she never thought it was odd. The people of the Ten Kingdoms ranged in a variety of colorings. Charmaine had even heard stories of women and men in the Sixth Kingdom with green hair. That was one thing she loved about the continent, what she admired so much about the world Dalton was trying to build—people were to be accepted, no matter how interesting they might be.

Interesting people were spell-binding; the world could do with more of them.

Vanellope stepped backward, and Charmaine noted the number of onlookers in the court who had picked up on their conversation. "Your King, Charmaine, is to be a good one. You are very lucky to live in this kingdom, with a good-hearted person seizing the throne out of necessity."

Charmaine nodded, taken aback by her sincerity and ferocity. "He is the King of Snow," she proclaimed.

"That he is," Vanellope commented, a smile quirking up on the side of her face. "It is not easy for new monarchs to make headway in the world. Particularly this world, so rooted in differences and borders."

She stepped forward, close enough so that only Charmaine could hear her words. "But if he acts like he did this night? He will be just fine."

Vanellope stepped back, holding out her hand as a woman Charmaine did not realize was behind her took it with grace. The woman had dark skin and long black hair braided down her back. She wore a matching white silk gown, but she did not wear a crown. Instead, she wore silver glitter on her eyes, which Charmaine had also adorned on more than one occasion at court to enhance her look. The woman smiled at her and bowed in respect. She leaned in to kiss Vanellope on the cheek, and the queen's skin flushed light pink.

Charmaine could not help but smile; they were radiant.

"I bid you farewell, Charmaine." Queen Vanellope looked back toward the throne, as if expecting Dalton there any moment. "Tell your King the people of the First Kingdom are welcome in the Ninth, *always.*"

"Thank you, your Majesty."

Queen Vanellope walked by with her partner, parting the crowd as they went. Randolph brushed up against her bare arm before she looked at him. His brow was furrowed, his amber eyes pensive.

"What is it?" Charmaine asked, concern lighting her voice. He had seemed on edge in the last few moments, more so than usual for him.

"Nothing," he said darkly.

"And why don't I believe that?"

Cold, bitter air swarmed around her, and she turned to see the culprit standing before her with a wicked smile on his lips.

"I am going to cut in, Randolph, if you do not mind."

"Not at all," he whispered as he turned away and was lost to the crowd within seconds.

Dalton's chilled fingers suddenly found the bodice of her gown, and they began to dance rapidly to keep pace with the strings of the music. Charmaine looked around, trying to keep from making eye contact with the King of Snow. She knew if she looked at him, she would feel the utmost power of the draw.

"Do not look at me while I have you in my grasp," he whispered softly.

"Can you read my mind?" she said with a chuckle.

"No, but you are not looking at me, and I want to keep it as such . . . Not that I do not want you to, because believe me, I do."

"Are you sure we should be dancing like this?"

"What did Vanellope want?" Dalton asked, clearly cutting to what he wanted to know.

"Nothing, she was being friendly."

"None of the rulers in the Ten Kingdoms are ever *just* being friendly, Charmaine."

Frazzled by the intensity of his hands and the lack of eye contact, Charmaine replied with the last thing she remembered Vanellope saying. "She told me to tell you the people of the First are always welcome in the Ninth."

After a heartbeat, he replied seriously, "She knows something. She has to."

Turning to face him, unable to take the pain of the draw anymore, his icy hands detached from her body. Before she could meet his dark blue gaze, he was already halfway across the ballroom.

***

Lawton Thornwood desperately needed a glass of wine, though he abstained. He was supposed to be working, after all.

Smoke and ash filled his senses. Without even craning his neck to the side, he knew who now stood beside him on the outskirts of the ballroom.

"Ah, Randolph. Are you enjoying the party as well?"

"No."

"Good to see you are having fun, my friend. Good to see you are having fun."

"Likewise," he said with a huffed breath.

"I cannot wait until all these people are *gone,*" Lawton said, exasperated.

Feeling utterly bold this evening, he put his head against Randolph's shoulder. Anticipating a jerk reaction, or even a shove, Lawton was shocked to find that Randolph did not budge an inch.

"Likewise," he said again with a laugh.

A continuation of his boldness, he asked, "Do you like Elena Leclair, Randolph?"

Randolph craned his head to meet Lawton's askew gaze. "Why would you ask such a daft question?"

"I saw you dancing with her last night. It looked oh-so-intense."

"We were merely speaking."

"About?"

"I do not *like* her."

"But you like her?"

Randolph sneered and shoved Lawton off his shoulder with a snarl. "I do not *like* her," he said with vehement enunciation. "She is the Queen of the First Kingdom and the Princess of the Fourth. She is the sole heir to her kingdom and a great . . . person. Have some respect, Lawton."

"Mere curiosity. I have not seen you ever have such . . . intensity with someone."

The top left of Randolph's lip curled with distaste. "I am a human, you know. I have feelings, despite my continued attempts to shove them away."

"For . . . women?"

"You are odd this evening, Lawton."

"Making conversation," he said with a flirtatious eyebrow raise.

"I believe in all forms of love, Thornwood, if that's what

you're getting at." He paused, a tattooed hand running over his face in exasperation. "I believe I could love *anyone*."

Lawton opened his mouth to reply something snarky, but unbelievably, Randolph continued with a deep breath in. Chuckling, he pushed on, "I have not quite had the time to fall into anything with anyone."

Lawton's features softened, and he felt bad for being so pushy with Randolph. "I apologize, Eniar. I was merely curious, that is all. I did not mean any harm by my pestering. If you are not ready to speak of such personal things with me—"

Randolph held up a hand, silencing him. "Despite how utterly annoying you are, I do consider you my friend. I am learning . . . I am learning I need to be pushed sometimes." Putting his hand on Lawton's shoulder, he said, "I hope one day, when I am steadier on my own two feet, and the world is not overrun by forces we cannot see—only anticipate—that I can find someone who meets me stride for stride."

"I hope that too," Lawton said with a rather sad smile. "I hope that too."

FOURTEEN

egrouping, Randolph stood outside Charmaine's chambers, waiting. Athelred was with her, adjusting her gowns and no doubt making her suitable for the continuation of trials and tribulations. She had requested to go back to her chambers to freshen up, and Athelred had taken her back with him.

Athelred had been utterly insistent that Randolph was not to be in the chambers. Although there was logic to the denial of Randolph—a knight—being allowed in her chambers, he could not help but think the young lad was hiding something. It was bizarre enough that Charmaine kept Athelred as her manservant, going against custom, but it was another thing entirely for him to be so oddly shifty in demeanor.

He had been forced to speak with the boy on more than one occasion, typically in reference to his unprofessional behavior. Though Randolph was not a model citizen himself, at least he had the decency to *act* like it. Athelred was shifty, his gaze never quite meeting Randolph's when they spoke. Normally, such behavior would not condone as much as a second glance for Randolph. However, these times were not normal, and neither was Athelred's disposition.

Randolph had volunteered to speak to him on account of Charmaine, for she feared if Dalton were to catch wind of his peculiarities, he would be sacked by the new King.

Randolph leaned against the wall of the hallway, his mind reflecting back to his most recent conversation with the servant. He had spilled tea all over Charmaine's chambers, particularly saturating her bed, after she had merely asked him how he spent his evenings off.

"Is there something you wish to tell me?" Randolph had asked.

Athelred's eyes shifted from side to side, a silent refusal to comply to conversation with Randolph. "No, sire," he whispered. "I merely wish to serve his Majesty in any way possible."

"And you did that best by serving the King's friend by spilling tea all over her personal items?"

Athelred shifted uncomfortably on his feet again, his eyes darting left and right. "It will not happen again, sire," he said softly with earnest.

Randolph, clearly, had not believed that nothing would happen again. Though for the sake of Charmaine's feelings—and the boy's—he was willing to speak to him on more than one occasion.

Charmaine did not have much consistency, especially given her relationship with her last servant, Gwendolyn, who had lost her head. He understood that need for constant reassurance and to be kind to the servants, for they were a large piece of what made the castle life what it was.

However, Randolph could not shake the feeling that Athelred was not who he proclaimed to be. Yet, he could find no proof. There was no need to bring forth these suspicions to the King, not yet. The next time there was an indiscretion, he might not have a choice.

The door to Charmaine's chambers reopened, and she

emerged again with her serving boy. Athelred crept behind her leisurely, and upon seeing Randolph still standing where he had left him, he straightened.

There was that incessantly annoying disposition, returned like a mask upon confrontation with a member of the King's close circle.

Randolph rolled his eyes, making sure Charmaine knew he was doing so. She grunted in displeasure, her gaze sympathetically going back to her serving boy.

"You cannot save them all," he whispered so low that Athelred would not be able to hear her.

"I know, but I have to try," she replied, her violet eyes suddenly haunted.

"Dalton would never do to him what Ronan did to Gwendolyn," he reassured her as they parted wordlessly from Athelred. "You do not have to put up with a shit servant simply because you feel badly for his lack of skills."

Charmaine turned her head to face Randolph, linking her arm through his as they walked. "What I did not do for Gwendolyn was protect her. She had that dagger somehow, and I do not know to this day why she had it. I did not help her. I simply did nothing while she lost her head."

Randolph paused, his voice thick with emotion. "I know what it is like to blame yourself, believe me. But you cannot live in the past; you have to try to move forward."

"I *am* trying," she said firmly.

"I do not mean with James. The death of a family member is different. That is a wound that cannot heal. But Gwendolyn? I fear that some fates cannot be changed and should not be dwelled upon."

"She was my friend."

"And may she rest in peace, but do not blame yourself

for things you cannot control. How were you to know that the dagger had magic?"

"You know very well that I could have picked it up. What is the saying, 'Those with magic are drawn to magic?'" She paused as if she made a connection. "Maybe that is why I am so drawn to—"

"Drawn to?" he interrupted.

"Never mind." She shook her head back and forth. "Let us walk back to the festivities."

Randolph decided to push onward with the conversation, despite getting the sense that Charmaine was not ready to venture there yet. "You know, I understand why you two get on so well."

Charmaine's lips twitched, her pale cheeks turning pink. "And to whom are you referring to?"

Randolph nearly rolled his eyes, but kept them in place out of fear of losing her in this conversation. It might be the only chance he had to get a true sense of what in the name of the Ten Kingdoms was going on. "Dalton Saphirrus, first of his name—"

With a jolt and what sounded almost like a squeal, Charmaine threw her hand over Randolph's mouth. Stunned speechless, he tried to mumble against her delicate hand, nearly tasting the blue gemstone that she wore on her finger.

"What are you doing, Charmaine?" he mumbled.

"Shh!" she hissed. "You cannot go around saying things like that, Randolph!"

Removing her hand from his mouth, he barked a laugh. "I've never seen you so worked up." He chuckled. "Ten Kingdoms! Are you always like this?"

Now it was her turn to laugh. Smiling, she collected herself by wiping her hands on her skirts. "No, but you cannot just go around and—"

"Ask my friend what I already know?"

"What do you know?"

"Nothing in detail, but your reaction to the question tells me more than I thought I would get out of you to begin with."

Running a hand through the front of her hair, she whispered sadly, "I do not know what it is between us, to be completely honest with you."

Randolph furrowed his brow. "Has something happened?"

He figured they had kissed on more than one occasion. The desperation in their gaze alone at the battle of Brinn was more than an indication to Randolph that something had passed between them physically. He had never pushed her to find out. He was only asking now because of the way she was around him, especially at the coronation ceremony. The funeral had been a gesture of kindness, but Randolph knew Dalton was not the type to give everything he had to someone out of the goodness of his heart. Yes, he was a good man with a pleasant disposition and a kind soul. But he was also a Saphirrus, and the Saphirrus line could be as cut-throat as they could be charismatic.

It was part of their charm.

"Not recently," she whispered. "I have been . . . in pieces, as you know."

"You are not broken."

"I feel like I could be."

Extending a tattooed hand, he touched her shoulder awkwardly. Cursing himself silently, he wished he were better at these sorts of things. He wanted to be there for her. He wanted to help her through this. But he also wanted to make sure she would not get hurt by this.

By Dalton.

"I know what it is to be in parts," Randolph said softly,

careful as always not to overshare. "I know what it is to be heartbroken, and to question everything that used to make you . . . well, you."

Her violet eyes shone with understanding, and she nodded. "You do not need to share with me if you do not wish."

"I wish to be here for you, not just as you work through the shattering, but as you work to pick up the pieces and put them back together."

She laughed, clearly shoving her emotions aside. "You are quite soft when you choose to be."

Lifting up the side of his mouth, he took a step closer to her and wrapped his arms around her. "I am not really a hugger," he said in an exhale. "But I will make an exception for you, always."

Pulling apart a moment later, Charmaine thanked him, then paused as if she was deciding whether to revert to the conversation or end it. "He has not hurt me, Rand. Not ever."

"I do not think he would, intentionally."

"You speak of him as though you have known him for a long time."

It was a mere observation, but Randolph worked to be still.

"I suppose I have known him longer than most," he settled on after a moment. "He is a Saphirrus, and they tend to all be the same."

"And how would they be all the same?"

"They do not hurt you, but their chaos does."

FIFTEEN

yril often experienced rage. It was a normal human emotion—concerning if one did not have the capacity for it.

He had been mad at Ciara on more than one occasion. He had rarely been mad at Cian, for he did not make many mistakes in life. But *Dalton?* Cyril had been mad at him so many times that he would have needed to bookkeep all his moments in order to get a specific count. In this moment, he was murderous.

He found himself chasing Dalton after the festivities of his coronation ceased. He had stared at him the entire time it was happening.

He had no idea what he had done; after all, he was only a boy. If he had been a better trainer and Thinker, they would not be entering the biggest disaster of their lives. If Ronan had been a father of any capacity, this could have also been avoided.

He was the King for all of a few hours, and all who knew him prior had already failed him. Cyril moved his legs as fast as they could go for a man of his age. His bones creaked loudly at his hips as he pushed onward.

The damn bastard was so nimble for a King, not yet weighed down by the crown.

"DALTON!" Cyril shouted as he turned to round the corner. He was done chasing.

Dalton paused, craning his neck backward as he stopped walking. He looked different tonight, somehow *less* angelic. Cyril scoffed. Leave it to this boy to be crowned a King and become human.

Cyril could see Dalton surveying him. *Was he angry? Was he serious?*

Cyril answered by pumping his short arms and continuing to power through his walk-run like he had been. Dalton's eyes widened at the wild gesturing and moving. Dalton knew Cyril was serious; however, he seemed rather amused by the fire that brewed within his mentor.

The boy probably did not think he could move like this still.

Catching up to him, Cyril grabbed him by the elbow, just as he did when he was a boy, and tugged him down the hallway to his chambers. They entered the great room, his white decor matching his physical attributes.

Cyril could not put his finger on it, but something in Dalton had changed tonight. Greater than what Cyril was about to discipline him for, yes, but something else had changed. Cyril blinked a few times, clearing his mind. He willed himself to not let his affections for the boy cloud him.

This was serious.

"What have you done, boy?" Cyril asked, getting closer to him, almost shoving him with the force of his words. He grabbed the front of his tunic, trying to shake him as if he was shaking the sense of this moment into him.

"I do not know. Oh, dear Cyril, what have I done?" He smirked, but his eyes betrayed him. As did his eyebrows. They were gray, white hairs permanently dusting the color of his hair.

He was scared.

Cyril released him, stepping back wildly as he tried to regain both composure and balance. He was not sure if anyone had told him about his changing features yet, so he relented.

"Dalton, my dear boy, you changed the vow. The King's vow." It was a term as old as Cyril himself. He would know. He was there when Cian instituted the vow.

Dalton blinked twice, his dark blue eyes recognizing the gravity of what Cyril said as if he had forgotten what he did. "I know," he said, barely a whisper.

"You . . . you what?" Cyril yelled, stepping back as he looked at him.

He really looked at him. This was the boy whom had been under lock and key, a boy whom had taken to a *commoner* rather than his Queen, a boy whom had no desires to rule their world. And he had changed the damn vow.

"I changed the vow. You asked me to repeat after you, and I said . . ." He straightened up, as if remembering the posture he had when he made the declaration. "*I do solemnly swear upon my life and the gifts given to me by the Gods, that I, King Dalton of the Snow Kingdom, First of His Name, will abide by the past lives of the Kings of Old, and will put my Kingdom and the one I love above all else.*"

"Dalton . . . You know this was no ordinary promise, no ordinary declaration of love?" Cyril asked, more quietly than he had intended.

This would be his downfall. This was the reason I was sent here all those years ago. I was supposed to protect this boy, keep this destiny from coming true. I failed him before he had truly begun.

"I might have had a broken life before this one, Cyril, but I know what I did. It is an unbreakable vow. If I sway from those words, I will die," he said it so matter-of-factly that Cyril felt sick.

"We can find a way out of this, boy. It will be tough, and it will be complicated, but we will find a way," Cyril answered, touching Dalton's hands.

Dalton smiled softly, appreciating the gesture with a light touch of Cyril's forehead to his own before removing his hands from his grasp. Cyril felt as though he were losing him, something he never thought he would experience in his lifetime.

No parent should have to bury their child.

Whether he liked it or not, Dalton was his, and he would always be his.

"I do not wish to alter the fate I have designed for myself," Dalton muttered softly.

"It is not altering if you make it up as you go, boy. None of us know the full extent of the plan which we are a part of." Cyril's temperature rose, the heat of the moment too much for his old heart to take.

His mind flashed back to the days of Cian following the death of his Queen. They had sat together for weeks, wrapped in one another's arms and praying she would find peace. He would learn there was no opposition in death. It was not until he had a vision of their beloved Queen, who came to him in his sleep to relay a message and a prophecy, that he learned what must happen. It was a prophecy of the King of Snows to come. Cian needed to continue the line *without* her.

If Cyril covered his ears and let his mind wander, he could still hear Cian break when he had spoken the truth to him. There was nothing Cyril could have done to prevent it, but the truth did not always set the man free.

Sometimes one was locked in chains.

Cyril swore he would never be a part of that type of

power again. The power that broke people. The power that destroyed people.

The power that changed *everything*.

"I need to make sure she is okay, Cyril," Dalton whispered.

At that, Cyril had no witty response. "Your power will change everything, boy. I heard from King Titan how you handled your meeting."

"Banishing Blarquenza from the First Kingdom might have been a little extreme," Dalton said with a smirk.

"I quite liked your style there. Blarquenza needed someone to bend his knee for a long time now. He is not old, by my standards, anyway."

"How old is he? Around forty?" Dalton said with a laugh.

"But he has been hardened to time."

"We all have in some way, have we not?"

Cyril was shocked by Dalton's frankness; he never spoke of his hardships under lockdown. "In some part, I think we are all a little broken."

"I think I am more broken than most."

"Yet, you are whole. You are our King. You keep us together. You—"

Dalton cut him off, standing straighter. "Cyril, you do not need to speak to me like we are in public. I have told you this before."

Cyril clenched his fists. "And I have told you before, boy, you do not get to turn off being King. It is your destiny! It is who you are—"

"I do not care about destiny, Cyril! Can't you see? I care about the people that I *love*, and that is all. I made that vow so I have one chance to save them or die trying. You should have heard Blarquenza in that meeting. He was baiting me, yes, but he was not wrong. Why did my father accept these attacks from the mercenaries? Why was this issue not resolved? Why have these attacks ceased? Why was it only the First Kingdom that was attacked time after time?" He took a deep breath, scratching the nape of his neck impatiently.

"We do not have answers to these questions, Cyril. I know you are trying. I know even Randolph is trying, but trying is not good enough anymore. We need someone to figure this out. I came at Blarquenza tonight because he threatened me, and therefore, he threatened the people I love. This vow . . . It is my chance to protect them— Elena, Charmaine, you . . . Ten Kingdoms, even Randolph is family after the last three months! This vow is my purpose. It is my legacy. And I will not fail."

Cyril softened. He did not need to look in the mirror to know his eyes were glassy. "My dear boy . . . You are enough. You have always been enough. Your value has nothing to do with the man your father tried to make you become. You were locked up because he was afraid. He heard of his end and thought he was playing Gods against destiny and prophecy. Clearly, he was wrong."

Unannounced, Dalton wrapped his arms around Cyril, throwing himself at the mercy of his comfort. Cyril stiffened and then relaxed upon the realization.

"Dalton, you are my King and my boy."

Dalton pulled back, as if he were shocked he had acted on impulse. He turned to his bedside table, lifting a wine glass that had been sitting there to his lips. "Then long may I reign, Cyril."

SIXTEEN

Dalton ran his hand through his hair in frustration three hundred and eighty-five times, grunted in frustration six times, and used an insurmountable amount of curse words at the pages before him. They were utterly maddening to sift through.

"I don't even know what I am bloody looking for—" he whispered to himself.

The marriage contract was one thing—a document built to fortify the relationship between two kingdoms—and he had no doubt he would crack that code. But it was the journals—this name he had been hunting for in secret—that would not leave him alone at night. He could almost feel the name he was searching for on the tip of his tongue, and he would get so close to saying it that he would awaken in a cold sweat.

Yet, when he opened his mouth to speak, nothing came to fruition.

"This is absolutely no bloody fun," he nearly growled, irritated beyond belief.

Before he could think for another moment, that little trickle of grief he had consistently ignored the last five years reared its nasty head at the forefront of his mind. Sticking out his hand to push it away, Dalton shoved any good memories of his dead family out of his mind. He refused to be shattered by the loss of parents who did not love him. He refused to fall into despair over a sister who had been lost for so long that Dalton could no longer remember the sound of her laugh, the length of her fingers, or the precise placement of the freckles star-dusted across her cheekbones.

Dalton was broken by many things and experiences, and despite his best efforts to remain whole, he was far from perfect.

"What the devil are you searching for?" A voice said behind him, cutting through the air like a sword.

Dalton whipped his head around, his crown-less head nearly spinning with the rapidity of the motion. "What the devil are you doing in here?"

Lawton stood before him, a member of his own knight's guard. If it was anyone other than a friend of Charmaine, Dalton would have dismissed him with moderate to severe frostbite.

"Hopping around," he said with a smirk, though his eyes were wary of all the pieces of paper around him. Clearly, he was unsure of what Dalton was doing.

Dalton found himself smiling, despite all that he was enduring. "I am feeling particularly charitable today, you know, with it being my coronation and all."

"Apologies for the intrusion, your Majesty. I assure you it was a mistake."

Dalton was not sure why, but he was telling the truth. "Mistakes can lead to grand discoveries." He paused, thinking of how he wanted to propose the question while remaining deviously mysterious. "How are you at reading, Lawton?"

Lawton looked as though he was insulted yet flattered, his blond eyebrows raising in inquisition. "Quite decent, depending on the source material."

"Diaries?"

Lawton motioned whether he was allowed to step forward. Dalton gestured to allow such a motion, and within a second, Lawton had crouched over the papers with him.

"What are you looking for?" he asked in earnest.

Dalton flashed him an unnecessary glare. He was not used to asking for help. "A name."

"That is useful information, your Majesty," Lawton said sarcastically.

Despite himself, Dalton chuckled, realizing the reason this knight was such a pain in Randolph's backside. He liked him already. "A name that has not been spoken in a very long time. We will know when we see it."

"And how will we know?"

"Because I am the King, and I said so."

Lawton shrugged his shoulders and muttered, "Seems like a reasonable explanation."

And they began to read.

***

They sat for hours.

"My backside hurts," Lawton complained.

"My brain hurts," Dalton chimed in.

"My eyes hurt."

"My soul hurts."

Lawton snorted. "While we are at it, your Majesty, my soul hurts too."

Dalton smiled, though he had to agree that his eyes too did hurt. With nearly trembling hands, he rubbed them so hard he was sure his eyelashes would fall off. "Let us give our souls a rest then for this evening. We looked long enough."

Lawton nodded in understanding, though he did not rise before the King.

"You are very special, Lawton Thornwood," Dalton said as he stood slowly. His knees nearly buckled from leaning on the marble flooring for so long. He was sure his kneecaps were bruised from the position he had remained in.

"I am?" Lawton asked in disbelief, that blond eyebrow raising again in distrust.

Good, he is right to distrust even his King.

"Despite all that I am"—Dalton gestured to his thin, pale body with a snicker, his voice dripping in sarcasm—"I have heard your name around the castle prior to this night."

"I was a part of the regiment that rescued the Grimes children from Brinn when it was burned down, your Majesty."

If Dalton were not experienced in the art of deception, he would have staggered at the mention of Charmaine and James. But he was practiced in demonstrations of neutrality, especially when the world felt as though it was burning down.

This was one of those moments.

"You served under the legion of Randolph," Dalton ventured, feeling rather daring.

"Yes, your Majesty."

"And how do you like him?" Dalton did his best to sound impossibly bored, but he knew there was power behind the loaded question. He wanted to know what Randolph pretended to be when he was out in the world with his men.

Lawton pondered this for a moment before replying with a clear voice, "I would take a sword for him."

"You would? And would he for you?"

Lawton did not pause before replying in earnest, "I do not know. I am not sure that I care, however."

"Hmph," Dalton mumbled.

Before Dalton had a chance to turn around and dismiss Lawton for the evening, he spoke again, this time a flirtatious danger laced throughout his tone. "Your Majesty, may I venture to ask a question?"

Intrigued, Dalton nodded.

Lawton laced his hands behind his back, his black velvet tunic shimmering in the candlelight. "It is about Charmaine Grimes, if I may inquire."

"What about her?" Dalton said breathlessly, unsure where this was going or why Charmaine's name graced Lawton's tongue. He knew they were friends, for they had clearly built a bond when Lawton and the legion rescued them from the border of the Second Kingdom.

Lawton's gaze lingered a second too long on Dalton's nearly white eyebrows. Dalton knew he was looking there because people had been staring all day. The whispers had been a constant background noise to his daily activities.

And this was the first time Lawton had *really* looked at him.

"Your Majesty, she means a great deal to me."

Dalton stuck a knuckle in his mouth to keep himself under control.

Lawton continued, "And I am not sure if she means as great of a deal to you."

Dalton was not sure if he was breathing.

Stepping toward his King, Lawton raised his hands in surrender. "And I only want what is best for her." He bowed his head, and as he rose, he whispered, "I am not threatening you, my liege, but if she is not to you what you are to her, then I will do something about it. That girl means far too much to me for her to live this half-life."

Dalton took his first breath in thirty seconds, ragged and icy. But regardless of being addressed so inappropriately, his reaction was anything but the way his breath felt. "I agree." With a smirk, he added, "I like you."

"Then this was quite the easy conversation," Lawton said, rising fully from his bow. "Thank you for letting me join you, your Majesty. I am sorry we did not find the name successfully amongst these dairy pages."

Finally. Dalton gestured to the doorway. As it clicked in finality, he sagged to the floor, whispering the name that had nearly jumped off the page hours ago in front of him, though he could not stop until Lawton was convinced they had found no such thing. Nobody could know—nobody could hear what he was about to say.

"Kai."

And Dalton swore he felt the castle walls rumble in response.

SEVENTEEN

The coronation had been beautiful, the spectacle of the century. Dalton had become who he was always meant to be, and Elena knew he had enjoyed it.

Yet, Elena Leclair rued this day.

Her kingdom, as well as the First, remained threatened by the ghost of the mercenaries. That was the reason she had come to the First, in order to please her mother and build an alliance between them and the Fourth.

She snorted to herself, muttering, "Nobody can say I did not strengthen the alliance."

Yet, a royal marriage, no matter how politically amicable it could be, was not a solution to all problems. If anything, it lit the pillar for spectacle and rumor. The world was built on foundations of power, and a marriage between the King of Snow and the heir to the Fourth Kingdom's throne was nothing short of a sight to be seen. Deep down, she feared her marriage to Dalton would heighten the tensions of the world, targeting her kingdom as the next place for the mercenaries to focus.

Her mother had not even bothered to attend her own husband's coronation, so she had not yet received what she had always wanted—acceptance. She had married the prince, now king. She had come to the kingdom upon a simple request to please and placate. She had willingly begun to detach herself before James died, accepting her place in the world as a potential ruling monarch. She even kept her two powers at bay, to the best of her ability, because she did not want to threaten her mother's throne.

Burying her face in her hands, she took a deep breath as her mind continued to spiral. Her heart was still broken, and she was unsure if it would ever properly heal. James, her mother, even Dalton . . . She had disappointed them all. How could one forgive her for duty, when she did not even forgive herself?

She had a bodyguard, one who she liked, yet she wanted nothing to do with him other than to play a one-sided game. Feelings were irrelevant to royals; rarely did monarchs have the opportunity to marry for love. Yet, she had never been one to make friends with anyone outside of the circle of kings and queens of the continent. This relationship with Greyson Althan, whatever it blossomed into, was foreign for her.

The fact of the matter was undeniable—princesses did not have friends. Especially not friends below their station.

Admittedly, it was a shame because Elena felt that she and Greyson could be good friends if a wall of power and titles did not stand between them.

Friendship with Dalton had become rather indignant as well, for it was as organic as taking a breath. But Dalton was another monarch, someone who understood the trials and tribulations Elena took on daily. He understood what it was to be throttled by society and not have the comfort of family to fall back on. Dalton and Elena were one and the same, despite having their heads screwed on differently.

Greyson was different altogether. He had built himself from the ground up, a knight who had shown his skill of his own accord. He cared for Elena's well-being, despite being a soldier assigned to keep her safe from harm, but it would never be enough. Elena was afraid she would never be enough—not for Greyson. He deserved a normal friend who was not plagued with troubles too big for the continent itself.

So, she cursed the day because she despised her life.

Picking up the document that laid before her, she read it out loud once more. "Dalton Naoise Saphirrus of the First Kingdom, wed to Elena Leclair of the Fourth Kingdom on the eve of Summer's end, dawning a new day for both House Saphirrus and House Leclair . . ." She exhaled, her hands shaking as she continued to read between the lines of thousands of words detailing her marriage, looking for a mistake.

***

"Your Majesty?"

Elena picked up her head from her arms to see her bodyguard standing at the forefront of her chambers. She had not heard him come in, so she was momentarily disarmed by his presence. He had changed since the coronation, now wearing a long black tunic and black trousers. His sword was still strapped across his back, as it was most times she saw him. Dark hair flowed to his shoulders casually, and his eyes pierced into her as he set the hard line of his jaw.

"Do you tell Dalton things about me?" she asked drowsily, standing up to fetch a chalice of water.

"It depends on what I am telling him," he said softly.

Her eyes flicked lazily over him as she poured the water into the cup. "So, you tell Randolph then, and let him decide what is important?"

Greyson swallowed noticeably.

"It's okay, though I would hardly trust Randolph to

make such decisions about classified information," she hissed, nearly laughing at her own irony, as well as Randolph's.

"You do not trust the head of the knights?"

She snorted. "I do not trust anyone who does not tell the whole truth." She took a drink from her glass slowly, not taking her eyes off Greyson. "My compass points true north. I might not always do the right thing, but I try to make a valiant effort to do so."

He said nothing in response.

She continued, "I want to do right by my kingdom. I must do right by my kingdom. Have you ever been to the Fourth?"

"No, your Majesty, but I dream of seeing the continent."

"Do you know what the continent used to be called? Sarridolon."

He smiled softly, the corner of his mouth raising ever so slightly. "Sarridolon? They do not teach that in the First Kingdom."

"I would assume not." She set down her chalice with a *clunk.*

"And why would you assume that?"

She sat back down, twisting the end of her red hair flirtatiously, despite her efforts to remain neutral. It was too much fun to play games when you had everything to lose.

"Because it was none other than King Cian who burned Sarridolon to the ground."

EIGHTEEN

itan's pink hair twinkled in the twilight as he stood beside Dalton. His hand rested on the new king's shoulders, while he whispered to him the joys of kingship, as well as the hardships.

"My entire first year as King was nothing more than political strife between myself and my youngest brother, Aithen."

"I remember Aithen. Is he still tragically short?"

Titan howled a laugh, his smile incorrigible and wicked. "A tragedy it is! I will tell him you said that."

"Get married if you so please, so I never have to invite him to one of these blasted events. I'd much rather deal with you." He shoved Titan playfully. It was good to be with friends.

Titan chuckled sadly. "I have not found the one yet, but I am looking."

Dalton raised an eyebrow. "Surely, there must be someone in your kingdom you are taken by."

Raising an eyebrow, Titan laughed. "Rather, I saw someone this evening I was taken by, but I am not sure how it would work."

"Someone from the First Kingdom?" Dalton could not hide his surprise.

"A young lad with blond hair and dark blue eyes. He was a marvel. He was with a girl with violet eyes and raven black hair, easing her anxieties is what I could see from afar." Titan stared off into the distance dreamily.

Dalton nearly choked on the air he breathed, knowing exactly who Titan meant. "One of my knights?"

"Ah, yes. One of your knights." He laughed. "Do not worry, I will not steal any of your military personnel. I believe I will be gone by the time the sun rises, but I will be sure to see you before I go."

Dalton blinked and shoved away all conversation he wished could be had. He knew who Titan was speaking of— the young knight Lawton Thornwood.

And he knew exactly who Titan had seen him speaking with earlier. But he could not talk about her. Not this night.

Changing the subject, Dalton chided, "Must you leave so soon?"

"The Sixth needs its ruler, as do the other kingdoms in uncertain times like these."

"How did you do it?" Dalton asked softly.

"Do what?" Titan replied, his white smiling blazing with curiosity and kindness.

"Become such a marvel, a strong leader," he huffed a sigh, his shoulders deflating on the exhale. "The First Kingdom has been invaded and terrorized for so long because my father never stood up to anything. He let these things happen. He was so passive."

"The First Kingdom needs a ruler with raw power and an iron fist," Titan said, causing Dalton to flinch. "But it also needs someone who understands what it is to feel terror, to be locked away, and shamed for who you really are. They need someone—as the world does—to lead the charge on whoever is responsible for the state of our world."

"Now I have to ask when you got so damn wise," Dalton said with a smirk. He balled his hand into a fist and gently pushed it up against Titan's shoulder.

"You will be wiser tomorrow than you were today. It comes with the crown."

"I did not know there was a job description that came from this position," Dalton said with venom.

"You will learn quickly what the rules are, and what the rules are not."

"Do you always talk in riddles?"

Flashing a dangerous smile, Titan replied, "Only when I do not know the answers."

Dalton laughed, his head tipping back as though he were howling at the moonlight. "So, you are essentially giving me all this advice, which is much appreciated by the way, then you are going to speak to one of my knights you find attractive, and then you are going to leave? When can I go to your kingdom and gallivant my way in such a manner?"

Titan giggled, his shoulder length hair glistening radiantly. "The matter with the knight is something I do not have time to speak of today, but I assure you it is far more pointed than just his good looks. He is ravishing, though, is he not?"

Titan clicked his tongue against the roof of his mouth, as if he were pondering something deeper than physical attraction. "As for visitation, you are absolutely right. How dare I come to your kingdom and do nothing but lounge and watch you battle for dominance with the biggest ass in the Ten Kingdoms?"

"Did I win?" Dalton asked, kinking his head to the side.

"Undoubtedly, Saphirrus. Blarquenza will be quiet for a long while after that display of power. I, for one, was truly impressed."

Dalton's mind wandered back to his fantastically devilish interaction with Blarquenza. He had been the epitome of true power then, like the legends of Queen Ciara in full rage. He wished he could have watched himself for he was sure he was magnificent.

Pondering, Dalton did not know how to ask, so he just did. "Do you have any gifts from the Gods?"

Titan's eyes twinkled with a deeper wisdom than he was letting on. Dalton could tell because he had been close with Cyril all his life. When Cyril knew something, his blue eyes erupted with expression. The blues became darker, as if the irises themselves were in deep thought. At this moment, Titan's eyes did the same thing.

"The Gods have plans for us all. I feel as though we need to remember them more clearly."

"Do you know their names?"

"The three that matter, yes. Though I do not suppose that the First Kingdom does? I quite love how this place is so Godless." He shivered, but Dalton figured it was for dramatic effect.

"I think we became this way after the death of Queen Ciara . . ." Dalton wondered aloud, trying to think back on his lessons with the Thinkers about the First Kingdom's history.

"Ah yes, the Queen of Fury rejected the Gods entirely. She said they did not wield the power of men."

"You speak as if you knew her," Dalton whispered, feeling oddly sentimental in this conversation and longing for Cyril's storytelling. Though he supposed the old man was off somewhere sulking at Dalton's example and vow at the coronation.

He would have to get over it eventually.

"The world is oddly divided on the manner of the First Kingdom, for one is either like Cian or Ciara."

Dalton put his head on his hands, shaking it as if he were trying to remove himself from this conversation.

"Oh Titan," he whispered. "We were having such a lovely time, and now you go off and mention the exact things Cyril has been blabbing into my ears my entire life."

Titan laughed, his hand coming to the top of Dalton's right shoulder. "The Thinkers are always right, I am afraid, in one way or another. They have told me something recently that is rather intriguing. I cannot wait to watch it unfold."

"I will never tell Cyril you said that," Dalton deadpanned.

"And I will never give advice or tell stories that don't have truth to them." Titan paused, surveying the sky above them before speaking once more. "My favorite of the Gods is the Goddess Karmonisa. She decided the fates of souls, of life and death."

"She sounds charming," Dalton said with as much sarcasm as he could punch into his voice.

"Ah, Saphirrus, your charm is a ceaseless wave pounding against the shore. Everlasting as it is damaging to those who just want to sunbathe."

"You are strange," Dalton said.

He turned to stride away, rather done with Titan's antics, when Titan said. "The Thinker at my castle, Riaus, told me a story once of how Ciara made an enemy of the Goddess, and Karmonisa worked against her as a result."

Dalton turned his head, an eyebrow quirked as if to say, "*And?*"

"Riaus could not tell me the rest of the story, but he did tell me that the Goddess is not one to make an enemy of."

Dalton whipped his head back and continued to saunter back into the castle. As he entered the threshold, he could have sworn he heard Titan call after him, yet he beat on.

NINETEEN

A sob escaped Charmaine's lips the moment she entered her chambers after the festivities.

She was crumbling, despite what Randolph told her about the fates and changing destiny. Maybe it was Gwendolyn's destiny to lose her head, but why did Charmaine have to be haunted by the memory? Everyone she knew at the castle—Dalton, Randolph, Cyril, Elena—they had all experienced more pain than most in the span of their lives. Although Charmaine knew she was not the only one in the Ten Kingdoms to experience grief, the only thing she could equate it to was her own.

It was crippling, to constantly be weighed down by the pain of it all.

As the door slammed behind her, she clutched her rib cage, trying to breathe through the tears. They poured down her cheeks, hot and sticky. Her nose was wet, and she was sure her entire face was red. All composure, all that work which she had put in throughout the last hours, was all for nothing. She had succumbed to her pain after all.

She groaned, frustrated and disgusted with herself. James would never want this type of pain for her. Ten Kingdoms— she did not want this type of pain for herself.

A shaking hand ran through the crown of her hairline, then down through the back of her curls. It was all she could do for herself in this moment, to keep the darkness off her face while she fell apart.

She keeled over, her forehead touching the ground of her chambers as her knees stayed on the floor. She breathed in the cold marble, welcoming the freezing temperatures to offset the heat of her meltdown.

Blinking and looking at nothing, she waited until her breathing became steady once more. Randolph's voice of reason played in her head over and over, and she utilized it to come back to reality. She did not know what it was about Randolph that calmed her down, but he always managed to do so.

Dalton was able to bring her back from the depths of her power, but rarely was he able to comfort her. She half-laughed to herself at the thought, nearly hysterical, but Dalton often brought about more anxiety than he intended. It was not his fault, though it was a part of his being. He was the King of Snow, and therefore, everything he did had gravity to it.

She could never tell him that, even though he knew it already. Charmaine would never subject him to more frustrations.

But Randolph? There was something comforting about his mysterious wisdom. Maybe it was the fact that he never tried to tell a joke amidst a serious conversation, or that not knowing anything about him somehow made his advice more welcoming. Randolph Eniar could settle Charmaine like nobody else.

Well, nobody else like James Grimes.

Closing her eyes one more time, breathing in the memory of her brother, as well as the prior conversation with Randolph, Charmaine rose to a young man sitting in her chambers.

She yelped, scrambling backward until her back collided violently with the wooden door. She turned quickly, her heart threatening to burst from her chest, when the voice spoke.

"Charmaine Grimes, I have waited a long time for this meeting."

Despite her mind screaming at her to run, she turned around and met the face of a young man who resembled nobody other than Dalton Saphirrus himself. His skin was tanner than Dalton's, christened by sunlight, whereas Dalton was touched by the stars. No freckles danced across his face in a constellation of random joy, but rather, he was the epitome of perfection. His straight nose and chiseled jawline were a match made by the Gods themselves, and those familiar, deep blue Saphirrus eyes burned into her like sapphires on Dalton's crown. He wore an all white tunic and pants combination, and he was barefoot.

Charmaine squinted, even rubbed her eyes to make sure he was real.

He was—though he was rather foggy, as if he were a memory, rather than a man.

"Who are you?" Her voice wavered.

"I think you know," he said softly, though his voice elevated the draw she knew too well. This was who she thought he was.

She bowed her head, refusing to utter the name of the King that had appeared before her. "What are you doing here?"

"I have been allowed to step back, to visit your memories while you sleep."

"I am not awake?"

Cian Saphirrus gestured in front of him, and Charmaine nearly gasped at her body laying on the floor.

"I am afraid you passed out," he said with sadness. "It is

your grief that binds us, allows you to see me just this once."

Just this once?

But instead, she found herself asking, "You are burdened by harrowing grief as well?"

He sighed, his blue eyes hauntingly like Dalton in that moment. Charmaine wondered for the first time how his story had ended, for it was never told what happened following the end of his Queen Ciara. She knew he had children, but there was often not context in the story. The life of Cian beyond Ciara was not one for bedtime stories for children. It made her wonder if it was more so the content of nightmares for adults.

"Every day of my life and my death."

"Did you die young?" She found herself blurting, then covering her mouth a second later. "I am sorry, I did not mean to—"

Cian smiled, his white teeth shining and a dimple appearing on the right side of his face. "No, I have chosen to remain young in death. It reminds me of the light, the better times."

"The Gods give you choices when you die?"

"If you earned them in life." He chuckled. "Unfortunately, there is not a lot of time for questions, Charmaine, but I have come to tell you one thing, and one thing alone. You must promise me that you will not tell a soul, not my grand sire, not the King of the Seventh Kingdom, and especially not Cyril."

The King of the Seventh Kingdom? How in the name of the Gods would I know the King of the Seventh Kingdom? And if I did, how would I explain any of this?

"I promise," she gulped.

"The dagger is the key."

Charmaine nearly fell over; her grief that had been

quelled by the presence of the former King in legends returned full-fledged. "What did you say?"

"Diamond Killer," Cian whispered softly, taking an angelic step toward her. "Diamond Killer is the key."

"I do not have it," she said.

She had not wanted anything to do with it since Dalton had almost given it to her in Brinn. She refused to touch the weapon that had taken Gwendolyn from her, convinced the knife was evil reincarnate somehow.

As if reading her mind, Cian said, "The dagger is not evil, but if you do not wield it, the people of the Ten Kingdoms will bow to the wrong man."

"The King of the Seventh Kingdom?" It had been so many years since the Seventh Kingdom had been involved in politics. Dalton had never mentioned their presence amongst the continent's world stage.

Cian laughed, his eyes telling a story of fire and rage, yet pride. "The King of the Seventh Kingdom is not the wrong man."

As though she had been dragged back into her body, Charmaine awoke gasping. Her face was swollen with the tears that had poured down her face prior to losing consciousness, and her head throbbed.

"What in the name of the Ten Kingdoms—" she managed to get out before she retched all over her chamber floor.

TWENTY

weat poured down the sides of Lawton Thornwood's face, the concentration causing him to grit his teeth, nearly biting off his tongue in the process.

Randolph had told him to train, therefore to work he must go. He should have seen this coming, for jumping could be a skill set that could be much more than a parlor trick. The thought had crossed his mind on more than one occasion—what he could have done differently to save James Grimes, for instance. He had been with James in that grouping. If Lawton had grabbed him, maybe he could have spared so many people their pain.

Though, he had never been able to take anyone with him when his power allowed him to jump. Not like Charmaine had taken Dalton when she disappeared.

He still did not know if he would be able to do that, if ever. But he did know if he could jump great distances, perhaps to other kingdoms and capitals, then maybe they could stand a chance. He would be given purpose, beyond his knightly duties, and he would finally be able to repay the First Kingdom for giving him such a gift.

He had not done it frequently, as of late, but he had

started practicing recently again as Randolph had encouraged. It could be useful, extremely useful, if played right.

Concentrating with all his might, he tried again. He jumped to the other side of the hallway, staggering as he fought to stand up straight.

He had jumped down this hallway seventy different times in the last hour, commanding himself to visualize and move without fear. It was maddening, the definition of insanity, to do the same thing over and over and expect a different result.

He had told himself that maybe the next time he would not feel as dizzy. Maybe the next time he would feel as though he was ready to try jumping further. But it was to no avail.

With a startle and gasp, he realized he was not alone. A tattooed hand came to the top of his left shoulder, and the voice of his legion head commanded him with one word.

"Stop," Randolph muttered.

"I only jumped seventy times," Lawton said with a grunt, falling onto his buttocks. "I was hoping to be done after one hundred."

"And how many times have you jumped in a row before this night?" Randolph's voice was laced with concern. He pinched the bridge of his nose, as if he were floundering on patience already with Lawton.

A piece of Lawton's heart thundered with chaotic energy when Randolph was exasperated. It made him feel loved, adored, and like he mattered. But the other part of him felt sad, lonely, and equally dismal. He did not know how to cope with the warring parts of Randolph's personality. On most occasions, he was able to take it in stride. Randolph had a harder life than most, and he harbored more secrets than most men could bear. But that did not excuse the symmetry of rejection and savoring that happened within him when the King of the Seventh Kingdom spoke to him in any capacity.

It came down to this for Lawton: he loved his friend dearly, and he did not want to see him in any more pain. He carried *enough*.

"Three or four. I have gone further than this, though," Lawton spat.

Randolph crouched down, with his brown gaze full of warmth. He smelled of wine and metal, as if he had doused himself in the liquid and then gone to training with the sword. Lawton closed his eyes, too entranced by the sight of his greatest friend.

"Let us be done, that is more than enough training for tonight."

A tattooed hand grabbed Lawton's, hoisting him to his feet. "I want to be ready. I want to help when the world goes to shit."

Randolph snorted. "It has already gone to shit. Let us hope when it explodes that we are on the right side of the blast."

***

Lawton ignored Randolph's advice, and after he left him, he tried two more times. Just two.

It was the same result. Lawton cursed at the unchanging results. It was maddening, to be able to hold this incredible gift, and have no idea how in the name of the Ten Kingdoms to use it.

Dabbing off his sweat-riddled face with a cloth, he reentered the castle to fall asleep. As the white corridor expanded around him, he was immediately overtaken with the scent of lavender and peaches. Scrunching his nose to get a better sense of what was happening, he nearly screamed as a body appeared behind one of the white marble pillars of the castle's hallway.

"I am sorry to frighten you," the voice said softly, in earnest.

"Ten Kingdoms, it is no trouble at all."

As the body stepped into the candlelight, Lawton stifled a gasp. It was King Titan of the Sixth Kingdom. Pink hair illuminated in the moonlight, skin twinkling as if it was killed by the stars.

"I am so sorry for the intrusion—I was leaving the courtyard."

"I wanted to introduce myself," King Titan said, extending a hand.

Lawton took it, surprised by how firm yet soft it was. His skin was like butter, warm and inviting. Shaking his hand awkwardly, Lawton bowed his head.

"I am Lawton Thornwood, a member of King Dalton's legion of knights, and a member of the First Kingdom."

"So proper," King Titan drawled.

Or at least, Lawton thought he heard the King of the Sixth Kingdom drag out his syllables in interest.

"I suppose the title is," Lawton said calmly, though his heart was pounding a hundred miles a minute. He was sure if he was like this for much longer, his heart would burst.

"I am Titan."

Lawton nearly burst out laughing, his informality so stark and refreshing.

"And am I to address you as such?"

The King had turned away, his vibrant pink hair glowing in the darkness of the tunnel. Though Lawton could still make out a dashingly white smile, enchanting. "You may call me whatever you like."

Lawton raised an eyebrow.

The King continued, not bothering to look behind him. "We will meet again, Lawton Thornwood. I merely wanted to introduce myself, so that the next time we meet, the formalities will not be necessary. I have many Thinkers in my castle, and I know as a result that you are very important. We *will* meet again. And we will become great friends."

And time stood still until that exact moment for Lawton, for something cracked within his chest as the pink-haired King walked away from him. A piece of destiny was free, about to wreak its chaos all over the world.

TWENTY-ONE

arinthya Faye Saphirrus felt the brunt force of the blade before she saw it. She had been sitting against the back of her bed, as she had for the past six years, when suddenly, the wind changed.

It had been howling outside of her chambers, but now it whipped from within. Before she could lift her gaze to meet the force of the breeze, the cool pressure of a knife was applied against the center of her neck. She welcomed the violence and whomever was holding the weapon. She silently prayed they would cut her throat and be done with it. She had been tempted to move her neck into the weapon, draining herself of her blood slowly, but paused out of curiosity.

Who had dared come to see her this evening?

She opened her eyes to see the familiar tanned skin of King Finn's manservant. His long dark hair was pulled back in a braid, his scarred upper lip pursed in a line of irritation. *Boy*, she had named him in her head. It had not been creative, but she had called him it nonetheless. All the names she knew were the names of people she had known in her past life, the one where she was royalty. And anything she had tried to come up with reminded her of someone from home.

And she never wanted to think of that place again.

For the past six years, *boy* had been attached to Finn's

hip, doing his every bidding and kissing the ground he walked on. She could not remember a time when he did not serve the mad King. She knew nothing about him, for they had never spoken beyond the duties he performed.

Whoever this man was, Carinthya hated him.

But not as much as she hated herself.

Three months ago, Carinthya had watched the Seventh Kingdom burn to the ground at the hands of the madman who had never *truly* died when Ciara had stabbed him with the immortal sword forged by Cian and Sean. The sword had taken his power, then put him to sleep, since he had made a deal with the evil Gods to restore the old ways and old kingdoms. To put the continent back under the rule of one leader would change the world's democracy and undermine every man, woman, and child in the Ten Kingdoms.

They had been lying low these last six years. She had sat idly as the dead king built up his army of allies. They had lurked in the shadows, and even though this attack had been so conspicuous, it seemed to her that nobody had discovered that it had happened. The Seventh Kingdom laid low enough on the radar, ostracized for many years with the king that had passed away and the son who had never taken up the throne.

Over the past few nights, she had closed her eyes and watched the Seventh Kingdom burn all over again. She could hear Princess Reine screaming in the chambers. Carinthya wanted to tell her it was useless. Finn would never come see her, unless she served a purpose. And it was best never to serve a purpose for Finn. He was not kind to his play-things.

King Finn did not care, just as he had not cared when the sword that pierced his heart killed his only daughter. Just as he had not cared when he captured an innocent girl of only sixteen, leaving her to rot in a cell to be used as collateral years later.

Carinthya wondered if her brother would recognize her.

"Carinthya," the servant boy hissed through the air. It was practically silent.

"I almost forgot you were there," she grumbled, opening her blue gaze fully to meet his hazel ones.

She was not afraid of this man, despite whom he served. She was about to spit in his face when she realized his gaze was clouded with grief and worry. She opened her mouth to ask him what was wrong—one of her good habits she had retained from growing up a princess—when he interrupted her.

"Your mother and father are dead."

He removed the knife from her throat, his dirty hands putting the blade away slowly. A tear slipped down her cheek, but she did not dare acknowledge it by wiping it away. Not now. Not ever.

"How?" It was all she could manage against the depths of her trauma.

"King Finn's men. Assassination in the First Kingdom."

"At the castle?" she asked, not sure why she cared. *They were not family. Not anymore.*

"In a town called Brinn. Do you know it?"

She nodded. It was not far from the castle, though she had never been to the humble villages outside of the confines of her court. "And what of my brother?"

"The King of the First . . . His ascension has come."

Carinthya physically slacked in her bed. Her poor brother, shackled to the crown and that Gods-forsaken Kingdom that had not seen glory since Ciara. She could scarcely remember the sound of his laugh or the precise blue of his eyes. *How was I to pray to the Gods for him when I could not remember what it was like to be near him?*

"I'm sorry, Princess," he said sadly. And she believed him.

"Why are you telling me any of this? Was it not when we took the castle that *you* were the servant designated to reinstate my chains?" Hatred filled her voice, and she realized in that moment how much she must have sounded like her father.

It terrified her.

"Because, Princess, we are to get out of here." His hazel eyes twinkled.

"We?" she asked, barely audible against the howling winds of the Seventh Kingdoms castle's confines. "I do not know you. For six years, you never glanced my way!" Apprehension erupted through her tone.

She had overheard from King Finn that this was where he had decided to stake his claim for now, as he planned to invade the Sixth Kingdom in the coming weeks. He had been calculating in the interim, and was in no rush to revive the kingdom which he had decimated with force.

"You and me, Princess."

"And why should I believe a damn word you say?" Her voice cracked with rage. She was trembling, beside herself with turmoil and mistrust.

"Because your brother is the King of Snow, and if we can get to him, we can be free."

Her entire body seemed to seize in that moment, her heart skipping a beat as his words doused over her like a cold bucket of water being dumped over her head. "What did you just say?" she hissed.

"Call me Callum," he whispered, backing away and lifting up his hands in a gesture of innocence. "Your brother is the King of Snow. I think it is best not to be here when King Finn finds out for certain."

II

The King Who Was Lost
and Has Yet to Be Found

TWENTY-TWO

ith a grunt of frustration and grit, Charmaine thrust the sword toward Randolph. Her weapon clanged against his with brute force. Her lean arms were aching, her back on fire as her shoulders screamed for release.

But she did not stop swinging.

Her hair was tied behind her in two long braids. It started at the crown of her head and worked its way back, not one strand out of line. Charmaine had been wearing her hair like this during their training sessions the past few days and decided she wanted to make it a new part of herself.

This refined version, one whom did not have a brother. The one where the girl was missing part of her soul.

Her legs ached for a moment to sit, catch her unsteady breath, but she wanted to keep wearing the leather pants Cyril had gifted her. It seemed stupid to anyone but her, but she was unstoppable in her battle garments. When she wore them, she was not a girl at the mercy of men. She was a woman who had the chance to bring men to their knees. And if she sat down, demanded a break, or showed any sign of weakness to these men—no matter that they were her friends and protectors—they would ask her to stop.

And she did not want to stop.

She wanted to say she only desired vengeance and the heads of the men who took her only family away from her. But she knew she was not there yet in her journey. Though, she could feel it on the horizon. The sadness and fear that had tainted the entirety of her life was washing away with the anguish that deteriorated in her heart.

Since the funeral four days ago, and the coronation three days ago, Charmaine thought of nothing but the innate source of her pain. It was not James who she resented, though she missed him every moment she was awake. Neither was it her own parents who had left her so many years ago. She had the time to sort out those emotions and come to terms with reality. It was the mercenaries, the soulless men who largely remained an enigma to the kingdom, despite causing so much terror.

She was blinded by grief, but she would not let anyone see. She would persevere, then she would find out more about the men who took her home and brother from her.

Randolph lifted his sword effortlessly, the dance of the fight easy for him. Charmaine tried to match his every move, committing it to memory, so she could hope to be as skilled as him one day. He fought better than anyone she had ever seen. His body was fluid, all lean muscle, and he sang the song of his long sword. Questions lingered on her tongue, as they always did, but she held back.

Charmaine had not yet tried to spar with Dalton. Due to Randolph's new personal—temporary—guard assignment to the King, he had not allowed such a thing to happen. Dalton had begged, insisting he could help her. At first, Charmaine had wanted Dalton over Randolph. He was a better listener and never held a sense of judgment over her, despite his power. But as she continued to work with Randolph, she was floored by his teaching skills.

He was serious; his amber eyes glazed over as he drank in each move she made. The first day they had done this, she felt so exposed in her leathers. It was as if she were naked, without a corset. His eyes ran up and down her visible body shape, for the purpose of the training, but she felt like every inch of her had been laid bare for him to see.

Over the next few sessions, though, Charmaine realized there was nothing to be self-conscious about. She had worn dresses more scandalous than these leathers, and they had been the dressings the world considered proper for a lady.

She scoffed, lifting her sword again, as Randolph prepared for the offensive.

"Remember your strengths, Charmaine. You have the element of surprise." He was talking of her invisibility.

She went beet red, and it was not from working so hard during the session.

"I cannot use that in battle," she whispered, stunned by his casual tone.

"Oh, yes, you can, and you will have to," a voice said from the entryway.

Her eyes wandered to Cyril, looking shorter today with his large, blue, Thinker robes on. "Do not think for a second that you are not able to use your gifts, not anymore, not in this Kingdom."

"Not in my Kingdom. Be who you were born to be, Char," Dalton said possessively, his dark blue eyes flashing with pride.

Dalton had encouraged her to embrace her powers since he declared his in front of the entire world. She was not sure she was ready for that yet, but she agreed to start training with Randolph and Dalton. She had trained with James when they were back in Brinn, and it had proved useful when disaster struck.

"And will you, my Majesty? Be who you were born to be?" Randolph asked Dalton directly, a playful and cruel smile on his lips. Despite his indignant attitude, Charmaine thought it good that he was having some semblance of fun.

"Will you, your Majesty, be who you were born to be?" Dalton shot back, drawing his longsword.

Randolph's charm disappeared off his face faster than it had appeared, looking at Charmaine with an expression that said, *'get out of the way.'*

Charmaine stepped off the ring immediately, eager to watch Dalton fight Randolph. She had seen Dalton fight before, during the mercenary attacks. He had used all his strengths—his lean build and speed. He was fast, moving with grace throughout the crowds of mercenaries as he ruthlessly cut them down. She tried to push the rest of the evening from her head and focus in front of her. Reflecting on the past constantly was exhausting.

Randolph had stepped forward, bowing before his King. Dalton walked into the ring and did nothing but lift his sword higher.

Asshole.

"Do not be nice on my account, Randy," Dalton said with a growl.

And then he slammed his sword into Randolph's and their fight began.

It was a clashing of noises so fast that Charmaine could barely keep up. Randolph dashed to the left, spinning as he missed a direct swipe to the side from Dalton's blade. Dalton laughed wildly, his white hair flowing behind him as he ran around the circle, jumping and twisting with utter joy. The fight brought him alive, set him on the course to who he was born to be.

The King of the First.

Charmaine gasped. Her hand flew over top of her mouth as Randolph sliced off a white curl on Dalton's head with his sword. He had missed the King's eye by a mere centimeter.

Cyril darted over to her side and held her hand. Except, he did not look worried. "He will be fine. I hope he gets cut up enough to realize who he is dealing with."

Charmaine laughed. *Who he was dealing with? This was Randolph, his guard! Cyril has nearly lost his mind.*

"I will get you for that, your Majesty." Dalton lifted his sword into the air once again. "I did not ask for a haircut today."

"You needed one, your Majesty," Randolph said with a laugh.

Without warning, Dalton's entire sword lit up with ice. He snarled, his teeth flashing like an animal. Cyril shouted at him, but she could not hear anything over the wind that picked up around them. He spun through the wind as its conduit, then turned around twice. With each full circle he made, a jagged shard of ice launched toward Randolph.

Randolph yelped, using his sword to cut each down at the last second. He looked at Dalton. Charmaine swore she caught despair in his eyes.

"You did not tell me you were going to use magic! You fool! You could have killed me!"

Dalton lifted a hand. Ropes of snow emerged from the ground without a precursor. There was no snow falling, no chill in the wind. The only indicator where the power came from was a small patch of snow on the dirt circle, which now had three ropes made of snow sticking out of it. Dalton closed his fingers, bringing Randolph down onto one knee. He strode toward him, rage pulsating through the air, and lifted Randolph's chin with a single icy finger.

Charmaine was not sure that either she or Cyril drew a breath. *What was Dalton doing?*

He lifted his knight's head. Charmaine could see the feral rage building within. Randolph was seconds from losing his shit. Calling Dalton a fool was enough of a mistake, but fighting back once he had already been stopped by his powers? It was a death sentence.

"If you want to be a King—or even if you do not, that is fine too—it can be rather dreary—you need to learn to be who you are, Eniar. Or so help me and the Gods, *I will make you.*"

And with that, he smirked, unclenched his hand, and walked out of the courtyard.

***

For all his dramatics, Dalton had effective methods for royally pissing off Randolph. The King blazed out of the training yard, all nonchalant attitude and not a care in the Ten Kingdoms radiating from him. Cyril had nearly dashed after him, yelling something about meeting with the council about grain for the border villages.

Randolph picked up his weapon and sheathed it. Wiping the sweat off his brow, he made a move to turn toward the entrance when Charmaine's soft hand grabbed his hand.

"You are not leaving, not until we talk, Rand."

His jaw nearly fell open. Charmaine had changed in the last three months, as had their relationship. But he had never received an order from her like that before. He liked it. She had endured horror after horror. To see her spread her wings even slightly gave him hope.

"Yes?" he said, unable to hide the surprise in his voice.

"What is going on between you two?" Her violet eyes blazed in worry.

Ah, there it is.

Charmaine was the fiercest of friends. He had seen it with her relationship with the King. They were rather inseparable, leaning on one another as darkness swarmed around them. He was happy they had one another. There might have been a time where it dawned on him that he could grow feelings for her. But he had never acted on them, especially when he saw the way Dalton reacted.

He cleared his throat, trying to be normal. Her frown and raised eyebrow let him know he was failing before he even began. Fantastic.

"You have been keeping things from me for a long time. Both of you have. I have been patient with it, out of curiosity that you have pushed me on anything that has happened in my past." She grabbed his hands, her thumbs tracing over his tattoos.

The gesture was not romantic in nature, rather, full of friendship. It had become their thing as of late, out of Dalton's eyesight, obviously. The King would lose himself if he saw her touching him so methodically, but it calmed him. As much as he tried to hide his past, Charmaine touching his physical reminders brought him peace—an acknowledgment, but not an admittance.

"I am sorry I have not been honest with you. Not completely."

"Can I ask you a question and you ask me one? A trade. You do not have to give me all the answers, not right now, but I need something, Randolph."

"I can try," he whispered, his gaze flickering uncomfortably to the ground.

"Why did you join the knights, Rand?" Her voice was quiet. He opened his mouth to answer, and she cut him off sternly. "If you say it was for the money again, you will lose your question privilege from me."

He chuckled. "Was it that bad of a lie?"

"It was the worst. I was not stupid then, even as a stranger to this court." She smirked, but worry blossomed behind her features.

She really did care about him, and it was that level of respect which kept her from pushing when he was not ready. Dalton, clearly, did not respect nor care about him. But whatever he did was working. Randolph's walls were coming down. *Maybe it was intentional?*

"You have been sharp since day one, Charmaine."

"Now answer my question, or I am going to be honestly concerned that you and Dalton hate one another on account of the draw between Dalton and I. And frankly, I do not want to be responsible for you two being driven against one another. It got old fast. And I hate being cold."

He let go of her hands, running two of them behind his neck. "No, it is not on your account, Char. I feel as though things between Dalton and I have always been rocky."

She raised an eyebrow, crossing her arms over her chest.

He smirked, knowing he was teasing more information than he was willing to give away. "But that is a story for another day. You asked why I joined the knights."

"Yes." Her tone exuded interest, irritation, and impatience all in one.

"I joined the knights when I was sixteen years old because I killed my father. I could no longer be in the Seventh Kingdom."

Her face paled, the flush from the training session immediately drained. She ran a hand through the top of her long braid, stopping when she could go no further. Her mouth was agape for no longer than a second as she realized she was reacting the way he expected. Like he was a monster for doing such a thing.

"You killed your father?" Her voice wavered, but she did not run.

Randolph held his breath as he watched her take in the information.

"I heard you were from the Seventh Kingdom from more than one person, but nobody ever elaborated." She paced back and forth in front of him.

He nodded, giving her a moment more.

"Why are you not speaking?"

He released his breath. "I answered your question."

She stopped, fisting her hands at her sides. If it were any other conversation, he would have laughed at her irritation, understanding suddenly what Dalton must feel when he messed with those around him. There was satisfaction in having fun and embracing humor. He would do best to remember that, to carry a piece of what made Dalton so begrudgingly infectious with him.

Once he dealt with all his shit.

"You are incorrigible!" she half-shouted, laughing. She shoved against his shoulders with all her might.

Randolph barely moved, but let her do it regardless. "You asked and I answered."

"Randolph . . . This is . . . I am sorry. I do not know what I expected."

"See why I told you it was for the money?"

She rolled her eyes, irritation and understanding mixing within the violet hue of her iris. "I hope one day you can tell me the rest."

"Word your question better next time, love."

She narrowed her eyes, but stepped forward and wrapped

her arms around him. "I am mad you felt you could not trust me with this."

He pulled back, holding her away at arm's length. "It is not your burden to bear. Never feel like you own this secret. I am the one who bears the marks."

She looked at his inked hands—a swirling garden that danced along his hands and arms. Recognition spread across her face again.

"What is your question for me, Randolph?" she asked in a soft voice.

There was so much he already knew about her. She had been quite open with him, and as much as he wanted to ask about her mother and father, he knew it was cruel to reopen closed wounds. Especially with James gone.

He unsheathed his sword and held it out for her to take. "Can you make this disappear?"

A dark eyebrow quirked up, but her violet eyes shone with the challenge. "I do not know."

"Oh, Charmaine, you cannot answer with, 'I do not know.' Imagine if I answered that to your question. You would have had my head."

She smirked, and he faked a flinch.

"I will try."

She grabbed the sword, her arm shaking slightly with its weight.

"Now, this is a knight's sword, Charmaine. It is heavier and has more ability than a normal sword. You saw me open the castle gates with one of these, but it can also cut through stone, and if you happened to have *gifts*"—he said the word carefully, not to draw attention to the heat that built within him at the mention of his power, then he cleared his throat— "you can channel it into the weapon, and it will not break like an ordinary weapon."

"So, it is a magic sword?"

He laughed, raw and real. "Absolutely, when you put it that way. Now take the magic sword and make it disappear."

"Okay," she said

He stepped in front of her and held up a finger, noting for her to pause. "I want you to make it disappear, but I want to see you. Every finger, Charmaine, you can do it."

"I have not practiced very much," she said softly.

"Now is a great time to start."

He stepped back and interlaced his hot hands behind his back.

She held the sword out, her brows furrowed in concentration. She breathed in and out, centering her control.

"That's it; focus your energy," he said softly, letting her guide her magic.

With each breath, the weapon evaporated. It started at the hilt, and inch by inch, the weapon vanished from the air with the utmost precision. It did not disintegrate into the air like Randolph had always imagined with her power, instead it faded away, like it was never there to begin with.

Randolph crouched down, watching his sword turn invisible in the hands of the girl who had never practiced her power. Not consistently, at least.

She opened her eyes, clearly still gripping the hilt of the sword, but Randolph could not see it. He wondered if she could.

But he was out of questions, so he would not ask.

"I did it!" she squealed, jumping up and down with the weapon in her hand.

He ran toward her, picking her up by the waist as she wrapped her hands around his neck. They twirled, all laughter and pride.

With a *clang,* the weapon hit the ground, the force so loud that Randolph nearly dropped her.

"You did it!" he said, excitement blazing within him. "It seems we need to start embracing, and stop keeping secrets from one another."

Recognition flashed across Charmaine's violet eyes, as if remembering something she could not place. She blinked, and the expression left her. Randolph was not even sure if he had seen it.

"That we do."

TWENTY-THREE

alton lived life as fearlessly as one could. He never looked where he was walking. He never thought twice before he spoke. He never considered the feelings of others before trampling over them, and he never admitted when he was breaking. But the past few days, he had been avoiding and letting it control him.

He had avoided Charmaine since he was crowned King. Yes, he had seen her, but he had not talked to her for more than a few moments, and never alone for long. Not since that evening at the tavern.

Honestly, he had been living as much a lie as anyone else. She had been so proud of him for finally claiming what was rightfully his. Excitement bustled throughout the castle at the sight the world had wanted to behold for years.

Beholding of his power.

It was not that he chose to live in this permanent state of games and dishonesty, despite it being in his nature.

Over the last three months, Dalton had defiled his state on the crown. He had not let the First Kingdom fall apart. His Lords and men had maintained all semblance of control during the transition of power. But he had been an absent ruler, and Kings who did not play a role on the continent's stage were not rulers at all.

He had found himself mostly comforting the one whom mattered to him most.

Charmaine Grimes.

They had bonded—thicker than thieves—after the assassination of many people in Brinn. She had been broken beyond repair, flashing in and out of invisible fury. She had nothing to cling onto. Her home was gone. Her people were dead. Her own brother had been snatched from her. All she had was her power, and Dalton was fully prepared to help her embrace it.

Dalton knew what it was like to be power shamed into nothing. He never wished the semblance of power build up on anyone or anything, even his greatest enemies. He reflected often on his outbursts following the Snow Solstice. He had turned the whole castle into a winter wonderland, and even given himself frostbite on more than one occasion. He had been unhinged, and even though it had been great fun at times, it was not the way of magic.

Since then, Dalton had become privy to what it meant to let the magic flow out—that difference of control. When it was intentional, it was like a breath of fresh air. He became lighter. A weight lifted off of him, and he could finally breathe again. When it was unintentional, it was as if someone were standing on his chest. He was heavy, pinned down, and on the verge of passing out. It had not happened many times, but once was enough of a warning.

Even with the powers of the Kings and Queens of Old, no one was invincible.

If Dalton dwelled on it long enough, he could pinpoint this as the reason for his attitude toward Randolph Eniar. The bastard had too much power and self-control for his own good. The Gods had given Randolph a gift as they had given Dalton, Elena, and Charmaine gifts as well. And all Randolph wanted to do was serve Dalton and the First Kingdom like he had allegiance that meant something.

But being able to blow smoke literally out of your nose was one of the most incredible things Dalton had ever encountered.

He would not admit that to anyone.

Especially Randolph.

Dalton had pushed him so hard earlier in the courtyard. Flexing his power in front of Charmaine had felt more than good, but Dalton wanted to push Randolph so hard that he erupted.

He wanted Randolph Eniar to explode in the fiery pits of hell.

In a good way, of course.

Dalton nodded to the onlookers in the throne room. Even when he had avoided the crown being placed atop his head, Dalton had embraced the people of this court and country like they were his family. He knew everyone, and with the Lords mastering everything under Cyril's watchful eye, Dalton had the chance to be the monarch everyone needed without claiming anything.

He strode onward, past the throne and down into the rose garden which had begun to grow again, despite the destruction that had besieged the castle. Terror gripped him as he saw Charmaine standing at the bottom of the stairs, her thin frame noticeable under her black silk gown. He made a mental note to give her servant Athelred a talking to, for continuing to make her wear these gowns like she was the King's prize. It was a new age, and women should wear what they wanted.

She was a treasure to Dalton, but he had a wife.

And he would do best to remember that.

In the last three months, nothing had happened between

them other than the blossoming of true friendship. Dalton had embraced her and all that she needed. She required someone to sleep with her at night, and to fight off the demons that came to her in her dreams. She required someone to eat meals with her, to make sure she did not forget to take care of herself. She required someone to remind her of the things she loved—strolling about the grounds and reading in the library. She had asked for all these things—for Dalton to be all these things—and he had happily obliged.

He reached out a hand as he bounded down the final three stairs, his long fingers gracing hers with the utmost respect and desire. A King typically did not bow to anyone, but he would always bow to this girl.

For whatever reason, the Gods had dragged them together with an invisible force. He would do best to remember this in the future as well.

"My lady," he whispered, planting a kiss on her hand.

"Your Majesty," she replied softly, her violet gaze dull today.

Dalton silently cursed himself for taking so long at the earlier council meeting and not sending someone suitable with charming humor to keep her company. There were so many damn meetings that he could barely keep track.

"I am sorry for the delay. Unfortunately, there was much to attend to." He sighed, taking her hand tighter in his grasp as they strolled through the regrowing garden.

"The King is never late; everyone else is simply early," she muttered to herself, that familiar boldness peeking through for a moment, like the first sunshine of the day.

"That is right, my lady, you were early. And I trust that your accommodations today were completely unsatisfactory. It will not happen again . . ."

She cut him off with a long, elegant finger touching the

center of his lips. "Nothing was unsatisfactory, and if it was, it had absolutely nothing to do with you." Her violet eyes glistened with understanding.

"Athelred is ass company, Charmaine. You need not lie to me." He smirked, but he was serious.

Athelred's jokes were terrible. He had run away from that beseeched servant more than he could count on one hand, and there had been a reason for that.

She barked a laugh, drawing her hand away and hitting him on the shoulder adoringly. "Dalton!"

"A King should be honest. That is my number one rule."

"And what is your number two rule? No bad jokes?"

He sighed, running a hand through his white hair. It had been clipped earlier this morning, the curls less wild and more Kingly. He imagined if he went to the portrait gallery and stood next to Cian, they would look almost identical, except for the white features.

"My number two rule is that I have to come clean when I have done something suspicious, berating, or immature."

She barked another laugh, her hand flying over her mouth in pure, unadulterated joy. It was electric, but Dalton was serious.

"I wish I was playing around this time," he whispered, sitting down on the scorched earth below them.

She sat with him, not caring to sit on fallen petals with her silk black gown. "I did not realize you took this so seriously, Dalton. I am sorry for poking fun where fun is not due. Is something the matter?"

He grabbed her hand, venom lacing his words. "Never apologize for having fun. That is my third rule as of right now."

She smiled, releasing his hand.

"I have to come clean about something I have done. I am

afraid you are going to resent me for it," he said, low enough that no one except her could hear.

"What is it? You frighten me."

He smiled softly, taking her hand. "When I was crowned, Cyril had me make the vow that binds all Kings to their servitude of the country. Now, many people do not realize this vow is not one to take lightly. They think it is purely ceremonial, but that is far from the truth."

"And your vow was bad? Dalton, I thought it was beautiful . . ."

He blushed, pulling away as he set her hands back in her lap.

He recited the vow like it was an imprint on his tongue, a stain which could never be washed away. *"I do solemnly swear upon my life and the gifts given to me by the Gods, that I, King Dalton of the Snow Kingdom, First of His Name, will abide by the past lives of the Kings of Old, and will put my Kingdom and the one I love above all else."*

"Yes, that is what you said," Charmaine said quietly, not registering the full impact.

"I changed the vow, Charmaine. I am at the mercy of those I love."

She kinked her head to the side, her dark hair falling over her shoulders.

He blew out a gust of frozen air, releasing the tension building with him.

Well, it seems as if I have to say it. Ten Kingdoms help me.

"The vow prevents the monarch from doing anything wild. Does it mean I have to be a good King? Absolutely not. But it is meant to ensure the King or Queen always does what they believe to be just and right. I changed the words because I have found people I love here at the castle. I have Elena, I have Cyril . . . I even have you. And I will not put my Kingdom above the three of you. Not at any cost."

Her cheeks flushed red, and fear blazed through her purple eyes. "Dalton, what happens if you break your vow? If your promise to the Kings of Old is not fulfilled?"

"Then I will die. I will be unfit to serve our world. I told you, Charmaine, my number one rule is—"

"I do not want to hear about your bloody number one rule! I cannot lose anyone else. This . . . This . . . This *vow* could take you from the world! We must find a way to reverse it. Cyril must know—"

"Cyril basically beat me over the head when I was done with the ceremony."

Dalton was practically seething with frozen power. He exhaled again, not sure why he expected this to go any other way. Of course she was upset. But he was determined to stick to his two new rules he had made up less than five minutes ago.

Well, three new rules.

He hoped his promises did not keep building, for he did not know how many rules he had to break to become a complete and utter failure.

"He must know something. What if something happens and you cannot get there to save the one you love? What if the mercenaries attack again and someone dies, James?" She stopped, her hand flying over her mouth as she realized what she had said.

James.

She had called him James.

"Charmaine," Dalton whispered, standing to meet her as she rose.

She backed up, her unbound hair spilling over her arms as she ran a ragged hand through it.

"Charmaine, do not punish yourself—"

"No, Dalton, do not punish yourself! How dare you stand where you are, after I believed in you, after I made a promise to let you heal me, and you tell me that you could be fated to die if you cannot make your match on this oath to Kings?"

"Well, when you put it that way," he whispered, trying to coat his voice in humor to break the anxiety pulsating off of her.

She hit him with her unbound hand, her anxiety changing into rage as she came to terms with what he was doing.

Was he seriously so beloved that these people could not bear to see him leave this world? They did not realize Kings died, right? Ten Kingdoms help him.

He stiffened with fear at having to tell Elena this news. He supposed he was saving the best for last, for she would surely murder him on site.

Without warning, Charmaine stepped toward the grand staircase and wound up the castle. She did not look back at Dalton, leaving her King standing there like a tree amongst the plains of battle.

He blew a stray piece of hair out of his face and dug his hands into his pockets as he made his way after her, careful not to be heard. She deserved to be alone, as much as he deserved to come clean and feel the wrath of being desired for the first time in his life.

And with that, Dalton turned without looking where he was going and tripped over a bed of fallen roses.

TWENTY-FOUR

oodbye, guests," Dalton said sadly to nobody in particular.

The guests of the coronation departed at sunrise. Titan had been the last to leave, mysteriously walking around with a stupid grin on his face. Dalton had tried to get out of him what he had been up to since they last spoke, but Titan only assured him not to worry about it and that he was sure the Gods would bring them all together again soon.

"Let us hope it is not for another funeral," Dalton had muttered.

Titan laughed at the ill-natured joke, then embraced his friend with a grand hug. Oh, how he loved having equally insensitive friends!

Standing on the precipice of the balcony of the half-rebuilt South Wing, Dalton tried to ignore how he had royally fucked up the day before. He had done what he had to do, finally being honest with Charmaine regarding the unbreakable vow. Yet, it had completely and utterly backfired on him. He could not say he did not deserve that reaction, for he was sure that if someone he cared about—for lack of a better term—told him he made a vow ensuring if something happened to them that he would die . . .

Well, it was no wonder she was so pissed off.

A sick, twisted part of him smirked at the notion that she did care about him, not that it was a surprise to him. Rather, it irritated him.

He could not have her, yet he wanted her so badly his hands shook when he got too close to her. He did not know what to do about it other than continue to ignore all the signs pointing to bringing them together, and continue to do the right thing by her and his country.

Duty was a royal pain in the—

"Your Majesty?" A voice sounded behind him.

Dalton lazily turned his head to see Greyson standing behind him. His red garb made him stick out like a sore thumb, for it was almost as fiery as Elena's gorgeous auburn hair. Dalton snickered at the thought of the two of them walking around today, while he wore that— two peas in a pod. Elena probably despised it.

Oh, how fun it was to watch her squirm with this assignment.

"Ah, Greyson!" Dalton chided, turning around to greet the young knight that did not irritate him in the slightest like Randolph did. "What may I do for you?"

"I just wanted to report about your—"

"My wife?" Dalton said, alarm raising in his voice. "Is she all right?"

"Yes, she's fine, your Majesty."

Dalton raised a gray eyebrow in question. "Then why have you come to speak of her?"

"I find she is . . . not in need of me."

"Interesting take on the situation." Dalton was trying to hold in a budding laugh.

A King *should* be professional, decisive, and strong. Dalton, however, in this moment, was none of these things.

He was rather shocked by the admittance, though he was overcome with pride for his friend for no longer requiring a watchdog.

"I did not mean to overstep, your Majesty. I just wanted to provide my input if that is appropriate."

In that moment, Dalton wanted nothing more than to tell Greyson he could return to his normal patrolling duties, but the prophecy and vow lingered in the back of his mind. He was not done living in the Ten Kingdoms, and he could not afford to take the risk.

After a moment of pondering, with all the kindness he could muster up, he said, "I appreciate that, Greyson. You have done a fine job with my . . . wife."

Greyson smiled, awaiting dismissal.

But Dalton could not give it to him.

"But I am afraid I require your services longer. I am still unsure where the mercenaries are, and I am sure they are still at large."

Greyson visibly sagged, and Dalton nearly fell over in a fit. He could not help himself from blurting out the first thing that came to his mind like he was Charmaine Grimes. "Is Elena unbearable, Greyson?"

Turning a sickly green color, Greyson looked as though he was about to heave up his last meal. "No, absolutely not, your Majesty. I find her delightful—"

"Delightful?" Dalton was having too much fun with this.

He was cruel.

Sometimes.

"She is . . . strong. Stronger than I think anyone gives her credit for."

Dalton stepped forward and put a cold hand on Greyson's shoulder. The boy stiffened, as though he had not expected Dalton to be a literal embodiment of his title.

"I know. You are dismissed, Greyson. I promise this arrangement will not last forever."

TWENTY-FIVE

n the late hours of the night, Randolph Eniar went to the darkest corridor of the castle's dungeons. He had started coming down here when Ronan died, for he could not unleash the fire that pumped into his veins with Cyril hovering so close.

Gods forbid, if he was discovered practicing his gifts, he might have to do something with them.

He stripped off his shirt, the violet tunic hitting the floor without a whisper of a noise. He breathed in deeply, bringing his hands to the center of his chest, palms touching. It had been like pulling teeth the first month he had practiced. The flames needed extreme encouragement to come out. He had not been able to make them greater than a spark until he thought of smashing Dalton's face in for nearly catching him in the courtyard the day before.

He wished no harm on his King in actuality, but it was always nice to dream of things no one could ever have.

He nearly purred as the familiar hum of his unattainable heat flamed in his hands. He pulled them apart and opened his left eye warily to see the fire he had created.

Randolph was gifted with the magic of flames, but for too long he had hidden in the shadows of the world.

He began to dance, his hands moving in harmony with his feet as he moved about the dungeons. He lit up every chamber he passed, his smile growing feral as the dragon beneath his skin came alive.

He had resented this part of himself, the part of his legacy that was destiny's gift to him.

A pang of guilt thrummed in his heart as he remembered his sister Reine, whom had never been gifted the fire he had awoken. A part of him always felt bad, even to this day, that he was chosen by the Gods over her. But a part of him was grateful too. It was hard enough to be a member of this continent, let alone someone whom had a gift that could change the fate of the world.

He did not think he was better suited than Reine, but something woke within him when he played around like this. He let it soak into his skin and danced around the dungeons like he was a child running amuck throughout the castle.

For something which had caused so much devastation in his life, his power now seemed primed. Ready to strike. Ready to play.

He came closer and closer every day to using it in public, to laying claim to what was rightfully his.

When James had died, Randolph promised himself that he would be better than the destiny he had been promised. He wanted to do everything he could to join in and work toward acceptance. But part of him knew it was simply too good to be true—one did not accept destiny just because it was laid at your feet.

It had to be claimed. And in order to claim it, he had to claim himself.

He spun again, laughing manically as he embraced the shadows within his heart. When he had first awakened his magic, he had been sixteen. It had ended in a banishment and a death. But now, there was nothing to keep him from exploring this part of himself that he had kept under lock and key for the past three years.

"Did you hear I have a third rule—that everyone is to have fun in my kingdom and never be shameful of it?" A voice said behind him.

Without warning, and without any semblance of control, Randolph unleashed the fire he had created. He yelled out, trying to shout a warning, but it was too late. It barreled at the voice without mercy. He shut his eyes as he feared for what he did.

Power erupted around him, smoke filling the air as Randolph charged forward to meet his match.

King Dalton stood at the forefront of the dungeon. Not a hair had been harmed on his head.

"Thank the Gods," Randolph whispered, falling to his King's knees.

"Get up, Rand. I want to see that again," Dalton chided, that irreversible smirk brewing on his mouth.

"What? I can never do that again. I almost hurt you! I could have killed you." Randolph was beside himself. Once again, he had become too comfortable. He let his guard down, and it had gotten him nowhere but more out of control.

"Do you know how many people I have hurt with my power?"

Randolph bowed his head as his King stepped forward, acknowledging his presence.

Dalton snapped his hand up, thrusting his fingers into the air. A blitz of snow came out of nowhere, lifting Randolph's chin without warning so Dalton could place his fingers underneath them. His hands were ice cold, but the intensity did not reach his eyes. They were a deep blue ocean of sadness.

"Stop bowing to me like you did my father. You know it is quite unnecessary."

"It is only formal," he gritted out. His teeth chattered as the frozen temperature left his cheeks numb. "You are my King."

Dalton released his face, his teeth bared in a snarl. "I am not your King, and you know it. Stop fucking running, Eniar. I have known what you are for years. Maybe I should be the one bowing to you?"

He bowed dramatically, and Randolph's ice-cold cheeks heated immediately. "You do not know what you speak of."

"You do not know how ridiculous you are. You do not think I have known since the minute you showed up at my father's doorstep, begging to serve in the name of the First Kingdom? You said your allegiance had switched, that your father was madder than a hatter, and you wanted to pledge yourself to goodness. I heard every word because I lurked in the shadows of this castle for five years. The night you showed up on this Kingdom's doorstep was the first night I had been out in two years without an escort. I heard you beg for your life."

Randolph stilled and did not even dare to draw a breath as Dalton continued mercilessly.

"I know you are the rightful King of the Seventh Kingdom, and frankly, I do not give a shit how you got your father out of the way. I know as well as anyone, and so did my grandmother Ciara, that in order to make the world a better place, sometimes bad Kings need to die. And your father was about as rotten as mine."

"You cannot mean that you accept my regicide?" Randolph could barely breathe.

"I do not accept it, you idiot. I pardon it."

"You what?!" Randolph laid a tattooed hand against his bare chest. His heart thundered.

"You heard me. I am the King of the First Kingdom, Inheritor of the power of the Kings of Old, and I pardon you for all the nasty shit you did three years ago."

"That is not formal, nor is it possible!" He shouted at Dalton, but he could not help it.

Dalton was maddening, his white hair stark against the moonlight in a way that had Randolph's skin crawling with fear. He had fully embraced his power, this way of life Randolph had run from for so many years. He was as jealous as he was terrified.

"What is it you do not understand about the way I want to run my Kingdom, Randolph Eniar?" Dalton stepped forward, snow flurrying around them as the wind picked up. "I do not want the formalities. I want the world to be a better place, and it will be because a bad King died. I did not kill him, but I wish I would have. I plan on making those who shirk their duties pay in blood. Do you want to pay in blood? If I had to guess, I would say you have spilt enough blood in your lifetime."

"You have no right to call upon me like I am a—"

"Like you are a King? Gods be damned, you are a King! You have been the moment since you took control of your own destiny and saved your kingdom from your father's darkness!"

"Dalton—" He could not get the words out.

"What happened? What did he do to deserve it? Tell me. I will tell you of my awakening."

"Dalton . . . I . . ."

Dalton sat on the ground, but not before forming himself a stool of ice to sit on. It rose so seamlessly from the ground that Randolph almost could not believe it had not been there the whole time.

"The Thinkers told my father of a prophecy. I will not bore you with the grimy details now, but I will tell you that it predicted all that has come to pass. It called for me taking the throne, these gifts being awakened, a Queen at my side . . . Father would hear none of it. And when he made a move to take me away from this place, away from Cyril and this castle, I lost it. I battled fiercely, but the result was the same. I was locked away until Father decided I was of use. I am still not sure about the inner workings of his mind. He was more lost at the end than I realized."

Randolph envied how easily Dalton could speak, the words always captivating and full of life. That was how a King should be—a force to be reckoned with in every sense of the word. Randolph could not entrance anyone, let alone a crowd of people.

Ice shattered behind him, and he looked down to see a stool just like Dalton had.

"Sit, Rand. I insist."

"You are incorrigible, you know that right?"

"It is one of my finer qualities." He snickered.

"My sister was in danger," Randolph said.

Dalton leaned forward, drinking in all that he had to say. Dalton knew just as well as Randolph that this would only be said once.

"My father had a knife at her throat, threatening to force her into a senseless marriage with some lesser man. Some disgusting man. One I do not even have the courtesy to remember the name of. He was cruel and foul. My father did not care, though, he merely cared about getting rid of her. My sister was more than just the heir to the crown—she was a threat to his ambition. My sister had no ambitions of marriage, or even the crown. She was only a girl, merely thirteen at the time. And I felt so helpless . . . the fire just poured out of me."

"Trauma awakens the deepest of beasts."

"So, I stabbed him. I blitzed him with all that I had, the

power just as incorrigible as you." Randolph smirked, despite his best efforts. "I took him from this world and left my sister as I ran. The guards were shouting at me that I was a child of the Evil Gods. I still do not know what that means. They said I should have never been awakened, and the Prince with the brown hair was dead to the world."

"So, you ran to my father?" Dalton's eyebrows were furrowed, a puzzled expression plain as day on his face.

"I ran to the only place I had ever heard of growing up that was just and fair."

"The Kingdom of Cian?" Dalton smiled softly.

"My name is Randolph Cian Eniar. I wanted to serve the land I bear the name of."

"Well, my name is Dalton Naoise Saphirrus, and I do not wish to serve the Tenth Kingdom like its bitch."

Randolph laughed, his head tipping back senselessly. He nearly forgot he was with the King of the First Kingdom.

"I only wonder now if I was meant to serve you, since you have the powers that define my middle name . . ."

Dalton stood up, throwing his hands down as his ice stool flattened into the ground. Randolph was in awe of the powers he exuded. He knew he had practiced more these past few months, but this felt different. Dalton was gifted.

He would never let him know that, though.

"I am tired of you serving me, Randolph Cian Eniar. I want you to serve yourself. I know you are a good man, somewhere underneath that baggage you wear on your skin like armor. You helped Charmaine when I could not. You helped my father when I did not see he was lost. You murdered a man who was a tyrant."

"Do you reject my service?"

"I reject you in general, but I do not denounce you." Dalton smirked, his white teeth flashing.

"What are you saying then?"

"I am saying you are free to choose. You can keep living this lie, or you can take power where it is your birthright."

Randolph's fire built within him, and he pushed it down without hesitation.

"You need to go home, Randolph, and claim what is yours."

Flames burst from Randolph's fingertips. He groaned, blowing them out one by one. He looked up at Dalton, who was utterly entranced by the continual demonstration. "There is absolutely no way I can go back there."

"And why is that?"

Randolph rubbed his eyes with his fingers, which had cooled down immediately after the burst of flames. "I would not be accepted."

Dalton huffed a laugh. "Acceptance is a fear I understand all too well. My advice is the following: you do not know if you will be rejected until you try."

"How are you so free-flowing, flexible, even? Your own father locked you away for five years out of fear of what destiny predicted you would become." Randolph sighed. "I do not know much about destiny—or at least I do not anymore—but how did you find the strength to get up again and again, despite the weight you bore?"

Dalton smiled sadly. "The answer is simple, but sad. I did not want him to win. I *could not* let him win." He took a step closer to Randolph, his aura icy.

Randolph guessed he was projecting his powers ever so slightly to get a rise out of him. Some things never changed.

"Despite having nothing going for me, I had a lot to live for. I had desires, and I still do. I held onto my dreams."

"Which are?"

He smiled, a curl falling over his dark blue eyes. He

looked more ethereal against the darkness of the dungeons, as he did when he was in the council chambers. They had the same black stone foundation—Randolph guessed it was left over from the days of Queen Ciara. King Cian clearly had not transitioned those parts back to white by his own power. If Randolph had to guess, he figured it was intentional. If that were the case, it was rather genius—to leave the memory of your Queen in the parts where one would need the biggest reminder of their love.

"I have always wanted to be loved. Not by my people—that is not what matters to me. My biggest fear while I was locked up, dear Randy boy, was not the fear of commoners or lords hating me, nor was it my own mother and father. I knew those people were lost to me. It was the distress of those who I never thought would abandon me, and what would happen to me if they did."

"Cyril would never leave you," Randolph offered as comfort.

Dalton placed a hand on Randolph's shoulder. "When you are suffering alone at the cost of a madman, you will believe anything." He stepped back, his eyes dancing with that captivating amusement that Randolph was growing accustomed to. "If you will not go home, you should write her a letter."

Randolph blinked. "Who should I write the letter to?"

Dalton quirked up an eyebrow. "You do not need me to spell it out for you, do you? I know you are an intelligent person, despite what you may act like sometimes."

Randolph fought the urge to smack his King on the side of his head. "She will not answer. I cannot imagine she has given me a second thought, since I abandoned her and shackled her to a seat of power she was never meant to have."

"Trust me," Dalton interrupted, "When someone you

love leaves, you never put them out of your mind. Not for good. Write her the blasted letter. If she does not get anything from it, I assure you that you will."

And with that, he spun around, heading to exit the dungeon.

"Where are you going?" Randolph asked, rather in disbelief that Dalton had wanted to speak to him for this long. So personally too.

He turned his head back to look at Dalton, his eyes still glistening. *Did he ever not find life amusing?*

"Leaving you to your practicing. It is late," Dalton said. "I hope you find it within yourself to write the words you have been keeping in for three years. You know where to find me if you need any guidance on apologizing. I have much counsel to offer on the subject matter."

TWENTY-SIX

andolph sat in his chambers—a place he never wanted to be for more than a few moments if he was not asleep—and he wrote *the* letter.

He had been a ball of nerves all morning, completely overtaken with the daunting task of reaching out to the person he had lost everything for. He was not looking for understanding. He did not give a damn if she saw who it was from and then burnt it, never to think of it again. He had to tell her that he was alive, that he thought of her every day, and that he would do what he did one hundred times over if it meant she would continue to live as she was now. How hard could that be?

He knew she had taken the seat of power three years ago, and she had never taken the title of Queen. His one goal, if anything, was to take the weight off his own shoulders and get her to claim what was rightfully his. He did not know why she had not conquered it for herself. There were Thinkers at the castle who could help rally the Seventh Kingdom's council in her favor.

He could think of nobody else worthy to wear the King's crown than his own sister.

So, he sat in his chambers, quill in hand and black ink in reach, and he wrote.

Dear Reine,
It has been three years since I last laid eyes on you, and I
hope the years have not been too long.

He threw the paper aside. And he wrote again.

Dear Reine,
I am not good with words.

He nearly smashed his head on the desk.

Dear Reine,
I have no words for the man I have become, and the choices
I made are ones that I have looked back on in the last three years
in nothing but shame. You do not need to reply to this
correspondence. Frankly, I think it would be harder on us both
if you did.
I have wanted to write this letter since the moment I ran
from all the damage I caused you and our family. I do not take
it back. Our father was a cruel King and a crueler man. I hated
him then, and I hate him still. He tortured us, tried to mold us
into monsters.
But I get a sick sense of satisfaction that we are both alive,
and he cannot touch us again.
I did not want to write to update you on my life, for it is not
my place anymore to guide you and tell you how to live yours. I
wrote to you because I have something I need to tell you, and I
need you to listen.

He paused, nearly laughing at the spitfire coming from
his quill. But it was perfectly hot, so he continued, despite not
knowing if Reine would read for this long.

I relinquish my claim to the throne as the King of the Seventh Kingdom. Please accept this as my final token of service to building the life that we both deserved from the beginning.

His hands shook uncontrollably, but he fought to keep his script pristine, so Reine would not think it a forgery. She would know his handwriting anywhere.

I do not require a reply. Hearing from the courts of other Kingdoms that Queen Reine now rules in our father's stead will be enough of an answer for me.
Take care of yourself.
I love you endlessly,
Randolph

He sat back and admired his work. It was not perfect, but Reine would understand how hard this was for him. Not in the namesake of the throne, but for the sake of reaching out his hand one last time to touch hers.

He grabbed the gold wax on the edge of his desk and the light blue envelope that would hold his last conversation to his sister. He laid it in gently, afraid of smudging what he refused to write again. Closing the letter, he stamped it firmly and let the finality of his title rush off of him. Back to the dungeons he would go, for he craved the release of magic, high from the relief that coated his veins.

TWENTY-SEVEN

andolph's father's voice thundered through his head as he blasted another flame from his fingertips. *Fire could be beautiful, if wielded with grace instead of force.*

He breathed in the heat slowly, taking in all that was alive and dangerous. There was strength in his ability that he was quickly learning, besides the obvious danger and gorgeousness of his power.

Fire could in fact be beautiful, if wielded with one's heart instead of their head.

Without warning, he threw his hands out. Not even a second thought crested the surface of his mind before he realized all that was to leave him had already done so. If there was one thing Randolph sought, it was control and his innate desire to conquer the flames. When he built them from within, he felt them winding up and down his veins. They were prepped for their voyage into the world around him. Yet, when he released them, he lost all control simultaneously.

However terrifying it might be to create something and then let it be free, Randolph could not go without acknowledging the smile that spread across his face. It was life and power wrapped into one singular motion. It was as natural as swinging a sword, as speaking to a beautiful girl. It was his soul, every last piece of it.

Memories danced before his very eyes with each flash of power, the prior stronger than its predecessor. He saw the Seventh Kingdom alive with parties of his childhood, his father and mother sitting in the gardens with him and Reine as happy children—he fought the tears that threatened to fall from his amber eyes as he shoved away what little happiness in his life he could cling to.

The heat that swirled around the dungeon soaked his back with sweat. He was thankful for the solitude, for down here it was just him and his flames.

And he was King of them this night.

Going again, he thrust his hands out, never tiring of the freedom he and his sister had been forced to hide as a child. He strangely related to Dalton in that way, for both of their fathers tried to suppress their gifts. The difference was that Ronan was terrified of what magic unleashed could do, as someone who had no experience with it. Randolph's father, on the other hand, was a monster within himself. He wanted to control his children, utilize them as weapons one day. He had no fear about the power of the flames his children could produce, and Randolph did not blame him.

After all, a knife had brought about his doom.

Twirling once more, Randolph gave in to the urge to try something he had never done before. He spun twice, rapidly gaining momentum on the stone floors. His focus was unparalleled. In this moment, he was sure that nothing could break him from his concentration; nothing could keep him from his goals. With a grunt of effort at the last second, he lifted his foot into the air and channeled his inner flames in and out of his body.

The fire erupted out of his boot, defying all laws of sense

and shutting down all preconceived notions about what he was born to do. In that moment, Randolph fought back sobs over cheers because of what he realized.

The only one keeping him from being who he was supposed to be was himself.

***

Dalton followed Charmaine inconspicuously.

Although, he was pretty sure she knew he was following her.

She wound down the castle's corridors aimlessly, as though she were sleepwalking. However, Dalton knew by the way her head turned and her feet hit the ground in anxious anticipation, she was awake. He had been venturing to speak to her, to apologize, when he caught her roaming. Now they were part of a game, and he hated to lose.

He strode behind her at ten horse lengths, his distance a variable that made him feel safe. The effects of the draw were not substantial enough to compel him to do something utterly stupid, yet he was close enough that he could feel the reverberation in his chest.

Crossing his hands behind his back, he stepped after her stride for stride. Never getting closer, and never getting further away, Dalton continued to follow her as she made her way down the halls.

He waited, almost impatiently, for her to turn around and acknowledge him. But she did no such thing. She was relaxed, enjoying the stroll around the castle. He swore she enjoyed the solitude of this type of company. There was something in her body language and something in his heart that confirmed this.

They were like this for some time, pushing soundless boundaries and tampering with the rules of society. Yet,

Charmaine never turned around to acknowledge the smirk plastered over Dalton's face.

As they descended the stairs, he rounded the corner seconds after she did to a bloodcurdling scream.

The sight of Randolph spinning as a raw yell cut through the air knocked Dalton's breath from his lungs. Flames danced on the edge of the dungeons, the heat so intense that Dalton could not lash out his frozen power.

In his peripheral vision, Dalton saw Randolph pause, yet all he could do was run toward Charmaine. She had collapsed onto the floor, her breath ragged and her sobs so filled with pain that it was as if James had died again. Clutching her hands to her chest, she curled inward as if to protect her hands from sight.

"Let me see, let me see, let me see . . ." Dalton whispered, his freezing hands acting as a conduit to counteract Randolph's raw power.

She moved to answer him, but no words came out.

And Dalton's heart turned to ice as he saw the raw burns that encompassed her hands from her wrists to the tips of her fingers.

"Char—" he started, speechless, enraged, and terrified all at the same time.

With a flash, Randolph dashed up the winding staircase with one word ringing through the stones. The name of the person who could heal this entire situation.

Heal her hands.

"Elena."

TWENTY-EIGHT

ou are a bloody idiot—both of you are—you know that, right?" Elena shouted at Randolph as she exited Charmaine's chambers. "You could have killed her."

Randolph did not even lift an eyelash to meet her gaze. He stood defeated, his tattooed hands interlaced behind his back in pure agony.

"And you will not admit to me how stupid you are?" Elena laughed in dismay, her attention turning to Dalton standing next to Randolph. "And *you*—what in the name of Cian were you doing there? Charmaine walking into a disaster alone, I can believe. But you? Do you have absolutely no semblance of self-control?"

"It would appear not."

She rolled her eyes, her fury uncontrollable. "Well, you better find some. What if that had been you, Dalton? Burned by the King of the Seventh fucking Kingdom? The privy council would simply die if they found out we have been harboring another royal—one who does not have a clean record, I might add. They could have our heads for this!"

"I could envision worse scenarios," Dalton chided, blowing a curl out of his line of vision. "You have quite the mouth on you, my Queen."

"Could you?" Elena growled, ignoring his flirtatious and inappropriate comment.

"Yes. It could have been my father who discovered him, but no, he let him in, and now he is here to stay."

Elena turned her attention back to Randolph, who stood irritatingly silent. "Go."

And he went. Soundlessly.

She turned back toward Charmaine's chambers when the familiar icy chill breathed down her neck. "How is she?"

Elena paused, her hand on the door. "She will be fine. Randolph got me just in time."

Dalton sighed in relief.

Slowly, she turned her head around to look at him. He was a complete and utter mess. Dark circles loomed under his eyes, and what had become a near permanent frown encroached on his white brow line.

"You need to be more careful. Magic is accepted, thanks to you, but I do not think the world is ready for the royals to flaunt it." She paused. "The last thing we need is for the world to hear that a royal hurt someone."

"Noted."

"I mean it," she whispered. "You instill fear just as well as you bring about hope."

He bowed dramatically. Elena nearly hurled herself at him for his continual disregard for following the advice of others. If she did not know him so well, she would have killed him. This is how he dealt with hard things and trying moments. He covered his ass in humor and a wide variety of smirks, yet Elena knew he struggled at night with nightmares. He often spoke in his sleep, reliving his traumas and horrors that even she did not know. He never talked about them when he awoke the next day—whether he remembered them or not, she did not ask. She merely asked if he was okay and if he needed anything, to which the reply was always no.

Elena knew he was not fine. Far from it.

"Good night, Elena."

With a sigh, Elena turned to go back in to see the girl that was driving her husband up a Gods-damned wall. She knew he would have a breaking point soon; she just hoped Charmaine was not on the receiving end of his blast.

Nodding to Greyson that she was okay, he opened the door for her, and she strode in. Elena reentered Charmaine's chambers to find her sitting up in her bed. Her violet eyes were still pained, but Elena was unsure if it was from the burns that had graced her hands.

"Do you need another bout of my power?" Elena asked, moving toward the girl. It was eerie to be close to her. She looked so much like James.

Charmaine nodded, tears welling in her eyes. "Thank you."

"I am sorry. This must be overwhelming for you."

Charmaine sniffled as Elena washed her hands in the bowl beside her bedside table. "I am more upset that I was lied to. Again."

"By who?"

"I thought Randolph was opening up to me."

Elena nearly laughed, but she kept her composure. "I am sorry. I am not sure what you mean."

Charmaine adjusted herself uncomfortably. "I know we have not . . . we have not really gotten to know one another."

"The world does not like powerful women to be friends, nor does destiny."

Charmaine smiled softly to herself. "Destiny is *not* all, and frankly, I am beginning to tire of it. But I had full faith that Randolph was my friend."

"Very few people who wear a crown can be honest with the world and themselves."

"You and Dalton seem to be able to express yourselves quite clearly."

Elena pondered this for a second. "Some things more than others, it would seem."

"Did you know . . . Randolph as a child?" Charmaine's voice seemed far away.

Elena knew if she did not answer, the girl would not relent. She deserved some fraction of the truth.

"No. The Seventh Kingdom has never been forthcoming in their traditions and exploits. I knew there were two children in the Seventh Kingdom, yet I never visited. The First Kingdom was always the pride of the continent, of Sarridolon. My mother never had any ambitions but to marry into the best."

"I see," she whispered, her mind clearly elsewhere. "Did you love *him*?" Charmaine asked, nearly flinching when she realized the words came out. Her voice was the strongest it had ever sounded to Elena, though filled with ice and longing.

Elena touched Charmaine's soft hand with the utmost care, letting her healing magic flow into her again as naturally as it was to draw a breath. "I do not think the Gods gave us enough time to love one another, yet they showed us what it was to feel that type of connection."

Charmaine was silent, her violet eyes hard and never leaving Elena's stoic face.

Elena continued, suddenly aware it was not possible to admit truths to someone who was not able to hear them. And she was not sure she was ready to face them herself. "I felt that pain and joy of loving him. It was all-consuming. We were getting to know one another, yet I was dedicated to him for all that he was. I know that does not bring you comfort."

"It does," Charmaine interrupted, her gaze focused anywhere but Elena's face as she spoke quietly. "One of the last times we spoke . . . I was upset with him for pushing me out. He had you, or whatever the Gods had planned for you, and it was hard for me to dissociate from that."

The raw honesty took Elena's breath away, but she managed to reply nonetheless. "I am sorry if I made you lose time with him."

Charmaine took her hands and wrapped them around Elena's firmly. She smiled, though her eyes brimmed with tears and shattered the illusion that she was strong.

"James was a bright light. I am glad you had time with him, no matter how short-lived it was."

Elena held back a strangled sob, her eyes involuntarily watering. *Ten Kingdoms save her, she was not a crier.*

As if reading her mind, Charmaine wiped the tear that ran down Elena's high cheekbone.

"I have learned that feeling pain and letting it overtake you makes you just as strong as showing the world that you are okay."

Without warning, Elena threw her arms around Charmaine—and all that was left of James—and cried.

TWENTY-NINE

Dalton had never been so enraged in his entire life.

"You burned her, you bastard. I told you—"

"I did not mean to!" Randolph shouted at his King, falling to his knees in despair. Boiling tears ran down the sides of his face, his pain evident and etched forevermore onto his skin. "I am nothing more than mistakes, than a fucking bastard."

He held his arms out as though he were in chains. "Take me and lock me away if you may. I do not deserve to serve you. I do not deserve to be a ward of this Kingdom and be a member of your court."

Dalton looked down at the scattered papers around his floor as if they held the answers to the world. His blue gaze flicked upward, challenging and stoic. He looked very much like the portrait of King Cian in the Hall of Portraits at this moment, frozen in time as the king who saved the world.

Randolph hoped he could save Dalton from himself.

"The flames that poured out of her hands were an embrace of devastation and raw power, yet if they were held together by anything, it was a desire to do good." Dalton's voice seemed far away, though it was unmistakably his own that spoke the words.

"What?" Randolph asked, confused why he was not speaking to him directly.

Running a hand through his white hair, Dalton crouched down to meet Randolph's gaze. "It is something I read. In a diary." He paused, then looked concerningly mischievous. "King of Flames, I need your help."

THIRTY

arinthya held her tongue while King Finn went to work.

He goaded the Thinkers of his chambers, his three extensions of death he held at his right hand.

Phillis was a decrepit creature, long and thin. He looked almost like a skeleton, his gray eyes sunken into his head and his lips constantly in a frown. Carinthya hated the look of him and frequently saw him lurking in the shadows of her nightmares. He always wore black fitted robes, never far from King Finn's side. Carinthya had tried to drive them apart on more than one occasion, but it was to no avail.

Phillis, it seemed, could not be cracked.

Meriki was small and plump, his bald head covered in tattoos of trees and whispering winds. He always murmured to himself and looked around as if he were lost. He got away from Finn as often as he could. She could hear him wail against the howling winds of the Seventh Kingdom's castle in the middle of the night. She was irritated the most by him because he was so lost all the time.

How in the name of the Ten Kingdoms did you find yourself shackled to the worst King the Ten Kingdoms had ever seen?

Her least favorite of the Thinkers was almost normal in

appearance, his gray hair unnatural for how young he appeared to be. He looked no older than her. His foxy smile and big brown eyes would be endearing on anyone else but a slave to the unfortunate king.

His name was Bairre, and he was an asshole in every meaning of the word.

He strode through the palaces they had inhabited over the years without any semblance of humanity. Shadows twirled around his fingers and feet at all times, a gift from King Finn himself. He never spoke to her, only flashed her devilish smiles and preyed upon her weaknesses. He had stood by too many times while Finn tortured with his dark power, thus making her lose all respect for him.

So, she held her tongue like the good little princess she was, as the three of them stood around Finn, who held a blue crystal ball in his hands. He never let it go, carrying it with him at all times. She had no idea if the bastard king slept, but if he did, she knew for certain he would have slept with the thing. It spun, a mixture of beautiful periwinkle and sapphire. She would not have known where it came from if she had not seen it in Thinker Eben's chambers as a child.

It was the crystal ball that belonged to Cyril during the reign of King Cian and Queen Ciara. It had gone missing over a hundred years ago.

And it was sitting in the lap of a madman who had no qualms about using it to destroy the world.

"When are we going to strike?" Phillis asked, his nasty, long fingers smoothing down his dark garb.

Meriki looked at the ball with hungry eyes, as he always did. It appeased Carinthya to note that Meriki was the clear idiot of the trio. He babbled like a baby and never did anything but cry when he was alone. A sick, twisted part of herself was overjoyed at how much of a disaster he was.

Even after all these years, Phillis did not give an indication of who he truly was. He had no hobbies. He did not seem to get off on the pleasure of other's pain. She wondered where in the Ten Kingdoms he came from in his prior life.

But she did not ponder too hard about Phillis because the one who concerned her the most lurked behind them, constantly seething. He was pressed up against the wall now, his large frame towering against the stones of the Seventh Kingdom's castle. The shadows spread out around him as he clearly contemplated something. If only she could go over to him and—

"Carinthya, dear, come here and tell me what you see." King Finn's voice whipped through her focus like lightning.

She walked over silently as fear overtook her. She knew how this would go. She would meet with the King, look into the ball, and see nothing. And then she would be punished for it.

The same routine had gone on for six years, and even though it was getting old, she was used to it.

Familiarity was easier to deal with than the unknown, so she still walked forward, even though she knew it was a bad idea.

"Yes?" she asked, peering into the blue orb before her.

"Tell me what you see, darling," he purred, with Ciara's shadows flooding around him.

She opened her mind, hoping to see what she always hoped for: images of her family, the people and the world she had left behind. But every time she looked deeper and wanted it more, she was left with staggering disappointment.

"I do not see anything," she said sadly.

"Look harder," the King commanded.

Meriki snickered behind her, and it took everything in

her soul not to kick him where it hurt. Instead, she centered herself. She breathed deeply and closed her eyes. She sensed Bairre get off the wall and sweep toward her, but she tried her best to ignore his ever-looming dark presence.

She blinked twice when she opened her eyes and silently commanded the orb to finally give her what she wanted.

Almost on cue, it lit up before her. She was not sure if the others would see, so she tried her best to remain neutral. Playing a part had become easy over the years, so she willed her face to remain stoic.

It was easier said than done, however, because the image that exploded before her was the single thread of hope that she had wished to see every day for the past six years.

A young man with white hair danced in her former castle's ballroom. He was on the arm of a woman who Carinthya had met before. She had sweeping red hair and the most beautiful dark skin. The young man laughed and drank champagne as he swung her around like a child. The other men and women in the ballroom looked at them as if they had lost their minds, but Carinthya felt the joy that blossomed from them. The girl was wearing a white dress. A tear fell from Carinthya's eye before she could stop it.

Elena had gotten married to a boy with white hair, and they were celebrating in her family's throne room.

The image continued to play out. Carinthya found it difficult to get a clear picture of the boy she danced with. He was light on his feet, and there was something so familiar about him that Carinthya almost pressed her nose to the orb to find out. But she held steadfast, afraid that one wrong movement would bring about her doom.

Elena and the young man spun again. Carinthya nearly fell over as the vision closed in on the two of them. Pale skin, freckles like a constellation of stars, and the deepest blue eyes flaunted before her. It took everything in her not to cry out, not to scream and fall to the floor in agony.

Why is his hair white?

Elena LeClair had married her brother Dalton, and they were dancing.

She refused to blink, willing her tawny eyes to continue staring at the stage presented before them. She could feel the tears falling, but she prepared for what would become of her when she refused to tell Finn what she saw. She would keep this from him, this piece of happiness in the world.

And then she saw a girl enveloped in darkness with raven black hair and violet eyes. She was there, then she vanished, evaporating like clouds did from the sky when one was not paying enough attention. *Who was this girl?*

The image melted away with the question, and Carinthya was left gasping in the arms of Meriki. She almost vomited at the smell of cake that radiated off of him, and she wondered without context why in the world he smelled of such a rancid thing. Carinthya hated cake.

"Ten Kingdoms, Carinthya, what did you see?" King Finn's voice cut through the air like an arrow toward a target.

"I saw nothing." She spat, her face wet from tears.

"She is lying," Phillis said without amusement.

"Carinthya, darling, you must tell me if you saw the girl with the violet eyes." He was so close that he was nearly kissing her.

Carinthya blinked up at him, unyielding. She wished she had a weapon so she could stab him and take his life from him once again. Maybe the world would get another one hundred years of reprieve before he came back to haunt them all again. She refused to tell them of Dalton, to tell them that her brother had white hair and a wife she had known since she was young. She refused to put them in danger. And they looked so happy.

She would never take happiness away from anyone, and definitely not her brother.

So, she nodded slowly, and Finn extended his hand to help her up.

"Thank you, Carinthya. You did well."

***

She awoke in someone's chambers, her gaze fuzzy as the sunlight peeked into the bedroom. Carinthya never imagined that this castle—one she had come to hate—could be so beautiful this early in the morning. Cascading on the red furniture and paint, the sun danced.

And despite her best efforts to remain negative, she had to acknowledge that it was beautiful.

Where in the name of Cian am I?

"Carin?" A voice sounded to her left quietly.

Without warning, Carinthya extended her fist and clocked someone in the head.

"Carinthya! Oh, Ten Kingdoms! What in the world? Carin, it is me!" The voice was exasperated and full of fear.

She opened her eyes, rubbing them ferociously as she took in the surroundings of the chambers.

The floors and ornamental decorations were a ruby red. The walls of the chambers were a stark white, enriching the heat of the room. There were gold accents everywhere; the entirety of the chambers was utterly enriched with a display of prowess.

She hated it.

She rubbed her eyes another time, just to make sure she was not imagining this place, then looked to her left to see her attacker.

"Ten Kingdoms, Callum! I did not know it was you . . ." She slid off the bed, panicked. She had hit her only friend and ally.

She was a disaster.

"It's fine, Carinthya, I should not have startled you."

"Why in the Ten Kingdoms have I been brought here? Whose chambers are these?" She was yelling, but confusion wracked her. She could not recall falling asleep.

"Bairre brought you here . . . He said you passed out and you needed a place to sleep in peace."

"What the fuck?" she whispered with dismay. "Oh, I am so sorry. That was so unprincess-like of me. Callum—"

"You are not sorry." He smirked, the corner of his mouth lifted with flirtation.

She wanted to blush at his expression, but instead found her body hot with irritation. Bairre had touched her, and she had not noticed? And why was Callum reacting so calmly?

"No, I am not. But I am sorry that Bairre touched me. He is despicable—"

"He is not as bad as you think. I personally think Phillis is the worst of the three."

She laughed, despite her confusion and heating body. "Meriki is definitely the worst. He smells like cake at all times, and I hate cake."

Callum snickered, his hand finally leaving the red mark that Carinthya had left on his face. "Who hates cake?"

"I do. Maybe if we live to make it out of here, I will tell you why."

His hazel gaze darkened. "I am working on it."

"You better be. I saw something last night in the orb, and it solidified that I have been here long enough."

"Six years is a long time, Carin. You never should have been taken here."

"When did you start thinking it was okay to call me Carin?" she asked, her blue eyes flashing with irritation, as well as adoration. She was not sure about him, but time had proven over and over that he would not harm her.

And she really needed an ally.

He flinched at her words, but he recovered quickly. He touched the tip of his tongue to the scar that ripped across his face. She wondered often where he had gotten it from, if it was in this life or the one he lived prior to coming here. She had plenty of scars from her life before being in King Finn's clutches. But they were not visible.

"I will not do it again, Princess."

"Do not call me that either," she said, despite her best efforts to remain neutral. "I have not been a Princess in a long time, and I will not be one when I return."

"You never know."

She shot him a death glare and fought off the urge to hit him again. She needed him, and she needed to not lose her head.

"So, what was it like to be in the arms of the biggest and baddest Thinker on the continent?" he asked after a moment.

She nearly choked on air as she shot out of the bed, searching for a glass of water. "I told you I do not remember it. I have never been close to him, and thank the cursed Gods for that."

"He told me to tell you that it was him."

She paused as she reached for the water chalice that had been left for them. "He told you to fill me in? How kind of him."

Callum rubbed his eye impatiently. She realized for the first time that his hair was unbound. It flowed behind him wildly. She liked him like this, different from his normal pent-up look. It was nice to be free, in any capacity of the word. "I will be sure to let him know you are grateful, Carinthya."

She gulped down the water like a savage and refilled her glass with haste. "Wait, tell me why you are in here with me?"

"He did not know what state you would be in when you woke up."

She nearly drowned in the glass she was drinking. The water spilled down the front of her dress, and she nearly shrieked on impact. "What state? What in the name of the Ten Kingdoms is that supposed to mean?"

"You have been through an ordeal . . . I was told not to rile you up."

"Consider me riled, Callum." She walked over, water dripping from her chin and running down her breast like a savage woman. "Now you are going to tell me why you are suddenly best friends with the worst creature in this palace besides the King himself, or I am going to hit you like I mean it."

Callum lifted his hands in resignation. "I have been with the King for as long as I can remember."

Carinthya sat down on the cold floors as if she were listening to a bedtime story.

Callum continued, "It was nearly a decade ago. I had strayed too far from my village and was wandering among the border to the forests when I heard a few branches snap. I had been hungry, oh so hungry, and my family was in desperate need of a hunt."

Kinking her head to the side, Carinthya urged him to continue with her expressive gaze alone.

"You probably assume right—that it was not in fact an animal—but rather, it was a dark mist. It was cold to the touch, but I assumed there might be some sort of mystical power to it, something I could harness and sell in a larger village than my own. To my surprise, it was a man who stood at the center of the forest, a man I had heard tall tale after tall tale about for my entire life."

"King Finn," Carinthya whispered softly. "It was King Finn in the forest?"

Callum bent down so he was eye level with her and replied, "That it was."

"What was he doing?"

"Practicing."

THIRTY-ONE

alton and Charmaine entered Cyril's chambers in silence, though neither of them was better for it. They had requested to meet in neutral territory.

There were no words left for Dalton, no other ways to apologize and ask if she was okay. Dalton did not think Charmaine had any words left. He braced himself as she shut the chamber doors with her bandaged hands softly, knowing she would ask for all she had not received. They had been doing what they always did, dancing around real life. And now someone had gotten hurt in the dalliances.

"I do not have words right now." Dalton's voice was lethal.

Charmaine's lips quivered in rage. "That seems abhorrent, considering I have never seen you speechless."

He raised a white eyebrow as she stepped closer, tipping her chin up to look directly into his blue eyes. He noted that her violet eyes were full of raw emotion; he noticed sadness and curiosity all in one, entangled together in a fight for dominance. Looking back down at her, he refused to give into her irritations with him.

Her bound hands were clasped in front of her casually, as if Randolph had not just accidentally burned them beyond repair. Dalton silently thanked the Gods that Elena had the gift of healing and that he was married to her, therefore he could command her by law to heal Charmaine. Although he knew she would never refuse him, or refuse James's sister anything, he felt better screaming at Elena to *fix her*. To fix all that had happened.

Pushing away the resurfaced emotions, he would apologize for his insecurities later. And it had been so long since he had fought someone other than Cyril and Elena. He wanted to relish in it for a moment longer without the intrusive thoughts of the world.

"I am mad at you—I think."

He raised a white eyebrow instinctively, aware she was goading him. Shock reverberated through him at her words, for Charmaine was always direct but never *mad*.

"Did I do something to offend you?" he asked carefully.

She smiled crookedly, an expression he had seen on his own face one too many times. It almost unnerved him—if there was a part of him that could still be surprised.

"I find out about the fact that Randolph has power, which I did not know because you kept it from me—and yet you ask if I have something against you?" She took a step closer, her chest nearly touching his own.

The draw nagged at him, against his own heart, and his breath became rapid amongst the quiet as he waited for her to continue.

Ten Kingdoms save me. Why did this happen? Why could he not be normal?

"I thought you were my *friend*," she hissed. "You were there for me every moment I needed you when James—" She paused, not finishing the sentence.

The word 'friend' cut into him worse than any dagger could.

"When James died, you were there for me every moment I needed you. And now I find out that you *knew* what Randolph was hiding from me, from all of us, and you expect me to be collected? Dalton, I trusted you. You told me there were no more secrets."

Her breath came rapidly as she continued to ramble through her rage. "You knew, and you did not say anything. The number of times I told you that I felt trapped, the number of times I told you that nobody could understand me but you. You told me there were no more lies between us—"

"You feel betrayed."

With a bandaged hand, she lightly hit him on the chest. "You of all people could have told me."

"It was not my secret to tell," he whispered.

"You could have told me *something*."

He blinked slowly, choosing his next words carefully. He knew she was reacting as such because of her brother—because she had lived a life of broken pieces and undesired power.

Of all people, Dalton knew what it was like to live with a gift he did not want.

But this was merely a manifestation of the true reasons she was so upset. The reason he had avoided her, the reason he had spent every waking moment with her while she grieved before he took the crown. It was the reason he was following her the past evening, mere horse lengths away.

"This is about the vow, is it not?" he asked, ice threatening to burst forth from his fingertips.

"It is not just about the stupid vow, Dalton." She reached out a bandaged hand slowly, as if to take his own.

"I cannot touch you. We have not talked about it since you left me in the garden, Char." He took a dignified step back, jerking his hand away.

She stepped with him. "Why?"

"Because I am King."

"You are full of it, and you know it." She took another step as he moved backward.

"Because I am married." He stepped back, his shaking hands now laced behind his back.

"Dalton," she protested, moving toward him. "Your excuses are not—"

Lifting her hands to cup his face, she paused a mere centimeter away. He knew she could feel the vibrations of the draw. Her violet eyes widened in wonder and shock as they registered the emotions flooding between them. She did not touch him, yet she might as well have.

"I cannot touch you because when I do, all that I am holding onto will be taken from me."

She lowered his hands, centimeter by centimeter, until they ran through her black curls. "What does that mean?"

He sighed at her question, knowing damn well she knew what he meant. "Do not make me say it."

Resigned, she took two steps back toward the door. "I am tired of being left in the dark."

"Some weights you must bear alone, Char."

"I wish you would let me in! You do not need to do everything by yourself!" She was nearly shaking with rage.

It was taking everything within him not to touch her. Reassure her.

He could not.

"You were there for me for so long—let me be there for you in the same way. Your trauma is valid, Dalton. Your life is worth something too."

"I am sorry." He moved toward the door, defeat lining every word. "I cannot be what you need. Not anymore."

"Dalton," she called after him.

He turned his head once more. With one final exhale, he said, "You cannot fix me, Charmaine. Nobody can. I am best left on my throne. Alone." Walking through the door, he began to stride down the long hallway, his shoes clicking incessantly against the marble.

Mad with irritation and the thrum of the draw telling him to turn around and banish all that he was entitled to—to give it all up for her—he paused. Erratic, he grabbed his left shoe, then the right shoe, and threw them to the ground like a toddler.

He heard murmuring up ahead. Without glancing up, he knew servants were whispering about him. He made a mental note to dismiss all claims of madness tomorrow, though he found himself not caring against the political nightmare that was all of *this*.

Clearly, he felt something for Charmaine that was beyond the mortal feelings of friendship. What he felt toward her was more than some draw of mystical energy which he had yet to figure out. No amount of library digging was getting him anywhere, at least regarding the draw specifically.

And yes, he had left her in the dark, but he was protecting her. He wanted her safe beyond all measure, and he carried with him nothing but pain as a result.

Leaving his shoes behind without a second thought, he stampeded down the halls of his castle like a banshee. He could hear the whispering growing, for it was most unusual for him to be so disheveled amongst his casual swagger and sarcastically confident persona. But if he had heard his opulent and Kingly shoes click on the floor one more time, he would lose control and blizzard the entire castle before the first natural snowfall had a chance to come.

Elena's voice cut through the air like an arrow, breaking

his stream of consciousness. He could hear the worry in it, obviously directed at his lack of shoes. "Dalton, wait!"

She came up behind him, lacing her hands through his as naturally as the sun rose every morning and set every evening. He breathed a little easier with her touch.

"What is wrong?" Her dark brown eyes glowed with concern.

In normal circumstances, Dalton would have lied, or even said something irritatingly cryptic. But there was no sarcasm laced in his voice as he answered, "Raven black hair and violet eyes."

Elena's face saddened. "Is she okay?"

Dalton thought on it for a second before replying, "I do not think she has been okay for a long time."

"Are you okay?"

Without hesitation, he whispered, "I do not think I have been okay for a long time, either."

"Then we have that in common, oh dear husband," she retorted, her smile faker than Randolph's life here in the First Kingdom.

"We need to divorce, Elena." His voice was stern, so much so that she nearly tripped over her navy velvet gown which flowed behind her like an ocean.

"Now?"

"We need to read that contract. Look for hidden provisions. There is no way your mother and my father did not lace that thing with something we could use to break free—"

"I am on it," she said, control exuding from her posture. Clearly, her composure had been restored after a momentary lapse. "But is this something we need to do this very second? Dalton, I know you do not love me like that, but this is advantageous for both of us as we . . . figure it out." She paused, waiting for a response from him that did not come.

With a sigh, she replied, "Do not worry yourself with one more thing. You have more than enough on your plate."

He snorted, as if she even knew the half of it.

They continued down the hallway and past the throne room, their destination none other than to continue wandering. It was as if walking would give them the answers, or at least, they both silently hoped so.

After a moment of continual walking and awkward gazing around, Elena did what she always did. She spoke her mind. "You know it is okay to let other people in, Dalton. She will not see what you truly are and run."

"She might," Dalton whispered.

That fear he had never admitted to anyone could only escape in the presence of his best friend in the Ten Kingdoms.

"She might see the parts of me that used to cry myself to sleep, the parts of me that broke me and had me begging Cyril to sleep with me, while I waited to be let out of my room for the first time in weeks. She might look at all of that, and refuse me. Refuse my . . . friendship." The word nearly made him gag.

"She is not fragile, Dalton. Gods, you and Randolph act as though she is made of glass!" Elena rolled her eyes.

Dalton was rather in disbelief that Elena was scolding him like this. *A comparison to Randolph? Nearly unforgivable.*

"Her brother died, her mother died, and her father died. She has nothing, and she did not always have the cushion that your life provided. If anything, this is the best she has ever lived."

"You speak as if you really know her, Elena, but I know you two barely talked until Randolph hurt her, and you healed her."

Elena paused, grief flashing over her eyes. "But I knew James, and they are one and the same. Trust me."

"I am a King, Elena. I cannot subject her to this life of courtly dancing and being in this Gods-forsaken castle. There is a whole world out there, a life and other Kingdoms that we have not explored."

"Have you asked her what she wants?"

Dalton found himself speechless at her question. "Not exactly," he whispered.

Elena raised a fiery eyebrow, a smirk on her beautifully full mouth. "You might want to try."

THIRTY-TWO

he matrimony between House Saphirrus and House Leclair was no union of love on the dawn of a new era, rather it was a curse to bestow on both of them. For they loved one another, but they were not *in love* with one another.

It drove Dalton mad to see his best friend in so much agony, but it also drove him mad that she refused to meet him halfway on anything. His earlier conversation with Charmaine hung around his neck like a heavy chain, yet he could not bring himself to bring it up amongst the two of them. They had their own problems, and he refused to burden someone else with the pain of his suffering. Continuing their conversation, they made their way to their private quarters away from wandering ears and eyes.

"Dalton, I need more time to convince my mother of Ronan's madness." She was pleading, her eyes flashing in pain.

"What do you mean you need more time? Elena, it has been three months since my father died! Cyril has all the evidence we need to present it to the council and show what we had planned all along. It will probably not be enough for a divorce, but it is a great start. This union has kept you safe. Our engagement and marriage has worked out divinely for both of us. But the council will start asking things of us, now that I have officially taken the crown. They will pressure you for an heir. These are things that you do not need, Elena. You know you are welcome here. You can marry for love this time—"

"I need more time. I am not ready to speak to my mother about this."

"Your mother is not the ruler of this Kingdom. You never have to return to her if you do not wish. You can stay here—be *just Elena*, like you have always dreamed."

"Dalton, her reach is vast. The moment she comes here, she will know everything. I cannot bear the scorn of her judgment. You know what it is to be controlled by a parent. She made me this venomous villain . . . this person who could never achieve perfection."

Dalton sat down abruptly, taking her hands in his. "Elena, you are no more a venomous villain than myself. And you are certainly more perfect than I could ever dream of being. You cannot let people control your narrative. You are stronger than me. You have two powers. It is incredible. And you have always embraced them."

Her face became pained, and she pinched the bridge of her nose with irritation. Her long finger nails grazed her cheeks as she wiped the tears that had begun to fall unannounced.

"What's wrong, darling?" he asked.

"I am lost. The first night I healed James—the first night I met him I should say—he and I shared something I had never experienced before."

Dalton's jaw ticked, and he held back an inappropriate comment. "Go on," he urged, praying Elena was not about to be vile.

"When I was healing him, my magic took over. And I saw . . . visions."

What in the Ten Kingdoms was going on?

"You had visions?! Who started them, you or James?"

Cian save him, did James have a secret power like his sister? Did she keep this from him? He would understand, of course, but he could not hide the pain he felt at her not trusting him.

Although, he had no room to talk.

But he was King, and if his father taught him anything, it was that Kings could be hypocritical and get away with it.

"I do not know. I never had them before I healed him that first time, but I also never asked him if he had power. He never said anything to show me that he had experienced them before that moment. We were both rather in wonder."

"What did you see?" Dalton asked, fear creeping into his voice without malice.

It was so rare to have any type of Cipher or seer abilities. Even Thinkers were becoming rarer by the day.

"I do not think we always saw the same things, but it only happened when we were together. We were just getting to know one another . . ." A sob wracked her body.

Dalton extended a long hand, checking before he touched her to make sure it was not ice cold. "What did you see, my darling?"

"I saw death. A funeral. I did not know what any of it meant, Dalton. I never did. I felt the pain, though, the loss and the love."

"And you did not tell anyone?"

"Cyril knew, to an extent."

Dalton's blood boiled in his veins.

Of course Cyril would keep this from him.

It was probably attached to some Godsforsaken prophecy that he could not share with anyone yet.

"I also saw a child," Elena whispered, grief clouding her

eyes beyond repair. "Do not look at me like that, Dalton. It clearly did not belong to James."

"What about this child? Elena, I am so sorry. You should have come to me."

She snorted. "You had enough going on, D."

"You know I am not made of glass."

"You and I are forged of the same blade. We can endure." She was curt in her tone, that familiar Elena energy seeping back into her moment by moment. There was his girl. His wife.

"He had dark skin like myself and the same brown eyes. He was being crowned on more than one occasion. I knew I was with him too; I just did not ever see myself. I never saw James with him, which was terrifying. I do not know who he belonged to, but I knew it was a son. And I knew he wore a crown."

"Which crown?" Dalton was panicking, despite his best efforts.

Elena was like his sister. The Gods could not have planned for the two of them to be blessed with a child? They were both messed up enough on their own, and this marriage was a culmination of his father's will and his dominion alone.

It could not stand.

"I do not know. It could be yours. It could be ours. It could be the Fourth Kingdom. It could be any kingdom."

"I hate destiny," Dalton murmured.

She smiled softly, the whites of her eyes reddening from the tears she had cried.

"They say our gifts are from the Gods," she whispered, so low that Dalton almost missed it. "I do not think so at all. I think they are more like a curse."

"Elena—"

"I am serious! Look at what happened to Ciara—you

know the story—the shadows that awakened within her destroyed her. She murdered her father, then she was lost to them in the end, after falling for the power that runs in your veins."

"She knew love, Elena. The world was terrified by her only because of what the world could make her be at times. Cian knew the real Ciara. Ten Kingdoms, Cyril knew her!"

"Cyril loves too easily," she said.

"We all love too easily. And do you know why?"

"Enlighten me, my husband."

"Because we deserve to be loved."

THIRTY-THREE

awton had many things going on in his life.

The first was that his best friend was the biggest asshole in the First Kingdom.

The second was that he was undoubtedly attracted to said asshole, and he could do nothing about it because that friend—and asshole—was his boss by definition. And it was just attraction. In no way did he have actual feelings for Randolph, other than acknowledging his physical beauty.

The third was that Lawton had been writing letters for hours to the King of the Sixth, and he could tell no one about it. Letters transferred by owl were rather slow, so there had been only a few exchanges between them. They communicated by poems, it would seem.

The fourth was that his best friend, boss, and irritatingly handsome asshole friend knew about the one thing Lawton never wanted anyone to know about.

His powers.

Lawton could jump from place to place, a gift which never lost its allure for his conniving mind. He was not ashamed of his gift; if anything he relished in it. But there was danger in power, especially power which could not be controlled.

And Lawton would never be on a leash.

He sat on a bench in the rose garden, flipping his First Kingdom knight's sword like it was nothing more than a toy. He knew, of course, that it was not. But the mindless task of wielding it from side to side helped him focus sometimes.

It also connected him to his father and all the hopes and dreams he still held onto.

His father had been a knight in the First Kingdom's guard and had raised Lawton himself in Thallgan. His father had been a good man, one who cared about the well-being of his kingdom. Lawton dreamed of his mother, even to this day, but he had no information on her. His father had refused to tell him anything, saying it was a world of heartbreak and anguish. He had remarried, a lovely woman from Thallgan named Jacqueline.

Lawton still visited Jacqueline on occasion, especially since his father had passed away. She was not his mother, but she was all the family he had left. Not even she knew his secret, one which had erupted when he was fifteen years old when his father passed away. It did not matter that she did not know. It was nice to be able to jump to see her whenever he wanted, not having to make a theatrical disappearance like so many of his comrades did when they went home.

Laoch once had begged the King for reprieve, and he was only able to when he convinced his brother to send a note that their sister was dying. Of course, the King did not want to look like an unfeeling lunatic—although he was—so he had granted the visitation. Laoch had gotten a whole two weeks off, slimy genius.

"Ah, Laoch," Lawton said to himself. "I hope to see you soon, friend." They had been on their separate quests since the King had made James and Charmaine his wards. They should have finished up by now, except it was hard to tell because Lawton did not know the specifics of the quest. Maybe he could jump Randolph some wine, and he would tell him later.

One of the worst ideas I have ever had. I must try it.

The night had been cold. Death had loomed over his village home. It was waiting for his father to pass so it could claim another good soul for its taking. Lawton's father had been older and had faced more disease, famine, violence, and death than the ordinary man. He had survived the reign of two Kings—Arthur and then his son Ronan. And he had served them valiantly.

But natural causes took his father from the world so unfairly, with years left to serve the world he loved.

Jacqueline had been with him, holding his hands and telling him that they loved him as he left to go elsewhere. Lawton had waited for the light to leave his father's eyes, terrified of what a world without his father would mean for his future, before he had stood and left the house. Jacqueline understood the pain of loss, and the weight which the death of his father would put on Lawton, so she did not follow.

Not following, as it turned out, seemed to be destiny's intervention.

Lawton had torn outside, fighting a yell and a scream at the Gods as he had blitzed through his house to the streets of Thallgan. He did not know where he was headed; he did not even know if he was going anywhere. He just knew he had to be out of that room. The stench of death had clouded him, overtaken his senses and rocked his faith.

He had to go anywhere else but the house where his father had just taken his last breath.

He ran into the streets, fighting the emotions which surfaced to break him, when his hands began to tingle. He stopped, touching his face as he tried to figure out what was wrong with him. Dizzying, unabashed, twisted pain laced through his arms and legs at once. He seized from within, unable to cry out or scream. He moved to take a step forward, to get to anyone who could help him, when he fell forward into nothingness.

He ripped through the stars, blackness and sparks of light flying through his vision without consent. He closed his eyes, but to no avail. His senses were impenetrable to reason. There was something else at work here—he just did not know what.

Without warning, he landed with a thud, face first on white marble flooring.

And he heard voices, unfamiliar and dignified.

"How in the name of the Ten Kingdoms did I get into the castle?" Lawton whispered, wonder and pain blitzing through him at once.

He looked around, the long hallway unabashed in its regency. He had only been here two times before—as a boy with his father on business—but he would never forget it. The white marble floors glistened, and the gold accents were as vibrant as they had been in the years prior. The stained glass window images were so detailed they nearly danced. Lawton had been as in awe then as he was now.

He was in the castle, but how did he get here?

Suddenly, a figure turned the corner.

"Shit, that is the King!" Lawton hissed as he dove behind a white pillar.

He stood there, breathless, as he fought the urge to scream. The King had raven black hair, his eyes blazing with unadulterated rage. He wore all leather, looking like midnight as he walked through the illuminated halls. He was unyielding, clearly walking with purpose to get somewhere else in the castle. How was Lawton supposed to get out of here if he did not know how he got in?

The King strode past the pillar that Lawton was behind without a second glance. Lawton held back a snicker, triumphant in his deceit. He slid down the length of it until his back hit the floor, and he exhaled deeply.

Without warning, the sensation picked up again, his mind thrust back into the unknown.

He landed with a thud not a second later, uncontrolled as his knees raked the pebbled ground outside of his home. He blinked twice, nearly slapping himself to make sure it was not a dream. He touched the ground before him, feeling the solidity, before he leaned over and vomited everything in his stomach.

***

Jumping back into reality, Lawton dropped his sword with a clang. He looked around, trying to play it off like he had meant to do such a thing. He sheathed it and made his way toward Randolph's chambers, looking for someone to bother, and itching to write a letter to a certain pink-haired king.

THIRTY-FOUR

allum entered King Finn's chambers as loudly as he could, making his presence known to the man who had robbed him of his life.

"My King!" Callum yelled enthusiastically, bowing so dramatically that one could only assume he was serious.

"Callum, what do you have to report on Princess Carinthya? How is she after the trials and tribulations of two nights ago?"

Callum cleared his throat, careful not to lose his mind when he spoke to this sham of a King. "She is doing fine now, your Majesty. Bairre brought her to my chambers like you asked, so she could awaken and not be as irritable as she normally is."

By all accounts, Callum would never describe Carinthya Saphirrus as irritable, but he knew it would please the King. So, he did so, even though it hurt his heart.

King Finn frowned, and Callum's heart nearly leapt out of his chest. He did not care what Finn did to him, for his life had been lost to the wheel of time a long time ago. But he did care what happened to Carinthya.

Much more than he cared to admit.

"And how did she take the news?"

"What news, sire?"

"That her brother is the King of Snow?"

Callum nearly froze. It took everything within him not to drop his jaw. How could Finn possibly have seen?

"I have eyes and ears everywhere, Callum, lest you forget the range of my power. I have had spies in the First Kingdom for weeks, as I have looked for the girl with the violet eyes."

"Your Majesty—"

"I am not finished." King Finn held up a long finger.

Callum noticed in the light of the room that King Finn looked more gray than usual, his second form of life less bright than that of a normal person. It was not natural to die by shadows and then come back. Maybe it had taken its toll on his body.

Hopefully, it was taking its toll on his body.

"I have been suspicious, but have not been able to confirm the rumors which surround the boy. Ronan's mind was so hard to infiltrate that I have not seen much of anything the last five years."

"You infiltrated the King's mind?" Callum nearly fainted with the realization.

"I merely saw into his mind; he never fully let me in. If he had, I would have seen this coming. Apparently, word has gotten back to me—the new King of the First Kingdom did a bit of a demonstration at his coronation." He held up a letter in beautiful script handwriting, folded precisely not to smudge. There was a letter on the table beside him, unopened, the envelope a beautiful light blue. "An owl delivered this just moments before I called to you, since I am assuming you knew."

"How would I have known?"

"Because you sneak out sometimes, Callum. I am not to be taken for a simple-minded fool. I am your King, and you have defied me. More than once. And you will defy me again if I let it stand."

Shadows twirled around Callum's feet mercilessly. Their touch was chaos and hurt in one. It took everything within him not to scream. King Finn stood up, moving closer to Callum with dignified slowness. He lifted his fingers, a piece of shadow touching the long scar that ran across Callum's collarbone.

"Do you remember when I gave you this?"

Callum nodded, doing his best not to show fear.

Finn leaned so close that Callum could feel his cold breath on his cheek. He smelled of ash and death. He was the embodiment of fear in this moment—the King who had taken his own daughter's life in the name of power.

"I am going to give you one to match, from your forehead to your jawline. When I am done, I want you to run back to your beautiful little friend and tell her what I know, and if you are planning *anything,* you will never breathe again."

"You took everything from me," Callum growled, though his hands shook violently.

"And I will continue to take, and take, and take, until everything is mine."

He lifted his shadows, and Callum began to scream.

THIRTY-FIVE

harmaine awoke with the burning desire to talk to her brother. She wanted to hug him, reach out, and run her hand playfully though his wild black hair. She wanted to lock eyes with him—a reflection of her own—and laugh about things that no longer mattered to the world. Crushing devastation overtook her when she realized she was no longer privy to the luxury of time with James. He was gone.

She had no more tears to cry, and she did not dream of these moments between them anymore. The first two months after his death, she had awoken screaming and had clung to anyone in reach for support. And she was right to do so. She had lost the one person who she called family, the one who swore he would never leave her.

But not all promises could be kept against the looming war. That was what this was, was it not? The beginning of something dark and twisted. Charmaine could not say for certain, but this omniscient energy brewing within the world was utterly dark and terrifying.

She was not healed, not even close, but she had stopped blitzing. Invisibility did not take her like it had in those first two months. One second, she had been there, speaking to

Dalton, then the next, she had been gone from sight. The first time it happened, he nearly lost his mind. The marble floors had been instantly coated with a sheet of ice, and he had called out for her as if it were the battle all over again. Despite her best efforts, her cheeks heated up, remembering the way he had brought her back to reality.

The King of the First Kingdom had kissed her and broken the curse she had placed upon herself.

She had come back to herself moments later, whole and alive. Dalton had been cautious not to have anything else transpire between them, especially since he was married, and Cyril did not yet have an understanding on the draw. But she had wished for a moment that he had kissed her again.

Charmaine had no place with Princes, and she surely did not have a place with Kings.

Dalton had become an anchor these past two months, a friend fiercer than any other she had known. He was there for her and understood what she was going through in more ways than she could imagine possible. He knew about her magic, and he did not shy away. If anything, he wanted to know more. He pressed her to train with him and encouraged her to let the change overtake her in moments where it flooded her senses, blinding her to anything else. Cyril had even chimed in, coming to her chambers with Dalton to help her as much as he could.

She could never repay him for what he had given her— her life back.

Grief still thundered against her soul every waking moment, and there was nothing she could do except endure the pain. She learned long ago with the deaths of her mother and father that time would dampen the wounds. Life went on regardless. The hardest part of losing a loved one was not waking up the day they left; it was standing up every time you remembered they were gone.

After downing a chalice of water, she quickly dressed, shimmying into a black velvet gown with thick straps and gold detailing. The swirls were chaotic against the shine of the fabric, rather not her style, but she adorned it anyway. She would rather those at court look at her gown than look at her anyways. Letting her black curls fall along her back loosely, not caring to give them a second look, she strolled out of her chambers.

She had gotten used to getting dressed quickly before Athelred had the opportunity to come in and swarm her with his awkward presence. She had nearly told Dalton about his outburst the other day, while she was indecent, but part of her felt guilty. In terms of society, she should be the one serving ladies, rather than having someone serve her. She was not a woman of noble birth. It was some miracle within itself that the King was . . . dear to her, therefore granted her stay at the castle.

Without looking to see if her door closed, she continued down the hallway briskly. Her hair was pushed over her shoulders with the wind that blew through the passage, and she noticed for the first time that the windows were open in the castle. The chill of fall air swept over her, and she wondered if it would become much colder soon. She had been dealing with so much that the normalcy of changing seasons had not been at the forefront of her mind.

Continuing down the hallway, eyes focused ahead, she prayed nobody would stop her as she made her way out of the castle. Turning past the rose garden, she came to the grand staircase that led down to the tombs of the First Kingdom. It was a graveyard, but one fit for Kings. Mausoleums and headstones ordained the land with the brazen glory of royal blood. In Brinn, anyone who was buried was simply at one with the continent, but here at the castle, those who had passed were marked in honor. Statues of Kings and Queens of Old and flowers lain across the stones that represented someone who had been loved. She had never been bothered by death, never scared of it. She was only scared of being unseen and lost to the span of time.

Her dress dragged softly against the grass, and the rose garden from above carried down the beautiful smell of flowers. She approached the headstone cautiously, afraid of awakening her brother from his slumber.

Here Lies James Grimes

Brother, Knight, and Dear Friend of the Crown

She stifled a gasp and fell to her knees. She grabbed the headstone with both of her hands and brought her forehead to touch it. She breathed in deeply, holding back a sob, and let a single tear fall from grace.

"I am mad at you for leaving me," she whispered, sure that James could hear her. "I am angry you did not stay with me longer. I needed you to guide me. I needed you to be with me and protect me. I am so sorry I failed you, Jamie. I did not save you."

Another tear fell, sliding down to her mouth. It was salty and bitter.

"I saved Dalton, just like you saved him and the King when we first arrived. I know it is what you would have wanted, even though I did not do it on purpose. I wish I could have dragged you with me—"

She took her hands off the headstone and brought them to her face, rubbing her eyes to erase the tears.

"I am devastated, James. But I needed to tell you what Father told me before he died, something which he made me swear I could never tell you. You are gone now, and I know you can hear me, so it is okay to reveal."

She smiled sadly, picking up her head to face her eternal brother.

"Father told me that I had to embrace who I was, and that the world would embrace me back. I still do not know what that means, and I have not thought about it for years. The other day, I was in the training yard with Randolph, and I swore I heard his voice again, but I could not make out what it was saying. When I awoke this morning, it was clear to me again, that final request. All I wanted to do was talk to you. I thought of it like it was just yesterday."

She stood up slowly, smoothing her skirts and running a hand through her raven curls. "I am going to try, James. I needed to come and tell you that today."

She bowed, pressing her lips to the top of her brother's tomb and turned. She nearly screamed at the man who stood before her, all darkness and flowers. He was dressed in leathers. His green eyes shone with regret and devastation that matched her own. He was holding a bushel of white roses, with one red rose in the center. He took a step forward, and she found herself running into his arms for comfort.

"Randolph," she sobbed, uncaring of how much he heard.

"I was not trying to eavesdrop. I brought these for him."

She pulled back, looking up at his tanned face in wonder. "You did?"

"James was electric, Charmaine. I did not nearly have the time that you did with him, but he left his mark on me." He touched the vine inked on his skin following James's death, and her heart thundered in her chest.

"I do not care what you heard—if you heard nothing, or

if you heard it all. You have seen it before—this grief and suffering I am going through."

He reached out with an inked hand and touched a loose curl which had fallen forward, tucking it behind her ear lovingly. "James asked me on more than one occasion to look out for you."

She nearly laughed. Of course he did. "Did you know he tried to get me to say yes to courting you once?"

Randolph snorted. "Oh, I am well aware. He told me it was a match of destiny, how we had all met in that pub and then found one another later."

"I would hardly call that a stroke of destiny."

"Is it not?"

"You once told me that you did not believe destiny is all." She raised an eyebrow, falling back into what had become her normal rhythm with Randolph. Their friendship had evolved so much over the last three months as well, despite the secrets which he no doubt kept.

Charmaine was confident—and always had been—that Randolph would tell her things on his own terms. It had always been like that for them, a push and pull of emotions that was easy on the surface. But they both struggled with the truth and the confidence of that truth.

"I think I might have been wrong."

She could not hide her surprise. "Randolph Eniar? Wrong?"

He smirked, but the mischief did not meet his gaze. "I might be more wrong than right."

"You are a good man," she said, leaning in for a second hug. "James trusted you immediately."

"James loved you and will love you from the beyond."

"Thank you, Randolph, for being there. For being my friend."

He pulled back, ruffling her hair affectionately, and walked forward to place the roses at the foot of James's grave. "I am so sorry I hurt you."

His shoulders shook, and with the snapping of something deep within her, she realized he was crying.

"No, no, no—" she whispered, throwing her arms around him in a deep embrace. "Randolph Eniar, you did not hurt me. I am healed. You see my hands, you see them—"

"I am not talking about your hands, rather I hurt your soul. I kept things from you, Charmaine. I kept them from *everyone*." He breathed out another sob.

She felt helpless against the stroke of time. He was unraveling, and she was not sure if she had ever seen someone with so many hard edges so utterly devastated.

"Randolph, I forgave you before you even unleashed your power. I only wish that you would have been comfortable enough to tell me."

He wrapped his hands around her waist, his hug both warm and heartbreaking all at once. "You do not know all that I have done, all that I have endured—"

"And you do not have to tell me. When I met you, we had a whole conversation so easily about wanting to tell one another our names on our own terms, that destiny was not all, and that it did not define us."

"I remember," he whispered, refusing to let go.

She wrapped her arms tighter around his neck. "Yes, and we had that taken from us too, running into one another hours later in the most dreadful of circumstances."

"They were quite dreadful," he huffed in a laugh.

She pulled apart as he did, taking her hands in her own. She gestured with her face to James, sitting below them silently, where he would remain eternally. "James was many things in life, but he could judge someone's soul. And your soul, Randolph Eniar? Your soul is power itself. Whatever it is that you have done, you have done so because you are a survivor."

She breathed through a sob, her violet eyes watering uncontrollably with all the emotion that swam between them. "And I am a survivor too. I think that the Gods, whatever and whoever they are, have shoved us together for a reason. We understand one another, despite not knowing much about one another."

Tears ran down Randolph's tanned skin, and he did not bother to wipe them as he said, "I am the lost King of the Seventh Kingdom. I abandoned my throne. I stabbed my father, and I came to the First Kingdom out of a desire for retribution. For a new life."

Shock pulsated through Charmaine, but she did not speak as he continued for another heartbeat. "My Kingdom was burned, overtaken by the mercenaries. My sister has not been heard from in months, and it is all my fucking fault."

"Randolph—" she started. "Randolph, you are not to blame. Do you understand me?"

"I appreciate your words, but I cannot absorb them."

"You do not have to, you idiot, just *hear* them."

He laughed softly, sniffling as his tears stopped. He looked at her like he was seeing her for the first time, his brown eyes full of life rather than their normal ominous gaze. "Do you remember when James wanted us to be together?" he asked with a laugh.

In an exhale, Charmaine threw her head back and laughed. "I think you and I, despite being so different in upbringing, are too alike to be husband and wife."

Randolph chuckled. "I know who is fit to be the other half of your soul."

Her cheeks reddened, and despite the pain she was

feeling, she smiled. "I know," she said sadly, gazing upon her brother's grave for yet another moment. "I think he knew it too."

THIRTY-SIX

arinthya sat at the foot of the bed in her chambers and picked at her fingernails incessantly. Two days had passed since she had awoken in Callum's chambers, without an idea in the world how she had gotten there. And then Callum had told her that Bairre was the one to relinquish her from the shackles of King Finn.

Even now, the memory flashed through her mind. The power in the sapphire orb had been all-consuming, cruel yet wondrous. Even now she could feel its clutches, days later. She dreamt over and over, in sleep and during the day, of the vision of Elena Leclair and her brother. She had tried not to think of him much over the last six years. She knew it was a ludicrous notion. Someone in captivity should think of their family outside—something to hold onto. But Carinthya was the opposite. If anything, over the last six years, she had suppressed all she had known from life before, fearful that Finn would use her love for her family against her. But he never had. So, Carinthya figured she had done a rather good job.

Until the other night, when she saw the two of them together and nearly dropped the mental shields she had built up over the last six years. They were alive. They were beautiful. They were powerful.

"Stop thinking about it," she said aloud, digging her thumb's fingernail into the tip of her pointer finger. "Stop. Thinking. About. It."

"Stop thinking about what, Princess?" A starlight laced voice said behind her.

Her neck snapped up, primal fear taking over. She pushed down her emotions, laying on the familiar Saphirrus sarcasm that got her through all difficulties. It was her greatest defense mechanism and her only power.

She turned to face the enchanting voice, and her jaw dropped open. The man that stood before her was drenched in silver light. His hair glistened in the candlelight, ethereal and bewitching, but this man before her was entrapping. He was soulless, as was the expression in his eyes. His straight nose crinkled in a twisted fashion of amusement, his smile devilishly endearing. His entire being in this moment was a paradox, and Carinthya did not care to understand one moment of it.

For the past six years, Bairre had not spoken one word to her. And now, he had called her *Princess?*

She had always been told she had her father's temper. She was quick to play it off, not wanting to adopt that part of herself as truth. But, in this moment, it was the only real thing in the world.

Carinthya exploded.

She shot off her bed and ran directly at the monster who stood before her. Thundering, her heart threatened to burst with fear. She had never been this consciously close to him. He was the most dangerous man she had ever met. King Finn terrified her; his power and reach were vast. But Bairre always hid in the shadows. And if Carinthya learned one thing in the last six years, it was that shadows gave one power, as did patience.

And Bairre had both.

"What did you call me?"

"*Princess*, now if you do not mind, can you please step back?" His brown eyes danced without emotion.

She did as she was told, his shadows flickering around her jawline, taunting. "I did not know you could speak."

He laughed. Until that moment, she did not believe he could make such a sound. "I can do much more than speak, Princess. I can also listen. Your boy . . . Caleb, I think is his name?"

"Callum," she interrupted. She did not know why she bothered to speak, especially to this monster. Maybe it was loneliness. Maybe it was fear. Maybe it was the opportunity to speak to someone who was not Callum, or his other two minions.

"Sure, Cal. Finn attacked him a few days ago and sent him back with a message, but by the looks of you talking to yourself, am I right to assume that he did not make it back?"

"Finn attacked him?" she asked, fear coating her tongue.

"Yes, Princess. Can you hear all right? First, you ask me about what I called you when I wanted to get your attention, and now you ask me to repeat myself again. Honestly, it is concerning."

Carinthya laughed, voicing the hysterics that consumed her. "Please, wake me up when I am dreaming, Bairre."

He froze, his brown eyes pleading with her for a second. She blinked, and the expression was gone. Wiped from his face. She must have imagined it.

She turned to sit back down, and Bairre was in front of her. She yelped, her breath stolen from her at his closeness. His shadows were wrapped around the room possessively, crawling up the walls with total freedom at his mercy. Her shoulders shook as she focused on her breath, refusing to show any lack of control. She bit on her bottom lip, avoiding eye contact.

"Listen closely because I can only use my shadows to silence the room from listeners once, and I am not going to repeat this interaction again. King Finn knows your brother is the Prince of Snow. Now, I am not sure what you know, Princess, but Finn is planning something. He has not included me on it, which is suspicious within itself. I need you to go to him the next time he asks, and keep this entire interaction under wraps. I need you to listen to Caleb when I get him back here."

The Sixth Kingdom, she wanted to shout. *When he took the Seventh, I heard him whisper that he wanted to take the Sixth next.* But she could not find the words.

"Callum," she corrected through her teeth instead.

Bitterness swarmed within her; she would not tell Bairre anything. There was no chance in the Ten Kingdoms that he would help her, despite what Callum had told her about him bringing her to his chambers. There had to be an angle for Bairre.

One did not just find kindness like it had been lost.

"I said listen closely, Princess. I am running out of time." His jaw was clenched, and a shaky hand ran through his gray hair impatiently. "I need you to listen to that boy. He is under strict instructions."

"Strict instructions to what?"

"To get you home."

She gasped, falling backward on the bed as a gust of wind blew her black hair over her shoulders. Why was he helping her? What was his motive? She blinked, ready to ask Bairre another question, but he was gone.

THIRTY-SEVEN

hile Dalton attended his weekly council meeting with the Lords of the First Kingdom, Elena met with Cyril to discuss opportunities to divorce him. Greyson had come with her, despite his protests. She wanted to have him near; his quiet support was becoming essential to her survival at this castle.

She was not sure what to make of that yet, but she was grateful for his service and friendship. Something had changed between them the night of her bath. It was not a romantic development, for Elena was not ready for that with anyone, but she had felt like herself again. It was refreshing to breathe in her usual sarcasm, her hard headed attitude fitting like an old glove. And he had taken it in stride too, not once tripping up on her tone or indications. He simply went with it. She needed people around her who she could trust, and since then, she trusted him.

Therefore, she had no aspirations or timeline for her own coronation, but she hoped to be divorced before it came to that. It would be much harder to divorce Dalton and get it approved by the Thinkers if she wore any crown other than her own. If her coronation was set—and it would be soon— her mother would come to the First Kingdom.

Just the thought of seeing Maria here, dining with the people of this court, sent tremors throughout Elena's whole body. Her mother was ruthless, cunning, and utterly genius. She would do anything to get what she wanted, and Elena did not doubt for one moment that what Maria wanted was a hand in two kingdoms.

Elena was so proud of Dalton for standing up to Blarquenza at the coronation's council meeting, just as proud as she was that he had unveiled the truth of his heritage to the world at the ceremony. But with great power came great responsibility and greater expectations. By simply being himself, Dalton had transformed into the legacy of Cian. She had heard Cyril whisper on more than one occasion that they were more similar than anyone would ever know. The admittance charmed Elena, yet it terrified her.

Legacy was a burden that only royals knew, and more often than not, they did not carry the weight of it well.

"You probably have mere weeks until the Lords of the council propose that we move forward with your coronation, Elena," Cyril's sharp tone interrupted her thoughts.

Ten Kingdoms, help me.

"Weeks?" she asked, her mouth agape. She twirled the curls on the end of her auburn hair incessantly, a nervous trait she had seemed to develop in the past few months.

"Weeks if we are lucky. I asked Dalton to sniff it out today at the council meeting, without calling attention to it."

Elena palmed herself in the face with her hands. "Surely, I am doomed if you asked *Dalton* to be subtle. Ten Kingdoms, Cyril, could you have a worse plan?"

Greyson's large hand touched her shoulder subtly, and she craned her head to meet his emerald gaze. He smiled softly, reassuring. "I am sure the King would not put this plan in jeopardy."

She released a breath, oddly patient with Greyson, despite her usual temperament. He had been a member of the guard for quite some time, and although he had been assigned to her for months, he had rarely interacted with Dalton. She was not sure what he knew of him, other than what everyone knew of him. She found his optimism and lack of knowledge of Dalton's antics to be rather charming—he was innocent to all but what Dalton was to the King's Guard.

"Forgive me, Greyson," she said as she painted her nicest expression on. "But you do not quite know my husband as I do."

"He is the King. I am sure he will take care of it."

Was this what it was like to be a member of the King's Guard? Unyielding in loyalty to the royal you served? She thought of Randolph. *Maybe Greyson is how a knight is supposed to be. I suppose Randolph was not fully a knight, given his true identity.*

"Yes, Elena, I am sure he will take care of it." Cyril smirked. Something fluttered in his bright blue gaze that Elena did not care to acknowledge.

She groaned, placing her hands on her red gown. Her gown was form-fitting today, velvet, with a low back and thin straps on her shoulders. The neckline was relaxed, bunched up naturally as the fabric formed against her body shape. She paired it with a simple pair of earrings and the most subtle crown she had publicly worn in a week. She was more than certain she had seen Dalton wearing this crown months ago, covered in leaves and diamonds, quite similar to the one they had placed on James's casket.

"Okay, let us play the hypothetical here. Dalton does what he is scripted to do." She flashed Greyson a grin. It was fun to play inside jokes with someone who did not understand at all. "And he fishes out that they plan to move to make me Queen in a few weeks. What is our angle? How do we break us both free without destroying our reputations?"

"Easy, we claim the madness of the King."

The original plan. Great.

"I do not think this will work as easily as we originally planned, Cyril," she said. "Dalton and I had discussed this on our . . . wedding night." Her cheeks flushed, despite nothing happening that night. She could feel Greyson's emerald gaze burning into her own, but she ignored it, continuing to look at Cyril.

"Why not? Do tell, your Majesty?"

"You do not have to call me that. I am just Elena most of the time."

"Most of the time." Greyson laughed.

"Sir Althan, was that a joke?" She nearly toppled over.

Who knew all he needed was one little explosion from me to open up? I would have played with fire a long time ago then.

"Stay focused, Elena," Cyril said, his eyes doing that weird thing again with the emotions. "Why. Will. It. Not. Work?"

"Because unveiling Ronan as mad would cause chaos. We are at an impasse here with new leadership, the revitalization of the powers of the Kings and Queens of Old, and frankly, despite what we all know, the Kingdom largely did not feel the scope of his anti-magical campaign."

Cyril cursed, realizing she had a point. "It would create more chaos for Dalton to navigate, especially since the Lords of the First were so terrified of Ronan."

"And if they were terrified, yet controlled, by a madman? Well, that would make them all—"

A voice sounded from the doorway, dripping in sarcasm. "Insufferable dimwits who wet themselves at the thought of my father's campaign against extraordinary people?"

Their heads snapped up to look at the King. He was adorned in leather pants and a bright blue tunic. He wore no crown today, and if he did, his hair was in such a state of disarray that Elena figured nobody would see it amongst the plethora of curls. Greyson stood to bow to his King, while Cyril and Elena merely raised an eyebrow. It took a lot within Elena not to acknowledge the look of horror on Greyson's face as they did not rise to meet the King of Snow.

Welcome to the monarchy.

"Exactly that," Cyril chided, irritation and love blitzing through each word.

Elena smiled at the arrival of her best friend. And husband. "What is the verdict? Am I to be your Queen?"

Dalton laughed, though his eyes did not leave Greyson standing particularly close behind Elena. "They had no agenda today other than pissing me off. To which, they did not accomplish. I am not so easily antagonized by the irritation of rich men who have never so much as lifted a finger other than to sign a piece of paper with their no-good names."

Cyril burst out laughing at the horrified expression on Greyson's face.

"You know my husband, Dalton Saphirrus? Sorry for the lack of introduction. You seemed to know him so well as the King of the First."

"We tend to be two different people," Dalton said with a crooked smile. "Although, that's neither here nor there." He pointed to his eyebrows, still gray from the white hairs which had transformed.

"We need time and a new approach," Cyril said, exasperated.

Elena felt for him—so much to figure out and not nearly enough time or resources. They had made no headway on deciphering the prophecy, figuring out the mercenaries' purpose, or the magical connections between Elena, Dalton, and the Grimes siblings.

"I will think of something," Dalton said softly. "I always do."

Elena stood to touch his arm, noticing for the first time since he strode into the room how exhausted he looked. His eyes were always alive with light, but his face was unnaturally pale, even for him. Dark circles blossomed under his eyes, and his jaw was clenched. Clearly, he was fixated on something. Bothered.

"Are you all right?" she asked.

He touched her hand, running his hand over hers in affection. "I am here," he said, his usual humor not ever-present.

"Being here is not the same as being good."

"I am working on it," he said, leaning forward to whisper in her ear. "I am glad you have made a friend out of him."

Taken aback, her dark skin flushed. She craned her head to the side, hoping Greyson did not see.

Dalton wiggled his eyebrows suggestively, his defining expression returning to his face quicker than it had left. He turned to face Cyril, crossing his arms over his chest. "Cyril, do we still have the marriage contract between my father and Queen Maria?"

"Yes, I would have to look for it among his documents, but we should."

"I want to read it, and I want you to read it with me. There must be something in there, an agreement or a piece of language that we can use in our favor"—he looked at Elena again—"Unless you want to become Queen of the First Kingdom?"

Her mouth fell agape, even though this was not the first

time he had asked such a thing. He had reminded her over the last few months that their situation was not a bad one. Most royals got a worse deal. They were best friends. But for her, it came down to the part of her that always dreamed of marrying for love. She had never been in love before, but she had seen it in her visions when she touched James. She could not shake the feeling that she was destined to feel something like that again, and for real this time. Despite how much she loved Dalton, and how this marriage elevated the Fourth Kingdom's status, she would never let go of the chance to find the love she had always dreamed of.

"You know where I stand," she said softly, refusing to break eye contact with his deep blue stare.

"Just checking, Elena," he said back, relief washing over his gaze. "Just checking."

THIRTY-EIGHT

lowing out a long breath, Dalton paused, cursing his predecessor for harboring so many secrets. Why did Cian leave the world if it was not perfect? The stories of the first King of Snow always mentioned his perfectionism—was that all a lie as well? All the journals he found detailed Cian's own accounts of his tumultuous rise to power. There were wars and battles, yes. But there was so much strife amongst the people of Cian and Ciara's time that it was a miracle she was an effective monarch.

Dalton was rather surprised that the world was not all sunshine and rainbows for the man whose shadow he walked in every day.

"This Gods-damned book," Dalton whispered to himself with blatant irritation. "Where in the name of Cian could you be?"

His hands delicately traced the spines of books in the library. It was one of many rooms that held the secrets of the Kings of Old, but Dalton had been in there many a time looking for answers to solve riddles that had stood the test of time. It would make the perfect hiding place for a journal, one the Queen of Fury could have hidden amongst the collections of her forefathers. He had been here time and time again, staring at spines and digging through books that meant nothing to anyone important, only to turn up empty-handed.

With his hands on his hips, he lifted his head to stare at the ceiling, as if he could will the Gods themselves to tell him the answers. The fact of the matter was that he was running out of time. Randolph became more erratic by the day—Dalton swore if he had to talk him off another ledge that he would drown himself in a pail of water. Elena clung onto the contractual language of their marriage to save herself grief with her mother, and although it was a deception he was willing to participate in, it was yet another distraction on an ever-growing list of problems. And Charmaine? He could not let the thought linger, for he had no words left to offer.

And it was *very* unlike him to be rendered speechless.

"Hmm," he hummed to himself, blinking in a silent farewell to the Gods. Extending his arms, he pleaded one final time. "Where is the Gods-damned book, Ciara?"

Without warning, the candelabras on both ends of the heavy wooden door went out.

"Hello?" he asked cautiously, taking a step in the darkness toward nothingness.

The wind answered, howling, and flickering the candelabra back to life.

Raising an eyebrow and kinking his head to the side, Dalton smiled as though he were greeting an old friend. The aura that washed over him was dark—yet full of light. It did not cloud his senses, rather it heightened them. He bowed his head, knowing who had tried to startle him and whose presence was there.

As he raised his head, he turned his gaze from the lit candles and made his way over to the bottom left of the bookshelf he had scoured many times before. He touched the spines as he always had. His long fingers danced across the titles in a mad dash for the diary which he now knew laid before him.

"Where are you, lovely?" he asked softly.

With a click of his tongue against his teeth, he did not hesitate before he pulled Ciara's diary from the shelf. He had found the name with ease with Lawton prior, but there was still so much left to be discovered. How was he to enter the chambers? Was he to be alone? What had the fearless Queen of Fury done to earn such ancient respect?

Surely, the Queen of Fury must have described her conquests with the supernatural in some context.

Or at least Dalton hoped and prayed she had.

As he flipped through the old book, Dalton chuckled , nearly pissing himself at the hysterical moments Ciara had chronicled about her life and King Cian.

Dalton put his finger at the top of one of the pages, laughing as he whispered the entry in the winter of Ciara's second year as Queen.

Today, I bested Cyril in a game of chess. His face was so incorrigibly angry that Cian was genuinely worried about his health. I assured Cian, the worry-wart and biggest thorn in my side here at court, that because Cyril is a Thinker, he is nearly impossible to kill as long as we do not dagger him.

He did not like my statement, voicing that he thought I wanted to dagger Cyril.

I assured him no; I did not want such a thing. However, if he was offering to take his stead, I would gladly dagger him.

Dalton found himself overcome with joy at the little notes and scribbles the Queen had documented throughout her reign. Dalton felt as though he were a part of the Cian, Ciara, and Cyril friendship. The joy and laughter practically radiated from the old pages. He read many scribbles like that, yet found no detailing of what he was truly looking for.

Closing the book slowly, careful not to damage its contents, he put it back on the shelf.

As he left the room for the afternoon to return to his courtly duties, Dalton found himself rather empty. Whether he would admit it or not, he missed the company of the Queen of Fury's mind.

And for the first time since he had known Cyril, Dalton shed a single tear for all that his friend had lost.

THIRTY-NINE

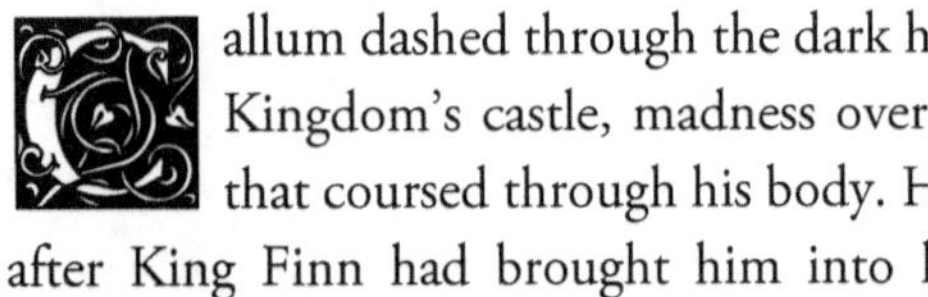allum dashed through the dark halls of the Seventh Kingdom's castle, madness overtaking every sense that coursed through his body. He had blacked out after King Finn had brought him into his chambers, lost himself to the whims of Queen Ciara's father's stolen shadows.

That was one of King Finn's best kept secrets, Callum had realized over the last six years. Finn had not only found a way to get a tangible foothold in the world, but he had stolen the shadows of his daughter over a hundred years ago when he plunged the sacred dagger into her heart. It had been ornamental—the dagger given to her by her father on the eve of her thirteenth birthday. Callum had learned it was a gift to celebrate her introduction into society, a weapon King Finn felt was worthy of a young Princess.

Callum did not know the full story, and he was not sure he ever would. He did not know when Ciara's dark powers had awakened, not specifically. He knew she had attacked her father with her shadows, then assumed the throne upon King Finn's destruction. The legends were muddled, but she met King Cian, and with his help alone, she overcame those shadows. No matter what story one was fed, one fact always remained the same: Queen Ciara died at the hands of her father and sacrificed herself along the way for the betterment of the Ten Kingdoms.

Blazing through the darkened halls, Callum lifted a hand to press on the temple of his head to stop the throbbing and bleeding. He had awoken, stiff and broken, only to know one thing.

He had to get to Carinthya.

He was hobbling the best he could. The shadows had entered his mind somehow, making him black out. He was not sure if he gave up anything he had known, but he was not hopeful.

How had King Finn found out Dalton was the King of Snow? And why had he been waiting to speak to Callum about it?

King Finn said he had eyes and ears everywhere, which did not surprise Callum given Finn's expansive paranoia, but it only made Callum wonder—*who were his eyes, and who were his ears?*

His chambers were up ahead on the left. He slowed to accommodate the thrust he would have to put into the door to get it to open. Breath ragged, he thrust his shoulder into the door and prayed to the Gods that Carinthya was there.

The door cracked open.

And she was there.

She sat on the floor at the foot of the bed. The silk sheets had been changed to black since he had last been in there. He knew it was an odd thing to notice—that she had been taken care of—but he was grateful for it. She was in a new dress too, Saphirrus blue, as he had called it so many times before in his own head. It matched her eyes, endless and dark, but so deep they might as well be a mirror of the midnight sky. Her sleek hair was draped down her back, hidden behind her shoulders.

As he entered, he knew he looked like hell because Carinthya had never been shocked by anything in the last six years. But at the sight of him, she gasped. "Callum, Ten Kingdoms what—"

He threw his arms around her, relief overtaking him at the sight of her. He was fearful that Finn would retaliate with her, especially given the news of her brother. "I am okay. I am okay."

She pulled back, putting her hands on either side of his face. She touched his jaw, and he winced. He had not gotten a good look at himself yet, but everything was aching and swollen. The shadows had resulted in the mental fog, but the physical pain? It had to be someone else. Finn would not risk getting his hands dirty by hitting someone who served him.

It was a form of self-preservation.

"You look awful. What happened?"

Callum wanted to tell her. He wanted to tell her everything he had learned over the last six years, but the King's message was loud and clear.

"Because you sneak out sometimes, Callum, I am not to be taken for a simple-minded fool. I am your King, and you have defied me. More than once. And you will defy me again if I let it stand."

"Bairre was here," she said, rambling like she did when she was anything other than utterly confident. "He told me to trust everything you say, to do as you told me." Her eyes were hopeful.

Callum willed himself to remain calm, despite the terror which pulsated throughout his veins.

"You can trust Bairre." It was the right thing to say. The only honest thing to say, and all he could say without saying anything.

He would not lead her down a path of destruction

because he wanted to play hero. She had to make it out of here. She never deserved to be here to begin with.

She nodded, not understanding, but accepting that was all he would give. "Do not leave me again, Callum."

"I cannot promise that," he said, standing straighter. "You need to promise me one thing, Carinthya. That you will listen to Bairre when the moment is right." He placed his hands on her shoulders. "You will go back to your kingdom, and congratulate your brother on ascending the throne. You will go back to the place you belong, and live out a long and happy life."

Her dark eyes flooded with emotion. It was almost unnatural on her usually sarcastic features. "Callum, you are scaring me."

"You do not know what he is capable of, Carinthya." He shook his head, the pain of the movement unbearable. He needed to show her how much this affected him. "He is the darkness of this world."

She blinked twice, absorbing his words. Her full lips parted slightly as if she wanted to question it, or make a joke, but she remained silent. "What did he say he would do to you?"

He leaned his forehead against her own, pushing his boundaries because he did not know when he would have another opportunity to speak to her like this again. It may be the last time.

I want to help you. I cannot tell you why, but I want to help you.

"You need to listen to Bairre," he uttered instead.

And with that, he left her in his chambers to find a healer.

FORTY

 awoke to the fires of Brinn, blazing as they took my mother away from James and I. He was holding onto my waist, his boyish strength enough to keep me from running to her. They had covered her in oil—mercenaries, we called them—ruthless men sent to find those with magic. They had to work for the King, for his newfound fear of magic was something which had spread across the lands. There was no other viable option. A King was the only one capable of inflicting such mass hysteria and destruction. And Mother was a Cipher, a woman whom could hold a Thinker position—if she were a man. She was dangerous, a threat to stability, and a rarity amongst the folk of the Ten Kingdoms.

They doused her, spit on her, and cursed her for not giving up anyone else in the village. They were not stupid men; they knew she could not be the only one with magical capabilities. They called her names, laughed at her agony, and thanked the Gods for a night without rain so they could watch her burn.

I watched her stand still, no fear in her gaze as she met mine for the last time.

She opened her mouth, only to mouth one word.

"Run."

***

Charmaine sat up, her hair plastered to her neck and her nightgown stuck to her back. She was saturated, the dream so vivid she could still feel James' hands around her waist, and the fire from the wood that had burned her mother alive.

She ran a shaking hand through the front pieces of her hair, as if trying to remake herself back into perfection, despite the chaos she had endured. Nausea overtook her as she made her way across the room to get a chalice of water. The white marble floors grounded her with their below freezing temperature on her bare feet, waking her up. She guzzled the water savagely, grateful for being such a disaster by herself.

Ten Kingdoms, what was that?

It had been years since Charmaine had thought of the night her mother died in such depth. It was a moment she had erased from her conscious memory, a moment she and James never spoke of beyond what it was. They had watched their mother burn, then they had done all they could to survive.

But there it was, that memory resurfaced. It had to have a purpose. Something like that should not be coming to the surface. Even when James died, she had not thought of her mother's passing in the nights that followed, so why now? Was this the work of her own subconscious, or was there something grander at work here?

"Cyril," Charmaine whispered without hesitation. "I must speak with Cyril."

It was the middle of the night, but she did not care. She had to speak to someone who could help her. She had never been this rattled by a dream before. And she knew the only person who could help her was someone who was like her mother, who could explain something regarding Thinkers and their realization.

She never had an inclination to ask nor reveal this part of her past, but she could not ignore the sweat on her back nor the pain in her heart.

What the hell did she mean when she told me to run?

Not even bothering with a nightgown, Charmaine opened the doors to her chambers and tore down the hallway to Cyril's chambers. She rounded the corner, her breath ragged and her arms pumping wildly. She knew she was manic and completely unlike her, but the terror was so vivid.

She was more afraid now than she had been that night with James.

With a fisted hand, she pounded on Cyril's door hard enough that he could hear her, but not hard enough that she would awaken the whole castle. Without a moment's hesitation, the grand white doors swung open, and Cyril stood at the threshold.

"I saw you coming," he whispered as he gestured her in with a hand. "Do not feel bad about awakening me. I was prepared. Sit down on the velvet chair. I will stand."

She saw the black velvet chair and obeyed without hesitation. She slumped back against it, her chest rising and falling with what she assumed was an acute panic attack. She used to feel that suffocating anxiety frequently as a child, the fear of not being good enough and being discovered was a constant debilitation.

"What did you see?" His eyes flashed with concern.

"Do you know who my mother was?"

He nodded, his blue eyes darkening. "I was wondering when we would discuss this."

"I had a dream, one which I do not hope to relive, about a night I have not thought of much since it happened. It was so vivid; the smoke and the oil all consuming . . ." She touched the spot where James's hands had wrapped around her waist. She closed her eyes, gulping. "I can still feel my brother's hands if I focus enough . . ."

Cyril stooped down to eye level with her, drawing her shoulders closer to him so she was sitting up. "What did you see?"

"My mother was turned in by someone who knew who she was. She was a Cipher, Cyril, a woman born with the same powers you possess. She would often say things to me as a child, but I did not understand. She put so much pressure on me, her practices misguided, and her love unabashed." She massaged her temples, willing herself to stay focused. "I saw her the night they murdered her—the mercenaries—I thought they were doing the work of Ronan . . . It was no secret that he despised magic."

"Ronan never issued the order to murder people with magical abilities in the kingdom. He tried to get them to work for him. Murder was only his cause if they practiced in forbidden acts against the law, like—"

"Gwendolyn," Charmaine panted. "Like Gwendolyn was found with the dagger that contained magic. It was against his code."

"Therefore, he enacted it. Charmaine, you are saying mercenaries killed your mother in the village, and the entire village thought it was a declaration of war on magic from the King?"

"I never assumed anything but that. The truth was not something we were hunting for. It was survival."

Cyril's eyes softened. "You poor child."

She took a deep breath, her eyes closing again with the weight of the memory. "She told me to run, Cyril. I remember it clear as day. I just saw it. Again."

"She told you to run?" He stood, pacing now back and forth.

"She looked at me across the town square, and she mouthed the word at me."

"What else had she told you, as a child? Were there any prophecies? Anything out of the ordinary?"

Charmaine bit back a sob, having not spoken of her mother in a long time in this capacity. "She was so hard on me, Cyril. My nerves were never a concern. She would tell me things that terrified me, and yet, she would tell me anyway. I knew she was a seer, someone who could see beyond this life and into the next, but as a child, nobody should be exposed to the truth like that."

"Charmaine, what did she tell you?" Cyril's voice was calm, but he had paled. He had been waiting for her to come to him about her mother, so he had to have known something about this prior.

Was it another piece of the puzzle they were missing? Was Charmaine's mother somehow more connected to the mercenaries other than just a misunderstanding regarding the King? Did Ronan truly have nothing to do with the death of innocents?

Charmaine took a deep breath, reciting from the depths of her memory, "It is you they shall bow to in worship."

Cyril leaned over, holding onto the banister of his grand, dark, wooden bed frame for support. He whispered manically as he seemed to run through a thousand different scenarios at once. He unlatched a hand from the bed frame, running it from his brow to his jawline dramatically.

"Cyril," Charmaine whispered, despite not being the picture of health herself. "Cyril, are you all right?"

His face turned beet red. His mouth moved to speak, but he could not. Charmaine had never seen terror across his face before, so she did not know what it looked like. She had seen anger, even disappointment, when dealing with Dalton and his shenanigans. But in this moment, the emotion Charmaine recognized was complete and utter rage.

He slammed his hands against the bed-frame like a child, followed by a plethora of curse words. "I cannot tell you," he said, utterly defeated as he sagged to the floor.

"Cannot tell me what?"

He threw his head back, exasperated. "I cannot tell you anything."

FORTY-ONE

Dalton blazed into Cyril's chambers with all the fury winter could bring.

"Where is she?" He spat, his dark eyes haunted.

Cyril grabbed him by the shoulders, shoving him out into the hallway with all his might. Dalton had packed on muscle in the last few months, since regaining his footing in society and personal affairs. He was still thin, his natural build unchangeable, but he was no longer frail, he was solid.

He was a King.

"She is resting in my bed," Cyril whispered, the door closing behind them. "Do not worry. I am too old for her, my boy." His eyes twinkled, but Dalton's only sunk further into despair.

"What happened? Why did you not come and get me the second she strode into your chambers?" He paced erratically, running a shaking hand through his white hair.

Cyril was rattled to his core, seeing the boy so affected by something completely out of his control.

"You needed the rest," Cyril said in his calmest voice. "A King cannot rule without—"

"A King cannot rule if he has nothing to live for!" Dalton shouted, his own volume causing him to shirk away from Cyril.

"Boy, you cannot protect her from everything that comes her way. She has experienced more trauma in this life than I am afraid any of us had realized before. She is healing, yes, but *just*."

"I felt it when I woke up this morning," Dalton said, his gray eyebrows furrowing. "I felt the draw and the *strain*. Was she terrified last night when she came to you?"

"Yes," Cyril said. He would not hide the truth from the boy. Not ever.

"My heart was thundering when I woke up. I could barely stand. I did not understand at first, that sense of *panic* . . ." He took a deep breath. "I have never felt like that in my life before, not even when I woke up in the throne room. I always knew I would have someone to look after me. I was never ripped from my home or a place I did not know. I have never known true fear, except for what I experienced this morning."

Cyril gulped, adding the extending circumstances of the draw to his ever-growing list of things to figure out. "I am sorry, boy. There was no time."

"What happened?" Dalton took a step forward, looming over him.

That sensation took over Cyril again as he moved to open his mouth—it was the same sensation Charmaine had been privy to last night. He could not draw a whole breath, his face reddening with a lack of oxygen as a warning from the Gods themselves. He was unable to tell anyone the truth, for the Gods forbid it.

"Cyril?" Dalton asked, helping him sit on the cold marble floor.

Cyril breathed out, silently promising the Gods he would not reveal the truth he had learned last night. "Dalton, I need you to listen to me very closely," he said between gasps for air. "I need you to remember what I told you all those years ago about me speaking a prophecy when the Gods do not allow it."

Dalton blinked, his blue eyes horrified, yet in wonder. "You figured out a piece of the puzzle?"

It is you they shall bow to in worship.

Cyril put a hand on Dalton's shoulder, already feeling the weight of saying too much. Of implying too much. Cyril nodded. Dalton closed his eyes, his head falling backward in exasperation.

"But you cannot tell me," he said, irritation and humor interwoven in perfect harmony. "Can you?" He snapped his head back up, his eyes suddenly haunted again.

"I am so sorry."

"We do not make the rules, Cyril. We are only forced to follow them."

***

After convincing Cyril to move to his own chambers, Dalton commandeered Cyril's room and refused to move from Charmaine's side until she woke up. Agonizing terror and fierce relief flooded through him in unison. She was here, and she was okay, but she was still broken. Tormented by her past, and magical conquests which would never cut her a break or give her a moment of peace.

Dalton held her hand with delicacy, afraid of alarming her when she awoke. It had been three hours since Cyril unveiled what he could, yet nothing, to him outside of this very room. Whatever it was Cyril had discovered, he could not tell anyone due to his Thinker position. The Gods had forbidden the utterance of a single word of prophecy. Cyril had tried, though, practicing forming the words at the cost of his physical condition. Dalton would have to check on him later as well. The constraints of Thinker laws were merciless. If Cyril spoke a word of his discovery, and the Gods still forbid it, he would die instantly.

And Dalton had not broken yet, not fully, anyway. But he knew there was no chance in the Ten Kingdoms that he could survive the death of Cyril.

So, he had to figure out this prophecy on his own—without Cyril or anyone else.

A part of him wanted to ask Charmaine *exactly* what had transpired between her and Cyril when she found him last night. But he was still haunted by whatever she had experienced. He felt all of it through the draw, or bond, or whatever in the name of Cian this was. He would not subject her to more pain; therefore, he could not ask her.

He would do as he always did. He would be King. He would be her friend. He would be the man, friend, ruler, sovereign—whatever he needed to be to stop the suffering. Whatever he needed to be to service the bond he had vowed to never break.

Suddenly, Charmaine began to stir. Her hand tightened on his as her violet eyes flooded open. Her eyes darted to the side, her eyes brightening instantly at the sight of his face.

"How long have you been sitting there?" she asked, her grogginess rather adorable, despite the terror that pulsated from her.

The warmth of her voice, that genuine kindness that radiated from her—it was hard to lie to her. But he did. "Not long, darling," he said softly, hoping to the Gods his eyes did not betray his voice.

He had gotten better at that, covering up his greatest tool for expression, but lately, it was harder to hide the shadows gathering within him. Especially after he woke up in such a panic, knowing it was all because of what she was feeling.

She sat up, huffing with the effort. With a jolt, she realized she was still in her nightgown and covered herself with Cyril's silk sheets. Her pale cheeks flushed pink, and she looked to the side to hide it.

Dalton smirked, clearing his voice and letting go of her hand.

"Where is Cyril?"

"I sent him off to my chambers to go back to sleep," Dalton replied. "He needs his rest."

"I will need to tell him later that I am sorry. I did not mean to disturb him."

Dalton smiled softly, leaning over to turn her head to face his. "He was not disturbed, just worried about you."

"Did he summon you?" she asked, worry etched into her features. "You look exhausted, Dalton. Did you sleep at all last night?"

Dalton laughed, blowing a stray curl out of his eyesight. "He did not summon me; I am a King. I summon myself."

At that, she cracked a smile. "Always making jokes." She paused. "I am still upset with you, but I am too tired to fight off your presence."

His heart cracked in two, yet he smiled at her acceptance that he would not leave her. He would never leave her. "Sometimes it is the only way to survive a day at this blasted court," he mumbled to himself before he could filter through his emotions. "I must be tired."

She smiled sadly, twisting her whole body so she faced him. "You need to sleep."

"I can sleep when I am dead," he deadpanned.

She flinched, and he cursed himself for being so blasted insensitive. "I had a bad dream last night," she whispered, urging him to come sit beside her.

It took all within him not to grow wings and fly next to

her, so instead, he moved slowly, cautious not to touch her bare skin. Or her nightgown.

"Are you okay?"

"I have not thought of my mother in years," she said, more to herself than to Dalton. "She was murdered by mercenaries, burned and refused to give up anyone else. I always thought it was your father who pushed the execution. As did the villagers."

"His discontent for the magical ran years before my own awakening." Dalton scoffed, hatred flaring within him at the mention of his father's legacy.

"But in my dream last night, I was back there. It was like I was watching it all over again, and I awoke just as she mouthed to me to run." She turned to face him, her violet eyes glistening with unwanted tears.

Dalton fought the urge to hold her, not knowing what would happen if he touched her based upon how the draw had affected him.

"I was not completely honest with you," she whispered, fear and deceit an agonizing pain in her gaze. "My mother . . . She was a Cipher. And according to Cyril, a powerful one. I do not remember much of her abilities. I do not remember much of her at all, except for the pressure she instilled on me. She never had room for errors when it came to me—no patience. It was not that she did not love me. I am sure that was where it came from, but she did not love me like she loved James."

She wiped a tear, and Dalton continued to listen. "I do not tell you this to make you feel even worse for me. My father died of illness. My mother was burned alive in our village. My own brother was taken from me by men who wanted the First to fall . . ."

"You do not have to explain anything to me, Char. I know who you are."

"She told me to run, but I did not. A small part of me wonders if all this misfortune I have brought on the people I care for . . . this whole castle . . . Was it because I did not listen? Because I stayed with my brother?"

The tether that had held Dalton back the past three months snapped. He threw his arms around her as she sobbed into the crevice of his shoulder, embracing her.

The draw was explosive. It hammered through him, pulsating and rejuvenating. He knew she felt it too, for her wracked sobs became silent. She pulled back after a moment, her tears neglecting to fall. With a long finger, he swept her raven curls from her face.

"I see you," he whispered to her, a mere inch from her mouth. It was the same line he had said to her when they had been attacked in Brinn, when she had truly lost everything.

She closed her eyes, breathing deeply through her nose before exhaling. Her eyes opened on the release, the violet pure and unafraid now.

Had the draw given her strength? What was the limit of their power when combined? Dalton was not sure if he wanted to know.

Taking everything he had in him, he pushed the draw's power down. He stood without warning, knowing he was not himself. He was never awkward, but in this moment, he knew it was precisely how he looked. He was fumbling, afraid, and terrified he would ruin all they had built together if he stayed a moment longer, wrapped in her arms.

"Dalton," she pleaded.

Of course, she recognized what he was doing. He was throwing up a wall, one that would keep her from getting hurt. He could not be who he wanted to be around her due to his duty. He could not admit it to himself.

What he wanted was forbidden. He had been foolish to

entertain the joy she gave him in the first weeks at the castle. He was a King, and Kings did not get the luxury of loving whoever they wanted.

"I will tell Cyril when I see him later that you were grateful for the bed in a safe place," he whispered, not making eye contact with her.

"Dalton," she started.

He opened and shut the door, disgusted with how he longed to hear the rest of what she had to say.

FORTY-TWO

propose we throw a ball," Elena Leclair said in front of the privy council.

Randolph nearly choked on the wine he was sipping.

Elena had organized for them all to be served hors d'oeuvres. She had been charitable enough to invite lesser members of the First Kingdom's society to the meeting this evening. The original council was present, as were three Thinkers. Cyril, Arao, and even Eben were seated at the table with the rest of the members. A few select knights had been chosen as well—Randolph, Lawton, and Greyson.

"Are you sure that is wise, your Majesty?" Lord Peach uttered nervously from the other side of the table.

Dalton raised a white eyebrow, and Lord Peach fumbled his wine directly into his lap.

Randolph had noticed the changes in the King's physicality, but he had yet to address it with him directly. He was not sure what to make of this budding relationship between him and Dalton. He could not call it friendship, but their usual strife seemed to have died since Dalton gave him the final push to write the letter to Reine. For being so Gods-damned goofy and irrationally bratty sometimes, the King knew a thing or two about coping.

He had meant to find Charmaine and see if she noticed as well, since the three of them had formed an unlikely bond of trust. Randolph was not sure what to make of any of it. Between Dalton nearly icing his head off in the dungeon, writing a letter to his sister, and seeing these physical differences in the King, Randolph wanted to speak with Charmaine to make sure Dalton was okay.

But Randolph also wanted to make sure she was okay.

"And what would the reasoning behind such an event be?" Cyril asked, leaning his chin on his fisted hand. Randolph could tell he was hiding a smirk from Dalton's less than subtle reaction to Lord Peach's attitude.

Elena's big brown eyes lit up with the challenge. She took a pointed sip of her wine, then swirled the glass before setting it down gently. She flipped her auburn hair over one shoulder, flexing the lean muscles of her arms as she straightened her posture.

Randolph was not sure he had ever noticed before that Elena was physically strong. It was no secret that she was absolutely stunning. All the men at Dalton's coronation nearly fell over at the sight of the First Kingdom's Queen. Warmth exuded from her in everything she did, even if she was berating and demonstrating how strong the depths of her power went. Randolph had spoken to her on more than one occasion, typically about duty. He never had a real conversation with her, now that he thought about it, but he had heard her and Dalton arguing before.

Randolph was glad he had never been on the receiving end of her wrath. Even the King of Snow had to bow to the mercy of the Princess of the Fourth.

She smiled sweetly, her full flips seductive and charming all at once. Randolph blinked and tried to clear his throat nonchalantly, but it only adorned a devious smile from Lawton.

"The First Kingdom has demonstrated a swift transition of power, while being respectful to the tragedies which have befallen our country and citizens." Her brown eyes flickered to the weaker council members at the table. "I propose a ball, so we can continue to relish in our recent good fortune, as well as show the world we are not victims of these harsh times."

Randolph looked to Dalton. He was smiling.

"And who will be invited to this ball, Princess Elena?" Arao asked softly. The Thinker was about eighty years old, recently arrived from the Tenth Kingdom as another voice of council for Dalton and Elena. Cyril had wanted absolutely nothing to do with Arao, and neither had Dalton. He had been sequestered to the library since his arrival, quite content with enjoying the expansive history on the Queen of Fury and King Cian.

Elena smirked, as if she had planned for someone to ask that question all along.

Dear Gods, the King and Queen of the First Kingdom really are a match made in hell.

"Everyone," she said firmly, as if it were the most obvious answer in the world. "What if we open our doors to the people of the Kingdom? Thallgan, Hammen, and any of the other villages we control here at the castle. I think it would be beautiful to mix society with the people we rule over." She leaned back in her chair, her arms crossed over her chest nonchalantly.

The men of the room gaped at her, Randolph included. All but Dalton were speechless, the idea so genius, yet so unexpected.

A deep voice spoke from the corner of the room, soft yet laced with judgment. "Elena Leclair, I cannot see how something like this would stand with your privy council," Eben whispered.

Elena opened her mouth for a rebuttal, her arms still crossed over her chest, but she was silenced when Eben spoke again.

"I, on the other hand, believe there could be not a better time in history to open the doors of this castle to the world."

Dalton looked like he was about to fall off his chair, his eyes wild and disbelieving. It was no secret that Dalton festered hatred for the Thinker who had so openly served and supported his father, but this support was uncanny. Forgiveness and gratitude nearly spilled from the King's soul onto the table.

Eben nodded in his direction.

"Then it is settled." Cyril stood. He smirked at Dalton, then turned his head to do the same to Elena.

Cyril was a master of politics, having served in courts for many decades. Since he stood, he had motioned for the King to finalize the decision before the council had a chance to protest. Randolph was not sure how Cyril casually juggled the side of ruling that nobody wanted, but he did it flawlessly.

The King of Snow stood quickly, on the receiving end of Cyril's telepathic movements. "It is settled then. We shall throw a party at the end of the week."

FORTY-THREE

Reine Evin Eniar's rage was positively lethal.

Her amber hair was raggedly plastered to the back of her neck, sweat dripping down the sides of her face as she fought the chains that bound her hands. Her leathers were itching, the chaffing raw against the insides of her thighs. She had busted her lip sometime during her last blackout—they had been happening more frequently as of late. Her anger was feral, unhinged. When it overtook her, no one in her path was safe.

When she figured out who was currently laying hands on her, they would die. She would make it hurt too. Charring their skin to a pulp was the only thing that allowed her to hold onto gravity, that dream of unleashing her violence upon them a sweet serenity.

"Do not even try to throw your flames in my face, girl," the disgusting voice purred. "These chains are older than I am. Your power will not do a blasted thing against it."

She snarled, baring her teeth like an animal. "You had better hope you never take them off then."

She swore the hands behind her flinched, and she smiled maliciously as they pushed her onward.

She had been locked in a cell in the dungeon for the past

three months. She was not chained, but the bars were magic. Impenetrable. She had tried on more than one occasion to unleash herself upon them—and whoever was on the other side of them—but it was to no avail. Originally, they had let her keep her quarters when they had overtaken her home. King Finn had wanted to grant her such a luxury. She saw through it, though. It was just another method of control. She was a prisoner in his keep, so she demanded that she be treated as such.

She would not live a lie.

A lot of things went wrong in Reine's life, but she would be damned if she went down without a fight every single time. Her brother, her father, her mother—her entire family had been taken from her. But she would rather be gone from this world than let some King who was supposed to be dead take over the one thing she had left—her Kingdom.

So, she held her head high—took in all that loneliness and made it raging fire—and welcomed the game she was about to play.

***

Carinthya sat in the throne room of the Seventh Kingdom and accepted defeat for the first time. She welcomed the game, the challenge that came with getting King Finn back for stealing her life away, but pieces of her were equally devastated and confused. She was destroyed in more ways than she could count.

And her only salivation was Bairre, since it was clear that Callum had abandoned her in some capacity.

She never cared about her safety, not once in the six years since she had been taken from her home. She did not know what she truly cared about. She had no purpose. No desires.

She used to think it was freedom, being reunited with

her family and her Kingdom. But the more she contemplated it, the more she knew that was a lie. Dalton had grown up, become the King of Snow, and she was left with nothing. Pride blossomed within her when she thought about her brother and all he was destined to accomplish. Tears almost fell from her eyes when she pondered too heavily on his marriage to Elena Leclair—the freedom to love and choose and simply be was almost too much for Carinthya. She had never experienced that before.

Her head snapped up at the rattling of chains, where her eyes met a girl she had not seen in months.

"You," she said softly, her mouth nearly hanging open. Her mind had not strayed to what happened to her, for Carinthya detached herself from all newcomers.

"Me," the girl said, attempting to gesture with her hands shackled behind her.

Meriki walked behind her. His small, plump frame was as hideous as always. He wore all black robes, nearly tripping over them. Phillis was already in the room with Carinthya, for he had brought her in. She had nearly screamed when he appeared in her chambers, his gangly, long frame as disconcerting as always.

The two of them were positively foul, but despite her best efforts, Carinthya had wondered where Bairre was.

She pushed him out of her mind and focused on the situation at hand. If they were gathering, it had to mean they were about to meet with Finn, which would not be good at all.

"Hello, Carinthya." Meriki snickered as he brought the brown-haired girl to sit on the floor. If the girl was bothered by it, she did not show it. She merely stared straight ahead, not bothering to give him the time of day.

Carinthya rolled her eyes. Meriki was an enigma. And not a good one.

"She is not in a chatty mood today. Seems her little boy toy got a taste of his own medicine the other day," Phillis said, clearly goading Carinthya.

She refused to take the bait, but she could not hide that his words burned some part of her. After he had left her in her chambers, alone and nearly begging her to listen to Bairre, he did not return. She had not even heard his familiar voice around the halls.

It was amazing to her that even after six years of being imprisoned by these individuals, their absences affected her. She did not know what Callum's goal was. He had only served King Finn and had never given her a second look. But something had changed in him, and maybe something had changed in her. He had taken a chance to protect her, to safeguard that piece of herself that had secretly hoped for an escape. She would not—and could not—forget such a thing.

Meriki moved to reply when the doors of the throne room flew open again, and Bairre and King Finn strode in. Phillis and Meriki bowed at the King's entrance. Carinthya and the girl could not be bothered to even blink.

King Finn wore a white silk tunic and black leather pants. His fiery red hair was tied behind his head in a slick ponytail. A blue sapphire crown was perfectly positioned atop his head, glistening in the starlight of the Seventh Kingdom's throne room.

It was an insult.

He was the ultimate insult.

Bairre, on the other hand, looked like a living nightmare. He wore the same black leather pants and a silk, dark green tunic. His skin was glistening amongst the red and black ambiance of the throne room, his own complexion absorbing the mystical aura of the palace. A black silk cape draped over his shoulders and tied at the base of his neck. He did not glance at Carinthya, but he might as well have. Her entire body was electric with the memory of their last interaction.

Princess, he had called her.

Mocking. Selfish. Uncaring.

Nonetheless, Callum had made a deal with him. That had to count for something.

"Ah, Princess Reine, how nice of you to join us this evening," King Finn said with a glance in her direction. She did not flinch. He stepped closer to her, lifting her chin to look at his face with a long, gray-tinted finger. "Look at me, child."

She did no such thing.

As the King continued to command Reine to no avail, Bairre looked directly at Carinthya, flashing her two fingers at his hip.

Two? What in the name of Cian does that mean?

She nearly shouted at him to demand an answer, but as soon as she looked at his face again, he had returned to ignoring her.

Insolent man.

She stood frozen, gazing upon the King becoming more and more flustered by Reine's disposition. Carinthya could practically feel the heat radiating off of her. Her amber eyes were blazing with flames, impatient and utterly disgraceful. Carinthya swore that Bairre was smiling.

"You will regret not following orders, Princess Reine," King Finn said, drawing out the words.

"I doubt it," she hissed back at him.

He turned fast as lighting, striking the side of her face with a devastating blow. Reine fell over, her chains not allowing her to catch herself. Carinthya was not sure she was breathing. She had never seen Finn strike someone before, despite knowing for years that he was evil. He had never been the one to lift a hand before her until now. Reine seized on the floor as she breathed through the pain.

Finn loomed over her like a banished God. "I wanted to tell you separately, but clearly, you will not listen." He spun around to face his three Thinkers and Carinthya. "I have something very special planned for this evening, and I cannot wait until it is underway. And it is all thanks to you, my beautiful Carinthya."

She froze. "Me?" she asked softly. "What could I have done to help you?"

"Oh, my dear, you do not know. That is the best part. It will happen tomorrow, but there will be chaos, so I wanted to tell you all now."

"Chaos?" Bairre asked, all emotion gone from his voice.

"The girl with the violet eyes . . . from your vision, Carinthya"—he motioned for her to recognize that was what she had seen—"she will be staying with us for a while."

The memory of the vision from the Saphirrus orb hit Carinthya like a wave.

"Am I to assume you did not invite her?" Carinthya asked, afraid of the horror she had unleashed by her admittance.

"I have been looking for her for some time, but she has always . . . eluded me." King Finn's voice was laced with hatred and desperation. "There is something I need her to do for me, but she has been under protection for quite some time." He stepped so close to Carinthya that she could see his individual dark eyelashes. His eyes flashed with menacing pain and iron will. "We can thank your brother's darling wife for the invitation."

"What invitation?" she asked, afraid of the answer, but unable to hide her thirst for knowledge. "If you hurt my brother . . ." She could not believe she had mentioned such a thing. Pain washed over her instantly. She had spent years avoiding thinking and speaking of her brother, afraid of putting the thought into Finn's mind. And now she had started a threat. She shut her mouth instantly, fearful of what she had unleashed upon him.

King Finn made a *tsk tsk* noise with his tongue and mouth. "Do not make demands of me, especially since we have spent so many years together."

She nearly vomited, but she could not take her eyes off of him as he continued.

"Your brother will be untouched . . . for now." He turned his body toward Reine, who continued to lay on the ground, unmoved since she had tipped over. "You, on the other hand, I might have to teach a lesson."

Slowly, he lifted a blue envelope from his leather trousers. It had been tucked inside his waistband, hidden by his white silk tunic. He opened it carefully, not touching the fine paper. "Dear Reine," he read properly. "I have no words for the man I have become, and the choices I made are ones that I have looked back on in the last three years in nothing but shame. You do not need to reply to this correspondence. Frankly, I think it would be harder on us both if you did. I have wanted to write this letter since the moment I ran from all the damage I caused you and our family. I do not take it back. Our father was a cruel King and a crueler man. I hated him then, and I hate him even still. He tortured us, tried to mold us into monsters. But I get a sick sense of satisfaction that we are both alive, and he cannot touch us again."

Carinthya had no clue who the letter was from, but clearly, Reine did. Sobs wracked her body, as did violent screams. She thrashed on the floor, her arms moving wildly as she tried to unbind herself. The sight was horrifying. Carinthya could do nothing but stand idly by while the girl suffered.

She knew what it was like to lose someone important to you. A tear fell from the corner of her eye in solace.

"I will kill him," King Finn whispered so softly that Carinthya almost missed it over the howls of Reine.

"You cannot! You cannot do this! Damn you! You have no right to take his peace away from him!"

Finn leaned down, and his daughter Ciara's shadows began to creep around the room. They slithered toward Reine, grabbing her by the shoulders and sitting her up straight again. The shadows whisked around Carinthya's feet slowly, as if deciding what to do next of their own accord. Carinthya had always been under the impression that Finn controlled them wholeheartedly, but in this moment, she was not sure. They looked free. They felt free.

"You will stay with Carinthya. She can teach you manners and what it is like to stay in line." He turned to face both of them, a wicked smile on his lips. "Won't you, my sweet?"

She nodded slowly, making eye contact with the sobbing Reine, and then everything went black.

FORTY-FOUR

n the days following Elena's declaration of the ball, Cyril managed to avoid Randolph at every turn. There had been a letter delivered to the palace from the Thinkers of the Tenth, and Cyril had been deeply disturbed by the news it held. The instructions said specifically that he was not to unveil the news until the day before the ball, and that it was only pertinent to Kings and Queens of the Kingdom to receive said news.

Well, it was addressed to the honor of the rulers of New Sarridolon, but Cyril was not ready to embrace that old culture yet and make it anew. The age of Cian and Ciara was over, and they had ended Sarridolon with the aide of the Gods because it had been a world that was no longer just and fair. It was almost like an Avalon now, a term that Cyril knew no person but the Thinkers would know. It was as fair and just as it could be, forged by the Kings and Queens of Old who spared it all to bring it forth.

Cyril pushed those old memories aside before they resurfaced, along with the rage and suffering that came with remembering the past. Rubbing a hand over his face, he took a deep inhale and made strides toward the King of the Seventh Kingdom.

***

"What do you mean it burned?"

"It is exactly like I told you, sir. The Seventh Kingdom went under siege three months ago. Maybe almost four now."

Randolph was lethal. "How am I just finding this out now?" Flames blossomed at the ends of his fingertips, destruction at the forefront of his bodily functions.

Cyril's face was nothing but earnest. "Randolph, I do not know. I only found out moments ago."

"Is that why she was not at the coronation?" His voice cracked, and he did not move to cover it up.

"Randolph, I do not know." Cyril's voice was softer this time, gentler.

It did nothing to calm the smoke pouring out of Randolph's nose.

There was alarm in Cyril's voice as he said, "Randolph, we need to recenter."

"I have lost everything," Randolph whispered. "Someone has taken everything from me."

"Not all is lost," Cyril whispered, his hand gently stroking the bottom of Randolph's tunic.

"How can you look at the world and say such a thing?"

"Because I have seen the world at its darkest moments. I have felt the world quake under my feet at the power displayed."

"And what?"

"And we will survive this because we did the last time."

A single, hot tear rolled down Randolph's cheek.

"What is going on in here? It is louder than a tavern!" Dalton strode into the room like the pompous ass he could be.

Whether it was intentional or not, Randolph did not care to stick around and find out. He whipped around so the king could not see any tears that had fallen down his face. All that Randolph had done thus far was bad enough: burning Charmaine, betraying his sister, losing his kingdom, living this life that he had cultivated when he was not doing anyone any favors.

It was too much for Randolph. He feared that this would be the culmination of all that he had endured.

Sensing that something was wrong, Dalton paused. It was rare that the King of Snow was rendered speechless, but it was not abnormal to see him change his demeanor in order to fit the needs of others. Despite all that Randolph despised about Dalton, there was much to love as well. But this was begrudging, and he would never admit it to him. Not as long as he would live.

"It seems as though the Gods have had their way with me," Randolph settled on, taking the Dalton approach to things. He spun around, his face clear of any sign that he had shed a tear. "The Seventh Kingdom has burned, and I have no idea whether my sister has survived as acting monarch."

Dalton paled, if it was possible for him to turn whiter. "How do we know this?"

Cyril answered for Randolph. "Intelligence from the Thinkers themselves and scouts from the outside kingdoms. It seems as though, almost four months ago, the mercenaries attacked the Seventh at full capacity. They had been living there ever since—"

"Living?" Dalton half-shouted.

"I must go," Randolph said bluntly, deciding then and there what must be done. "I cannot leave my sister to those rats—"

"Do not get hasty, Eniar. We do not know what they are doing—"

"THAT IS MY SISTER!" Randolph shouted, his voice

the harshest he had ever spoken. "You do not know what it is like—"

Dalton cut him off, an icicle somehow procured from his bare hands now pressed at his jugular. "You know I would do anything for my sister." His voice was lethal.

Randolph settled, his shoulders relaxing almost instantly with the disdain he felt for himself. "I am sorry, your Majesty—"

"Cut it with the 'your Majesty' shit. We will go after them, Eniar. We will." Dalton paced back and forth, his white eyebrows furrowed in a plethora of emotions that changed so fast that Randolph could not keep up with the emotional range. He was not sure he had the capacity to feel that many things that quickly.

"We will?" he said after a moment, barely hiding the surprise in his voice.

"The Seventh Kingdom has done the First many favors in the past. We will go to their aide."

Randolph opened his mouth to speak, but found himself incapable as Dalton shattered the icicle he was still holding with his hands.

"But we will not go this night. Tonight, we show our power. Tonight, we show them not to mess with the King of the First Kingdom and his friends."

FORTY-FIVE

even days had passed in a blur for Elena. This party—this project of hers she had come to call it— was all-consuming. She never did anything less than at full-throttle, and this ball was the distraction she needed from the permanent pain of the last three months.

James Grimes's death was a phantom wound at her side. It was constant, a feverish reminder that life was cruel and unyielding to the whims of destiny. Greyson had been a welcome distraction for Elena, as well as an unexpected friend. But he alone could not heal the slashes grief had put on her heart.

She sent riders first thing the morning after the initial council meeting to all the villages within reasonable walking and riding distance to the First Kingdom's castle. She cultivated thousands of formal invitations, white paper adorned with blue cursive that she had personally spent hours on. She wanted the people of the First Kingdom to feel that her invite was personal . . . because it was.

Despite feeling like she was shackled to the whims of her mother and the expectations of being a Princess, Elena did enjoy ruling. She was good at it. She relished in making others feel welcome or less than. The power of controlling the minds of weak men and uplifting the souls of women was a gift that Elena knew the Gods had given her. And being in the First Kingdom was significant for her.

She often wondered what her rule would look like if she announced to the world that she had not one gift, but two. Elena had no desire to undermine Dalton, especially in his own kingdom, but she knew it was rare for a ruler to be blessed with one gift.

Dalton's gifts, however, were legendary by association. King Cian had erupted in a moment of desperation. Everyone knew the epic love story between him and Ciara, and how his power aided her in saving the world. When Ciara's rule ended, Cian had taken the role of King and forged a world built on trust and love. His mere name was legendary, and very few people took it in vain.

For hundreds of years, the First Kingdom had earned its right to be just that—first. The rulers of the First Kingdom were known for their justice and salvation. The Fourth Kingdom had no such reputation. Although it did not bother her, it did mean something to sit on the throne of the First Kingdom and make decisions that could lead to real change on the continent. She would take the opportunity to serve one of the greatest kingdoms in the history of the world and do something great with her power.

This ball—this moment to touch the lives of the people of the First Kingdom—it was a brilliant plan of hers. She had thought about it for weeks and rather nervously approached Dalton about it prior to the council meeting. Of course, he had been nothing but supportive. He was excited to see her alive again, full of life, and wanting to make the world better. But he was also an idealist, who wanted to take full advantage of the opportunity to solidify the First Kingdom as forward thinking and accepting.

And this evening was the culmination of all that she had done. It may have been her last act as Queen Consort of the First Kingdom, assuming she could find a successful way to divorce her best friend. That was another reason she wanted to throw such an event. She wanted to find a weakness, something she could use to her advantage when they brought their divorce to the Thinkers.

Dalton, Cyril, and Elena had reviewed the contract numerous times, keying in for specific language that would allow them to break the binds that held them together. So far, they had not seen anything in the verbiage that suggested their wedding was anything other than for political gain. Elena had scoffed, irritation building within her to the point where she debated lifting the water from the jug on the table and pounding it against the wall with her power.

Since Dalton was more reasonable these days, he suggested she do something worth her while. She had breathed deeply then and left the room to plan the ball. It was good to throw herself into things that gave her purpose, rather than succumb to the self-sabotaging behavior that normally guided her decision-making process.

Lost in thought, she barely noticed Randolph had strode into the council room where she finished her final preparations. She had finished signing the final cards, which thanked the people of the First Kingdom for traveling to the castle to enjoy a fine evening with their court. It was a personalized touch, one that many would deem unnecessary.

If Elena had learned one thing in the last three months, it was that reaching out a hand was never unnecessary.

"Queen Elena," Randolph's stoic voice projected from the other side of the room. "Do you need any help with anything? King Dalton sent me to—"

She cut him off by raising a hand, but not without

smiling in his direction first. "Randolph, you do not know me like you know Dalton, but you do not need to address me as such."

He stilled, irritation radiating from his stiff form. "I am only trying to do my job."

Elena smiled sadly, feeling sentimental this evening. "I have known who you are for a long time, Randolph Eniar."

She moved toward him slowly. Her stiletto black heels colliding with the dark marble floors was the only sound besides Randolph's breathing. Her black velvet gown glided on the floor behind her silently, approaching him like she would approach prey.

She knew she looked beautiful this evening. She had nearly ensured it with the commissioning of this obscenely flashy gown. The corset fit perfectly to her curves. The neckline was strapless and showed off the curvature of her chest. The top of the bodice was decorated with a river of diamonds which glistened with every turn. The base of the dress had a slit that ran up the side of her right leg, though it was not scandalous. She looked powerful and regal.

Like a Queen.

His breathing quickened as she tilted her head to the side. He wore typical knight chainmail overtop a white tunic and the usual leather pants. She was tempted to grab the crown on her own head and crown him, for he looked preposterous playing King's Guard when she knew what he was. "Take it from me, your life will be much easier when you stop hiding who you are."

His jaw softened at the sincerity of her voice, but he did not move. Clearly rattled, he replied, "I will take it under consideration, my Queen."

She rolled her eyes, understanding why Dalton found

him so incorrigible at times. "I do not need anything else. I will be out in a moment."

He dipped his head, his amber eyes never leaving hers. With one final glance in her direction, he spun and left. Elena, rattled by much and nothing at all once, found herself drenched in irritation. Randolph Eniar was nearly more irritating than Dalton made him out to be.

She shook her head and rolled her shoulders back. Flinging her auburn hair over to one side of her head, she straightened her posture and exited the council chambers to greet the guests of her ball.

***

Charmaine was taking longer than usual to get ready for the ball. Typically, in the past, she had arrived on time. She had been punctual, focused on the party and even excited about it.

Tonight, she was none of those things.

She could not deny that the concept of the ball was perfect. When Lawton had come to tell her of Elena's proposition and successful commissioning of the ball, she had nearly burst into tears.

What would she have given to be invited to such a thing? If James were here, he would be swarming with pride for Elena. She was giving people, people like Charmaine, a chance to experience life. To not be outcast, lesser than, and forgotten. She was giving them a moment.

And Charmaine did not know how to express her gratitude over such a thing.

Charmaine and Elena were not close. Not in any capacity. But tonight, Charmaine planned to seek her out and thank her. It seemed like such an insignificant gesture, undeserving of such a small demonstration of appreciation with little reward. Elena was a Princess, and now a Queen. Surely, a thank you would not move her to tears. However, words were all Charmaine had. And she intended to use them properly.

Athelred had left her chambers moments ago. *Thank Cian.* He had dropped off a floor-length, form-fitting, white velvet gown . It hugged Charmaine's thin frame beautifully, allowing her to finally feel confident, despite all the weight she had lost. It was not that she thought less of herself regarding her body changing—grief took many forms—but she no longer felt like herself. For the first time since James was gone, she felt beautiful.

She had refused the jewelry Athelred had brought forth, as she always did. He always tried to push it on her, namely necklaces and bracelets. Per usual, she declined it all, but he seemed rather irritated by her decision this evening. She shrugged it off, for it was probably stressful to be a servant at that castle during an event of this magnitude.

She looked in the mirror one last time, noting the low neckline of the white velvet gown. She did not wear a corset, as most non-titled women did, but relished in the opportunity to gaze upon herself once more. The gown draped beautifully over the curvature of her breast, strapless and fitted on the bodice in a ruched fashion. The skirt of the dress was straight, yet hugged every curve of her lower half. It was the perfect length as well, no doubt hand-crafted by a talented seamstress with her precise measurements.

Dalton.

Smiling to herself softly, she blinked, admiring the green powder she had opted for this evening on her eyelids. It reminded her of the first ball she had come to and the gown she had worn. A sharp pain slashed through her heart at the reminder of her kind brother, who had sold his sword in order to get her a gown worthy of court. Her gaze flickered to the gown now, all black roses and sheer fabric, which hung in the corner of her chambers.

She hoped one day she would have the courage to wear it again.

But the decoration on her eyes was a good start.

With a final breath in and out, she moved to exit her chambers. Swinging open the door with all her might, she nearly screamed as she walked into a wall of a man. Glancing up, she found dark blue eyes and blond eyebrows quirked in amusement.

"In a rush, it seems?" Lawton questioned, sarcasm dripping through every vowel. "You are never late."

"There is a first time for everything." Charmaine laughed. "I haven't seen your promiscuous self around much of late."

"Me? Promiscuous?"

She tipped her head back and laughed. He was genuinely offended. "Who is it this time? A member of the court catch your eye?"

He smiled softly, his blue eyes darkening and reigniting so quickly with emotion that Charmaine figured she imagined it. They were walking down the hallway, after all. *Maybe it was a trick of the light?*

"There is no one in this court that I am interested in— yet what I truly want is unattainable."

She raised an eyebrow in question, but he would not give.

"Ah ah ah, Miss Grimes. I do not share my potential conquests." He paused. "But I want human connection. I want interaction. I want destiny."

"But you kiss and tell?" she questioned, rather overwhelmed that Lawton was feeling such a way.

"Absolutely." He smirked as they headed toward the throne room.

The sight was one to behold. Men and women danced freely, dressed in whatever they found most opulent. Men wore traditional leathers of the villages and simple tunics, while women wore their finest dresses.

Before she could stop herself, tears fell from her eyes. Lawton reached over silently and wiped them with his delicate fingers.

The throne room was decorated as if a winter storm had blazed through it. The walls and floors remained their typical white, but the snow that fell from the ceiling was truly captivating. On the perimeter of the throne room's walls, circular tables shone with opulent candles, foods, and drinks. It was so simply decorated that it felt like it always did—home.

Charmaine realized with a gasp that Elena had purposefully kept the decorations to a minimum. She wanted the people of the First Kingdom to see the First for all that it was.

Beauty, divinity, and blessed by the Gods.

"Come," Lawton whispered, grabbing Charmaine's shaking hands. "It has been so long since we danced."

***

Dalton met more people that night than he had met in his entire life.

And he adored it.

The people of the First Kingdom were hard-working, beautiful, and unrelentingly kind. Within the first hour of the ball, he kissed seven babies, blessed three couples to get married, met two people who named their children Dalton, and three more who promised their first born would take his name as well. He was not sure what he had done in his life thus far to warrant such support from the people of his kingdom. For someone who relished in public-speaking and wit, Dalton found himself without either skill in the face of his people's unfathomable gestures.

He spun to find another group of villagers to speak to and thank them for their travels and support, when his eyes caught a swirl of raven black hair and a white silk gown. It took everything in him not to fall to his knees right then and there, and begin to pray to the Gods.

Charmaine was a marvel, and she had no idea.

The people of the First Kingdom had obviously taken notice of her. Those on the perimeter of the throne room stood and watched her turn with the infamous Lawton Thornwood. They danced in harmony, full of life and laughter. They were one unit, laughing and smiling, embodying friendship. No part of Dalton was jealous, rather, he was enamored.

The music picked up, the strings chaotic. Yet they kept pace, swirling hand-in-hand like they were the only two people in the room. Those around them clapped to the beat of the music, and Dalton found himself joining in. They were relentlessly having fun, and Dalton wished the song would never end.

In the last three months, he had never seen her so alive. Since he had known her, he had never seen her so at ease.

Before anyone could see the King of Snow shed a tear, he wiped it away.

The song slowed, as did the clapping. And so did the two of them. Before he realized what he was doing, his feet carried him toward them. The crowd parted, speechless that the King of Snow had moved onto the dance floor. Dalton could nearly hear Cyril across the room, cursing him for acting so publicly.

Slowing before them, he bowed his head in greeting. They did the same. Dalton noticed Charmaine's gaze was full of emotion, while Lawton's blue eyes danced with a playful mischief. He never heard much of the young Thornwood, though his father had been legendary among the ranks of his grandfather; King Arthur's regime. He acknowledged him with a dazzling smile, returning the same exuberant expression.

Returning his gaze to Charmaine, he opened his mouth to speak. To his dismay, she stepped forward. She leaned so close to him that he could smell her lavender scent, intoxicating and sweet.

Whispering so low that Dalton nearly asked her to repeat herself, she said, "Meet me in the rose garden."

Then she strode off without another word.

***

Randolph was going to kill Lawton and find a way to get away with it.

First, it had taken him minutes to find Lawton, only to see that he had been on the dance floor. A stabbing pang flooded his heart when he realized he had been entertaining Charmaine, who looked elated to be in the company of friends. But irritation continued to flood him because Lawton was *supposed* to be working.

The First Kingdom did not have a good history with balls as of late, and Randolph did not want this to be a trend.

He beckoned Lawton with a tattooed finger when he separated from Charmaine and Dalton. Mischievously, he slithered his way over to Randolph.

"Yes, my captain?" he asked dangerously.

"We have a job to do, Thornwood. Let's go."

"Where are we scouting?" Lawton asked as he nearly jogged to keep pace with Randolph.

"I have men up here keeping eye, men in the gardens, and people all over the perimeter of the castle."

"So, why can we not enjoy the party?"

Randolph rolled his eyes, but he kept walking forward. They turned left and headed down the long stretch of hallway that led away from the South Wing of the castle. "We will, after we check the dungeon. And every other room."

Lawton halted. "The dungeon? Are you mad? Nobody will be down there."

Randolph continued to thunder forward. This was not an argument. The safety of people was not up for debate. Not tonight.

"Randolph, are you listening to me? Nobody is down there on a good day, especially not during a ball."

"We have to check every inch of this castle!" he yelled, his inked hands fisted at his sides as he whirled around to face Lawton. "I will not have our castle sieged again. I do not have time for your insolence or your jokes. You are one of my men. I trust you to help me because I fucking asked you to. We. Have. To. Check. Everywhere."

Lawton's blue eyes darkened with an emotion that Randolph knew all too well, despite it being a foreign one on his face—fear.

Randolph breathed deeply, his breath nearly smoking with rage and paranoia. "I am sorry. I did not mean to—"

"Yes, you did." Lawton shoved past him to walk toward the entrance to the dungeon.

***

Elena wanted to strangle Greyson for looming behind her like her own personal bodyguard.

In fairness to him, yes, that was his role.

Except he was single-handedly undermining all that Elena had worked to build this evening. Dalton got to walk free—not that she would ever take that sentiment for granted—but she was the shackled one.

She shot another glare behind her, making direct eye contact with him. He shot back a rather dazzling smile in return, clearly relishing in playing his role to its finest. She made a mental note to be obscene later—maybe throw a pail of water over his head—so she could get the point across.

You do not get under the Queen's skin.

Elena rolled her head from side to side, cracking her neck slightly, before she straightened her posture and made headway for more groups of villagers. Her hands were going to fall off from shaking so many hands, touching so many people. Her full lips hurt from smiling constantly, but it was the best pain she had ever experienced. To be loved like this, cherished, was the best feeling in the world. No wonder monarchs never gave up their crowns. Power was addicting, for all its wrongs and stressors.

A young woman stepped forth into her path, her brown hair tied neatly atop her head in a bun. She wore a yellow gown made of cotton, the corset cinched beautifully to fit her hourglass figure. Her amber eyes shone with nervousness and awe as she bowed to Elena. "Your Majesty, I-I just wanted to thank y-you for throwing such a beautiful ball. I-it has been an honor to attend."

Elena studied the girl, unsure how she wanted to proceed. She had learned so much in the last hour about people. Not royals or members of court—she knew how to interact with them. With other royals, one had to assert dominance and show strength, while keeping your true power a secret. With members of court, a ruler had to be ruthless, an iron fist capable of hammering down anyone or anything. With the people of the First Kingdom, she had to give them what they did not know they needed. This girl was clearly bold, yet nervous. She was appreciative, yet fearful of not being accepted.

So, Elena did the one thing that she felt deep in her bones the girl needed. Grabbing the sides of her black velvet gown, Elena curtsied to the girl. Waves of shock rippled from those standing idly by, for the Queen of the First Kingdom had bowed to an insignificant girl.

Except to Elena, each of these people were significant. And now she had shown that.

With a quick word of apology, she strode off past the gaping girl to enjoy the rest of the party.

FORTY-SIX

andolph's temper was explosive on a good day, but he felt more on edge after Cyril's detrimental conversation. The Seventh Kingdom had burned, and it was run by the monster who had begun to take everything from the world.

He pushed those thoughts away as he made headway with Lawton, letting his thoughts drift to other places of his life that were also a disaster.

Cursing himself, he realized he had meant to stop by Charmaine's chambers and speak to her—that seemed to be the cure for his misery as of late. But there was so much that plagued him, therefore the only solution he found was to ignore everything going on with himself altogether and throw himself into his work. He refused to acknowledge the possibility that his sister could be dead, and his kingdom had been ruined.

Hence he had forced Lawton to scour the dungeon with him during one of the most politically genius and important balls he had ever seen.

They walked down the winding and dark staircase, swords clenched in their hands. Sweat beaded at the nape of Randolph's neck as he moved to enter the full view of the dungeon before Lawton.

He was the leader of the King's Guard, even if he forgot sometimes.

"We scour the area quickly, check all twenty of the cells for weapons or anything else suspicious, then we can return to the party."

"I will take the left," Lawton said, duty-bound.

"And I will take the right," Randolph replied with a nod.

They separated, but Randolph swore he heard Lawton mutter, *"That would be the opposite of left, genius prick."*

Smoke blew out of his nose in one hot breath, and he silently embraced his power because of how it was able to calm him. It was no wonder that he struggled with his temper in the past, isolating himself and never wanting to stick out. But now? Now he could feel the power coursing through his veins and knew he was awake. It was a beautiful thing—despite the terror happening on this uncertain continent—to be at one with a small part of himself.

He pressed on, ignoring Lawton's other muttering he could not make out, as he always did. Making his way through the cells of the dungeon, he checked and then double checked. He refused to have any surprises befall this evening. There was pain, and there was suffering, then there was the guilt of simply being unprepared. He would not underestimate this invisible enemy again, no matter how silent and successfully elusive they had been.

Over the last day or so, he truly embraced the title at the forefront of his name. *King* Randolph Cian Eniar of the Seventh Kingdom. Yet, he refused to let go of the part of himself that had helped get him to this place. The knight was a piece of him that would remain forever.

"All clear on the left!" Lawton shouted as he finished his round, breaking Randolph's stream of consciousness.

Randolph grunted in acknowledgement. "I do not want to admit it, but it seems as though it is clear."

"Nothing to worry about, darling," Lawton drawled with his usual smirk. "I think for once we are prepared."

Slightly irritated by Lawton's lack of seriousness and being called *darling*, Randolph knew he was right. "I guess so. Let us return to the festivities and keep watch up—"

He paused. His amber eyes shot directly to the corner of the first cell he had inspected, the glistening of a small, sharp object illuminated in the candlelight.

"What in the Ten Kingdoms is that?" Randolph asked, while his heart pounded mercilessly in his throat.

He strode toward the object, inhaling a sharp breath as he picked it up. It was sharp, half of a circle on the bottom, with the top perfectly crafted into a point.

"Shit!" he yelled, nearly dropping the object. He recognized it immediately. "Shit, shit, shit, shit, *shit*."

"What?" Lawton asked, with the humor that had been in his voice gone. "What is it, Rand?"

Randolph unsheathed his sword, the sound all that could be heard in the dungeon. Holding the object between a tattooed thumb and pointer finger, he motioned for Lawton to take it from him.

Lawton held it, careful not to cut himself on the point.

Randolph lifted his sword, standing the hilt on the ground with precision as he lifted the piece to the tip of his own weapon. It was a knight's sword, forged from the fires of the Gods and specially gifted to those who held a position of power in the kingdom. It was the only way into the castle, besides a true royal opening it with their bare hands. The tip had to be inserted into the gates—that was the only way in unless Dalton was with someone.

It could not be true.

Randolph willed it not to be true.

And yet, a curse escaped his mouth, as he realized the small object and his own sword were a complete match.

FORTY-SEVEN

fter shaking one hundred more hands and smiling at one hundred more beautiful faces, Elena decided to retire to her chambers to freshen up before she rejoined the festivities. The next item on the evening's agenda was for her and Dalton to speak to the people of the Kingdom and thank them for traveling such lengths once again. Then she would extend the offer of rooms to them at the castle, because they had hundreds that were left unused.

She parted ways with her final guest, an old man who told her he had celebrated his eightieth birthday, and she made her way back to her chambers.

And of course, Greyson followed her.

When they were out of earshot from the crowd and out of sight from possible onlookers, she harnessed all her strength and slammed him against the wall. Using her forearm like she had been taught, she pinned him. Except he did not fight back, nor did he squirm. She cackled manically, for she had managed to stun her bodyguard.

"Did I ever tell you I did not need protecting?"

He groaned, but managed to get out, "Once or twice, your Majesty."

"You would do well to remember it, Greyson. Why are

you following me like a dog still? After I told you to back off—"

"It is an *order*."

She huffed a laugh, running her hands through the ends of her curls. "I am sick of people doing what their orders tell them. What about what is humane, Greyson? What about what is good for people? I can handle myself." She released him, realizing she had not let go of her positioning.

He leaned over, grabbing at his throat for a moment as he gained composure. His gaze met hers as he rose, sad and intrigued all at once. "I do not make the rules, your Majesty."

"Then who—"

Cyril appeared out of the hallway, making his way back to the party. "You make some rules, Elena, but you know it is your husband who gives the orders."

She flashed him a smile worthy of King Finn's treachery. "And where would my darling husband be this evening? I have not seen him in a while."

Cyril quirked an eyebrow, the whereabouts of Dalton clearly beyond him. "He is King now. I do not get paid to keep tabs on his whereabouts anymore."

"Do you get paid at all?" Elena retorted.

Cyril's expression softened. "Let him have his evening, Elena, and let him protect you. The King's Vow—"

She paused, her mouth falling open at the terminology. "The King's what?"

Cyril's eyes darkened and widened, shock radiating off of him at what he had admitted in three little words. "He did not tell you?" he managed to gasp out.

"Tell me what?" she seethed.

Elena whipped her head to Greyson, who sheepishly looked down at his leather boots. "What do you know?" she half-yelled at him.

Betrayal swept through her, as did haunting fear. She felt like her back was against a corner—secrets and lies plagued the world around her—and she had nowhere to run except directly at them. To confront them.

She whirled on Greyson a second time because she knew he could take it. Except this time, he was ready for her strike. He lifted his arms seamlessly, blocking each of her hits as if he read her mind. Within a few seconds, she was panting, breathless, and he had her hands behind her back.

"What do you know?" she half-sobbed, horror blazing through her as she realized something was terribly wrong. "What did he promise them?"

That one word. *Them.* The Kings of Old who had dignified the King's Vow to keep monarchs blessed with the role to hold true to their word. She had heard of its power, but it had never been a problem for a monarch before. *So, why was Cyril speaking as if she were somehow involved?*

"Safety!" Cyril yelled, exasperated. "He commanded that his reign was supported by the safety of those he loves, and in case you didn't know, Elena, that means you." He was breathless.

For the first time in her life, Elena was scared of Cyril. He loved Dalton more than anything, but he lived on a short fuse. Elena knew he had lost Ciara and Cian in his lifetime, and she could not comprehend the pressure he felt to be in such care of a monarch again. Her heart ached for him, for his pain.

And that amount of pain would never cease to stop terrifying her. She could not go through it again. She would not go through it again.

Rage festered within her—at Dalton for keeping this from her, at Greyson for following orders without filling her in, and at Cyril for not stopping Dalton from making such an assertion to the Gods. She was even mad at Randolph. He had looked her in the eye earlier and did not say a word. No doubt he was checking on her for the sake of the king.

And here she thought they had finally made strides toward familiarity.

Did Charmaine know? Elena did not speak to her often. Interactions with Charmaine were essentially off-limits due to her precarious draw to Dalton and avoidance of court gossip. But she was also the sister of James, the last living reminder he had been real.

So, no—she could not talk to Charmaine. Maybe not ever.

She had already lost so much. She would go to the ends of the continent, destroy the whole world in waves—she would do anything—if it meant her friend could live free of the shackles of his destiny.

"I am going to kill him," she hissed, struggling to break free of Greyson's grip.

"Your Majesty, I do not think that is a good idea."

"I am going to destroy him for thinking he can protect everything he loves. I am going to tell him what an idiot he is, and make him revel in it. I am going to douse him in cold water and—"

She paused her sermon of rage as a figure came into her vision down the hallway. He looked so familiar, but she could not put her finger on why.

"Ah, Athelred!" Cyril chided.

Athelred was Dalton's prior servant and Charmaine's current one. Elena recognized him instantly upon hearing his name.

Cyril gestured for Greyson to drop her hands, and he did. Shaking them out slowly to avoid catching Athelred's gaze, Elena hid them behind her back.

"Shouldn't you be out on the dance floor, assisting the people of the First Kingdom?" Cyril grumbled.

Elena felt a pang of guilt for the boy. He could not be much younger than herself, but she had heard from Dalton how he was utterly useless. Anger continued to burn within her, a steady flame of hatred and sadness, as she realized Athelred had been responsible for one of Dalton's last beatings as well. He had been sent to catch him in Thallgan and return him to the castle—and he had obeyed.

It was not as if servants had much of a choice when given a direct order, but the flames of disgust still clawed at her. Even if it was an order, there was a difference between right and wrong. Social class and occupation had nothing to do with making the right choice; that alone was in your heart to decide.

"I have been . . . busy," Athelred whispered mischievously.

Elena heard Greyson unsheathe his word before she felt it against her torso. The metal was cold, reflecting her face as he held it softly, parallel to the bodice of her gown. He had moved them against the wall, her body perfectly intertwined with his in the protective stance. He did not cover her mouth, but he did whisper one word that terrified her more than anything else.

"There."

Looking in the reflection of his knight's sword, she followed his gaze down the hallway back to the throne room. At first, she saw nothing. Irritation continued to boil within her blood.

And then it ran ice cold.

Black hooded figures—large men from what she could tell—walked amongst the people of the First Kingdom in the throne room. They wore long swords at their sides, though they did not touch them. They moved so silently that the people of the First Kingdom did not notice, nor did they disrupt the ball.

"Mercenaries." The word expelled three months of anguish in one breath. It took everything within her not to slump against Greyson's rigid body. Instead, she raised her head and made direct eye contact with the slithering being that stood before them. "Let go of me," she commanded Greyson.

To her shock, he did.

She strutted forward, grabbing the front of Athelred's tunic. She had never touched a servant in such a disrespectful manner before, but his smirk gave it all away. He was behind this. Or at least he had a clue what was going on.

"You listen to me very carefully. You are going to tell me what they are doing here, or you will—"

"You are not the Queen of Fury. I am not scared of you," Athelred hissed.

Elena stepped closer, letting her power rumble through her hands for the first time since she came to the First Kingdom. She had not unleashed herself in so long, her training on halt since she arrived and James died. She had not practiced with her water magic, let alone thought about it.

She had learned over the years that a monarch's greatest tool was a weapon that was not used most frequently.

His eyes widened, that boyish fear returning.

She smirked, relishing in it. "You will wish that I am the Queen of Fury when I am done with you."

"They just want her!" he snapped, breaking already.

"Who?" Cyril asked, his face pale.

"The Violet Queen!"

***

Charmaine wondered what James would think of her if he

saw her now. *Would he laugh? Beg me to seek counsel? Encourage me to seek my hand in matrimony to Randolph again?*

A girlish laugh exploded from her. She had been so bold tonight she wondered if she had been slipped root of the lily again. Her lips tingled with the sensation of the words she had whispered to Dalton moments before striding away. He had looked dumbfounded that she had initiated such a meeting, but she did not care that she had taken him by surprise.

She missed him. Through and through. And she did not like how things had been left the other night.

Her heart threatened to burst in two when she saw him standing there, laughing and clapping like one of the common folk. He was a damn good man and a better King. She did not believe for one moment that she was worthy of his praise, friendship, or even affection. But she would not let him push her away. Not anymore. Not ever again.

They had been through too much together. Too many secrets between them. Too many unknowns. *How could he not understand their world was better together? That when there was no fear, there was less suffering?*

She had no agenda for inviting him to the garden tonight, other than to tell him that she understood. He had nothing to be sorry for, while she did. She forgave him, despite her words of irritation when he spoke to her last.

She needed to explain that to him, before the common people left the castle and their lives returned to normalcy.

Striding through the rose garden, she touched nearly every budding flower. Her senses were flooded as she wound deeper into the maze, before turning and heading the way she came. It was a brief venture, but a beautiful reminder of the growth of the world. The vines were growing back thickly, since the healers had started to repair them, more so in the past few days. It was beginning to look like it had before, and that hurt as much as it healed.

As she rounded the corner and the vines began to dissipate, she took a sharp breath, nearly running into him.

"Ten Kingdoms, Char!" He laughed, his face exploding into a grin. "I did not know you were trying to play hide-and-seek."

She put her hands on her knees, nearly doubled over in a laugh. "I did not expect you to be here!"

"Clearly not," he said with a chuckle.

Standing up straight, she dramatically tried to fix her hair, ensuing a laugh from Dalton. "Thank you for meeting me, your eminence."

"I hate that," he said with a crooked smile.

"Do you?"

"I hate all titles of authority when they come from your lips."

Her mouth parted in surprise, the implications of his words jarring, especially since they had been having fun. "So serious already."

"I find myself more serious by the day it seems," he said sadly. "Another perk of the crown, I suppose."

"If it is any consolation," she said, gesturing for him to take her hand. "I think you wear it well."

He smiled softly, his dark blue eyes heavy. He looked less tired tonight, more full of life, but the weight of it all was clearly crushing. "I am trying."

"You are doing wonderfully."

"When I go back up there"—his gaze lingered on her lips a second too long—"I am going to tell the people of the First Kingdom that they are free. Free as they are to do magic, learn magic, learn in general. I do not want to rule over a land that is in fear of anything."

Charmaine did not have to look in a mirror to know her eyes were shining with tears. "A formal declaration? Dalton, that is . . ."

He had demonstrated his power at the coronation, a soft recognition of the power that coursed through his veins. But she had felt so seen in that moment, a pride blooming within her that abilities were accepted. She had never been fearful of Dalton, but she knew others would hear of it, and they would no longer be afraid too.

"You do not have to say it."

"No," she whispered, "I do. I told you the last time we met that I was mad at you. I told you that I had not forgiven you. I walked out on you. You laid yourself bare to me and told me you cared . . ."

She took a deep shuddering breath. "And all I could think about was the implication that you would leave this world to keep the people you care about safe."

"Char—"

"And you cannot do that to me, Dalton. That is soul-crushing. I cannot handle it."

He touched the ring on her hand—his ring—from the night of the root of the lily. "I did not realize you still wore this," he whispered.

"I have never taken it off since you gave it to me. It was a—"

"Promise," he finished.

Reaching into his coat pocket, he plucked out the dagger that Charmaine had not thought of in some time. The familiar dizziness associated with the memory flooded back to her at once. She nearly fell over with the weight of the dream. *Had it been real?*

"I care about you," she said in an exhale. There was release in the weight of the words, an underlying meaning that she knew he would be able to extract. "I cannot accept this dagger."

He smiled sadly and backed away from her. "I am married, and you should have it. You earned it in battle—"

"You are the King of Snow, inheritor of King Cian's powers, first of his name, son of King Ronan, grandchild of King Cian!" Charmaine shouted, her fists at her side. "I am tired of hearing what you are, Dalton. You are a human being. You are a person!"

For once, he was speechless.

She continued, pacing back and forth so rapidly she swore there would be tracks in the ground if she stopped. "You kept an eye on *me* every day that my brother died in some capacity. You were there when I changed in Brinn, and you brought *me* back. You are all that I think about, even when I am determined to not think of you. Your stupid smirk and your addicting wit are all-consuming to *me*."

She did not dare to look at him. "Ten Kingdoms, I told you I care about you, and your first response is to remind me of your political alliance to your best friend! What is wrong with—"

Cold hands suddenly gripped her jawline, her voice silenced by the taste of blueberries and snow. Dalton's hands ran through her hair, hungry to express pent up desires that no words could accurately describe. His Kingly demeanor shone through, the strokes of his tongue demanding and unrelenting. Desire swept through her as her misplaced frustration slipped away inch by inch.

In an answer, she ran her hands through his wild white hair so quickly that she knocked the crown off his head.

And neither of them stopped to give it a second glance.

He turned her with his hands, walking her back against the rose bushes, so they would be out of sight from the ball just feet above them. She laughed against his mouth, wild and free and *alive* for the first time since they had both taken root of the lily by accident.

"You vex me," he grumbled against the side of her jaw. "You do not know the depths of your power, yet you utterly control me."

A soft breathy moan escaped her at his words.

"I care about you too," Dalton said, pulling back to look into her eyes. With his thumb, he rubbed the center of her lips gently, his eyes full of desire. "More than you could ever know."

She nodded in reply, speechless. "I did not mean to yell at you," she blurted.

He tipped his head back and laughed. "Yes, you did, darling. I deserved it."

"Just because you deserved it does not mean I should have done it," she said with a laugh.

Cian save me, who am I around him? My anxiety always flees when alone with him, instead losing all sense of control.

As if he could read her thoughts, he said, "I like who you are around me. You are unafraid, unabashed. You are stronger than you know. I have said it before, and I will say it again."

Gripping her shoulders slightly, he looked her directly in the eyes. He was so close that she could see her own reflection in his eyes, her hair wild and her lips swollen from his kiss.

"You are stronger than you know, Charmaine. You just need to believe it."

She wrapped her hands around him, embracing all that he was. "I know this is not the draw," she murmured into the crevice of his neck.

"I know," he said sadly.

She pulled away from him, rather shocked at his grave expression. "I do not hate you for being married, you know."

"I am trying to rectify it."

She paused. "Rectify it?"

He rubbed the back of his neck awkwardly as he leaned over to pick up his fallen crown, though he did not put it back on his head. He merely held it, as if contemplating if he should carry it the rest of the evening. "I have not had much time to tell you—"

"Spit it out."

"Encouraging as always, Miss Grimes," he said with a laugh. "Elena and I have been looking for a loophole, a way out of our marriage. There must be some language that signifies this was more than a planned transaction to unite two kingdoms."

"And Elena?" Charmaine could not help asking. "Is Elena okay with this?"

"Elena . . . Elena will be fine." He quirked up an eyebrow. "She will never lose me. You should get to know her better. I feel as though you two have more in common than you are aware."

Charmaine huffed a laugh, but was reluctant to answer. She admired Elena and would forever appreciate the relationship she had with her brother. But Elena was a reminder of James, and Charmaine did not know if she was ready to confront that side of him. The side of him that did not confess he had started to fall for the Princess of the Fourth Kingdom, the side of him that at the end of his life, Charmaine felt like she did not know at all.

Instead of saying that, though, she muttered, "I will try."

"Good," he said softly, moving pieces of her hair out of her face. "She does not bite, you know. Not hard, anyway."

"Do you think you will marry again?"

Damn me and my mouth.

She was not sure why she had asked, nor was it

appropriate. Dalton was the King of Snow, and she knew where she stood in society. She was his guest, and although they had this thing between them, she never asked for anything more. She never expected more.

He froze, his eyes widening at her boldness.

"I am sorry, that was overstepping. I did not mean—"

"Yes," he said so quietly she was not sure he said anything at first. "Yes, I would marry again." Picking up the dagger which had fallen to the ground, he kneeled before her.

"Please, take this," he pleaded. "Every woman needs a dagger around here."

"But Gwendolyn—"

"Was a victim of my father's tirade."

The dagger is the key.

"What if it holds a power we do not understand?" Her voice was anything but neutral.

"Then we can work to understand it together."

Taking his hand with her left, and picking up the dagger with her right, she knew she held all the power in the world.

***

Randolph blazed up the stairs of the dungeon. Smoke poured out of his nose, the heat of his skin feverish to the touch.

The sword was a fucking match.

And they were all fucked.

Lawton trailed behind him with the same precision and speed. Randolph prayed nothing had transpired at the ball. That unfamiliar feeling blitzed through him, one he experienced often, but never called it by its name.

Fear.

At the top of the stairs, Lawton bent over to catch his breath. Randolph trudged on, despite the screaming of his legs and the sharp breaths he was taking.

Please be all right, please be all right, please be all right.

Flying down the hallway, Randolph approached the familiar sounds of dancing and laughter. He halted at the entrance to the throne room, expecting to see turmoil and death abound. Instead, he saw everything as it remained.

"Thank Cian," he muttered to himself as he bent over to catch his own breath.

Lawton pulled up beside him. "What in the name of the Ten Kingdoms was that?"

A voice murmured from the hallway he came from, a voice Randolph was not sure he recognized. "Psst!" the voice said, trying to get his and Lawton's attention.

Randolph turned and strode down the hallway toward the voice.

Before he had a chance to take another step, a feminine hand grabbed him by the collar of his tunic and dragged him into the room.

"Elena?" Shock washed over him as he gawked at the Queen that had shirked him from the hallway like he was a misbehaving child.

"It is him." Her eyes blazed with multiple emotions he had no time to read and place. "It is him. He is the reason James is dead. He is the reason Dalton is King."

Elena lifted a long, delicate finger to point at Athelred.

FORTY-EIGHT

ho is the girl with the violet eyes?" Princess Reine asked Carinthya.

She sounded bored, but Carinthya knew better. She had heard that same tone from her brother a million times before. He practically invented the pretending-not-to-care body language. If someone asked a question, they cared to know the answer.

"I do not know. I only saw her in a vision."

"And so you gave her up?"

"I told Finn what he wanted to know. I did not just *give up* information." Carinthya seethed.

A week had passed since she had taken up her new role of entertaining, befriending, and living with Princess Reine.

Reine was different than anyone else Carinthya had met before. She blazed with a fiery rage, did not converse unless it suited her as such, and seemed less like a princess than she did a warrior. Carinthya had tried asking her about the rather large rose tattoo on her arm, to which Reine told her she would rather die than tell her anything about herself like they were friends.

And that was the last time Carinthya asked her a question.

But Reine had asked Carinthya many since then, and she had answered them all.

"It sounds like you gave up information to me," Reine said, disinterest lacing every word.

Carinthya's blood began to boil, the irritation unbearable. "I told him something in exchange for someone else's safety. You will find that King Finn loves weakness."

"I am afraid I do not have any weaknesses."

Carinthya barked a laugh. "Sure. So, I did not see Finn read you a letter that you lost your Gods-damned mind over?"

Reine sat up, smoke nearly pouring out of her nostrils. "You do not know what you saw, Carinthya."

Carinthya sat back in her chair, rolling her eyes before she whispered, "I did it for my brother."

"You what?" Reine said unnaturally softly, her brown eyes suddenly less hostile.

"I confirmed the girl with the violet eyes was in the First Kingdom, so that I did not give up my brother's secret."

The white hair. The power. It was all too much for Carinthya.

She turned to Reine, her blue eyes pleading for understanding and acknowledgement. "What would you do for your brother?"

It was the first question she had asked her since Reine told her she would rather die than be her friend. She braced her shoulders, as if in preparation for an explosion from the girl.

To Carinthya's surprise, Reine turned her body to face her. Her round face was all steel, her amber eyes unforgiving and loving all at once. Not for the first time, Carinthya wondered what went on inside her head and what was in her heart.

Then the girl spoke, her voice like a crackling fire in the

silence. "I would burn the world down for my brother."

"What was he like?"

Reine paused, pondering the question. She seemed to loosen up as she thought more on it, as if the memory she was thinking of relaxed every muscle in her body involuntarily. "A pain in my ass."

Carinthya laughed quietly, almost afraid of expressing joy so close in proximity to Finn and his minions. "Mine as well."

"He was fiercely protective," she went on. "He would have ended the world for me to live a day better than yesterday—he practically did."

"My brother was unbridled chaos. He was always getting into trouble, and I had to bail him out with my father and mother on more than one occasion."

"He sounds a lot like me," Reine said, her brown eyes swimming with memories.

"I miss him dearly."

Reine stood and took a few strides toward Carinthya. With not as much as a word, she placed her hand on her shoulder and smiled softly. Carinthya found herself taken aback.

Without warning, Carinthya was shoved up against the dark castle walls of the Seventh Kingdom's chambers. A pale hand clenched her throat. She kicked out her legs to no avail as she fought to breathe. Vision blurred, she could not make out the figure before her, though she would not forget the voice anywhere.

"What in the name of the Gods have you done, Carinthya?" Bairre growled as he dropped her.

Gasping and grabbing what she was sure was a bruised throat, she nearly vomited on her own clothes as she fought to recover from the shock. Reine stood against the walls of the castle, paralyzed and petrified at Bairre as though he were some terrifying creature.

Leaning up against the bedframe, Carinthya gagged once more before raising out, "What the hell do you mean? What did I do?"

Bairre looked truly alarmed, his eyes betraying an emotion Carinthya had never seen on him, and one she had not seen in so long that she was not sure she remembered what it was called.

"What did you tell him?" His voice was strangled. Pained.

It was when he said it and ran a hand through his silver hair that Carinthya realized his hands were covered in bruises, as if they had been smashed over and over.

"What happened to your hands?" she whispered, taking a stride toward the monster who had tried to choke her.

"What did you tell him?" Bairre retorted.

"Who did this to you?" she half-sobbed, looking into his eyes and trying to understand him.

Nearly gasping again, she remembered the name of the emotion she had seen on his face, the emotion that was still there as he looked upon her.

Devastation.

"What did you tell him about the girl?" Bairre's voice cracked as he said it, all sense of the strength he normally exuded evaporating by the second.

"The girl with the violet eyes?"

"Is she with him?" He grabbed her shoulders with his black and blue hands, shaking them softly.

Carinthya nodded, afraid of what she would see flash in his gaze if she said yes.

"Damn you, Carinthya."

"I was protecting him—"

But it was too late, Bairre was gone, and Carinthya was once again shattered.

FORTY-NINE

harmaine and Dalton strode from the rose garden into the throne room. Ordinarily, Randolph would not give them a second glance, but tonight something was more than amiss.

Scowling at them from afar, he noted every detail of her and his King. Charmaine's cheeks were flushed pink, her raven hair perfectly flowing down her back. Her hands were at her sides, yes, but her left hand also hung mere centimeters from Dalton's. Dalton was a bit more precarious to Randolph, his blue eyes alight with fire. Randolph could see it from here. His lips were peeled back into their usual smirk, mischievous and wondrous all in one.

It took Randolph all of forty-five seconds to guess that they had kissed in the rose garden.

Fuck.

He did not have time for this. No time to be overjoyed. No time to be a confidant for his friend.

Well, either of his friends.

Athelred had confessed that the mercenaries would not harm a hair on anyone's head, as long as they got the Violet Queen. However, he did not know who the Violet Queen was, nor why they wanted her. Cyril had been ghostly pale the entire time, words escaping him permanently at the mention of this queen that nobody knew.

Rolling his shoulders back, Randolph stepped forward into the crowd to get them to safety discreetly. The people of the First Kingdom parted around him, as most people did when they saw him. There had been whispers for years about the Head of the King's Legion, dangerous and covered in ink. Clearly, those rumors spread, for people from all walks of life jumped to get out of his way.

He opened his mouth to call out to Dalton, not wanting to draw attention to Charmaine beside him and draw whispers, when a man dressed in black leathers and a black tunic stepped in front of him. He drew his sword and backed up toward them, lifting his weapon in warning.

"We came for the queen," he spat, his chipped teeth showing as he donned a disgusting smile.

Randolph put a tattooed hand on the hilt of the sword, his eyes widening at the fear that plagued Charmaine's face. Dalton had gone still, the temperature in the room rapidly declining, along with his tether to self-control.

"I would not touch that sword, pretty boy," another mercenary said, emerging from the crowd.

"Touch the sword, and you will all die."

"Randolph," Charmaine whispered in a plea. "Do not touch it."

Dalton grabbed her hand, clenching it tightly as he stood frozen in place. He had no weapons on him, for he had not wanted to intimidate the people of the First with ornamental displays of power.

Yet, everyone knew it was the power that coursed through his veins that made him so dangerous. A sword was only an addition to the strength he carried.

Change, Randolph mouthed to her. *Change and run.*

Her violet eyes danced from each of the mercenaries that continued to back up toward them, then back to Randolph. He knew there were hundreds of eyes behind him watching the situation at hand, yet he knew just as well that she was only looking at him.

Then she shattered his world with two words he never wanted to hear from her. *I cannot*, she mouthed.

"No!" he half-yelled, taking a step forward.

"Ah, ah, ah! Do not move," a mercenary from behind them said loudly, his voice dancing off of the throne room walls.

"THEY JUST WANT THE QUEEN!" Athelred yelled manically from behind him. "THEY WILL NOT HURT ANYONE ELSE!"

They all turned toward Charmaine, Dalton beside her no more than an ornament in comparison, and lunged. Dalton spun, shoving Charmaine behind him as ice erupted from his hands in one fell swoop. It jetted from the ground, sticking up like pikes on a battlefield.

The crowd gasped as he did it again, but it was to no avail. The mercenaries were skilled, clearly prepared for such an attack. It was as if they anticipated each move he made.

Randolph cursed as they ducked again, avoiding the power that shot through Dalton's hands. Charmaine cowered behind him, her eyes wide with terror. Randolph's heart twisted in two at the sight of her, reliving every experience she had with the mercenaries up until this point. He knew how it felt to be so frozen with fear that you were powerless.

But the mercenaries did not attack them; they merely avoided Dalton's reach. *Why were they not attacking them? Who is the Violet Queen?*

"Do not harm the King!" the mercenary closest to Randolph yelled over the sound of crackling ice. "He is not ours."

Dalton turned to face that mercenary and dove at him. Snow sprung from the marble floors, twisting in a personal-sized snowstorm. The snow was alive, wrapping itself around the mercenary's legs to keep him from taking another step. Dalton moved to do the same to the next mercenary, when he heard a bloodcurdling scream.

Charmaine was in the arms of the mercenary who had come up from behind him, strung over his shoulder like a limp doll. She was sobbing, completely frozen by everything that had happened to her. Her cries sang the song of her life affected by these mysterious men: her mother's murder, Brinn's destruction, and the death of her brother. It was a cry to every moment of pain in her life, all of them together at once.

"Move out!" the mercenary contained by Dalton's snow cried out.

The men obeyed, turning and running at once. The man with Charmaine strung over his shoulder ran out first, and as he turned, Randolph gasped. Charmaine's face was streaked with tears, her mouth open as if gasping for air. She was trying to scream, to make any noise.

Randolph could guess the name attempting to leave her lips.

Dalton lunged for Charmaine, only to be met with a sword by another mercenary who cut him off. He stopped, and with the blood roaring in Randolph's ears, he could not be sure, but he swore the King screamed.

"If you follow us, everyone in this room will die. The First Kingdom will cease to exist." The mercenary held a sword inches from Dalton's face, calculating and ready to strike should the king make another move to bring them down. "And as much as we would love to bring about that downfall, it is not our choice to make."

"Damn me to the dungeons for this," Randolph

muttered as he ran forward and grabbed the king by the shoulders, bringing him to the floor.

The king would never forgive him for this. Randolph could never forgive himself for it. But it was the right thing to do; the entire kingdom would be wiped out if these men were not bluffing.

And since he had known of the threat, Randolph had never known them to bluff.

"Let me go!" Dalton struggled underneath him, so fragile and broken in this moment that his own power was not within his grasp. "Let me go, Eniar! She needs me! They cannot have her! They cannot take her away from me—"

Dalton opened his mouth and screamed. Bloodcurdling, venomous, and gut-wrenching agony filled the halls of the most ethereal court in Sarridolon. Throwing his head back, he sobbed once more in finality. It was as if Dalton had opened the windows of the world to a winter wonderland. A blast of snow so cold and torrential swarmed around the ballroom, full of raw power with a heaviness that knocked everyone backward.

Randolph slid against his own will, abandoning the King, but not before a cold tear ran down his cheek. Opening his mouth to call out for Dalton, Randolph found that the words would not come.

It seemed that the power of snow had disarmed his greatest tool: his voice. And Randolph guessed the silence of the ballroom meant he was not alone in this. Freezing like the rest of the citizens of the First Kingdom, Randolph squinted to see the mirage of the King laying peacefully on the ground. If Randolph did not know any better, he would have guessed he was sleeping.

He watched the snow begin to fall slower. The storm calmed before his very eyes.

Despite every bone in his body telling him to run to his King, he let him sit up on his own. He needed to show the world who he truly was, and what Charmaine meant to him.

Inch by inch, Dalton rose before his Kingdom, hauntingly in the image of the Kings of Old who came before him. Lifting a thin hand, he ran it through the black waves which now fell in front of his dark blue eyes, and spoke so much like a seasoned monarch that Randolph was unsure if it was Dalton who stood before them.

"They will pray for me to shatter their souls once I turn them to ice."

FIFTY

TWO WEEKS LATER

airre had been selected for this task.

It was a paradox for him.

King Finn had been adamant Bairre alone should travel to the edge of the citadel to receive the package he had been waiting for. Bairre had not been privy to King Finn's maddening plans the last few months, since they had arrived at the Seventh Kingdom.

This life was a paradox for him.

On one hand, Bairre wanted the information, so he could manipulate situations as he saw fit. He could use his gifted shadows to his advantage, warping the emotions of others, and even removing painful memories from those who Finn had wrongfully harmed. He had done so for Carinthya once, when they had dragged her from her home. It hit him like a wall of bricks every time he thought about what he had taken from her, that rage that had settled like dust to time. He had not known her then, but there had been no way that Carinthya could have survived that type of pain, especially since it was clear Finn had no intent of returning her to the First Kingdom.

Not if Bairre had anything to do with it. His last act on this continent would be getting the Princess home. He was not sure when he had decided it to be his last act, but he was committed wholeheartedly. He was not as easily corrupted as the servant Callum was, despite the boy's good intentions. Finn had scared and beaten the shit out of him. Bairre could have erased his pain, made him forget, and forced him to be vengeful, but it risked putting Bairre in a compromising situation if he was discovered.

Bairre would not lose this opportunity, or any opportunity, when it arrived.

On the other hand, Bairre relished in the freedom of choice. With Finn preoccupied with this package he was waiting for and the impending girl that was to arrive to the castle, he had been busy.

When Finn was busy, he tended to become nonsensical.

And a nonsensical Finn made mistakes.

Mistakes were the key to Bairre's success.

Bairre reached the border of the Seventh and Third Kingdoms later than he anticipated, a carriage already waiting in his stead. He nearly snorted at the sight of the two mercenaries who stood before him. *Disgusting oafs.*

"Good evening, gentlemen. What is it that is so lovely and secret that King Finn sent me here all by myself?"

"Wouldn't you like to know?" one of the men said, his teeth particularly rotted.

In response, Bairre let his shadows flow out and caress the mercenary on the mouth. The man flinched. Bairre commanded his shadow to slam itself over his lips, silencing him. The man struggled against the dark power, trying to wriggle it off of him with muddled screams.

Bairre simply looked at his fingernails, ready for this

whole exchange to be over with, so he could get back to whatever it was that was not *this.*

"Are we quite done?" Bairre asked the other mercenary, who was much larger but no less stupid.

The man nodded and stepped aside as Bairre retracted his shadow and stepped toward the carriage. He swung the great black door open to be met with an unusual sight to behold. He had not known what King Finn was plotting, but he would have never guessed the gift he was about to receive was none other than a girl.

He peered into the carriage, her unusual violet eyes wild and her breath rapid at the unexpected sight of him. He raised a dark eyebrow at her in question, though she did not open her mouth to acknowledge the question. *What are you doing here, girl? What does he want with you?*

Bairre popped into the carriage, but not before banishing his shadows from his sight. He did not want to frighten the girl more than she already was.

More than she would be when they arrived at the Seventh Kingdom's castle.

"I am going to ask you one question."

He softly closed the door behind him so the mercenaries would not pry. They were oafs, monsters in their own right, despite their stupidity, but they were also dogs. They would tell Finn anything Bairre did, and he could not risk arousing suspicion.

Especially with Carinthya on the line.

"What is your name?" he drawled, leaning back casually not to alarm her.

"Charmaine Grimes," she whispered, her voice cracking as though she had not spoken in days. "My name is Charmaine Grimes."

DALTON AND THE CREATURE

andolph had a hard time picturing Dalton as he was now—the true heir to the Gods who gave the same power to Cian one hundred years ago.

The mop of black hair that flowed in front of his hauntingly dark blue gaze did nothing to help the matter.

They strode down beneath the dungeon with nothing but their tunics and leathers. The staircase had taken two weeks to find. They had been relentless in their searches through Queen Ciara's diary in order to find the passageway, and to confirm for certain the name of the voice Dalton had spoken of.

At first, Randolph had been furious that the King had kept such information from him. Though, despite his best efforts, part of him was grateful that Dalton had kept such chaos at bay until he was ready to find an answer.

The name had been laid bare in front of them, lazily written in her diary, as if it was a mere afterthought. It laid on the page so clearly that at first Randolph thought the Queen had signed her own diary, marking it with her stamp of approval, as if it were a legal document. Dalton had been impervious to such results. He spoke as if he knew the Queen, which disturbed Randolph greatly.

Randolph had always thought himself to be the greatest secret-keeper in the kingdom, though he realized more and more that perhaps it was Dalton that laid every night with his own troubles. Pushing the thought away, Randolph's hand went instinctively to his belt, to find that he had left his sword upstairs.

Dalton snickered, finding humor in the darkest depths of the world. "How many times have you done that since we began our descent?"

"A few," Randolph said quietly.

"Right, and I am not the King of Snow," he seethed with sarcasm.

The stairs became narrower as they walked, as did the temperature of the walls. Randolph had a few guesses as to what was down there, though Dalton had kept his own information under lock and key.

All he told Randolph was that this was the key to everything, and Ciara had left it for him to figure out.

"Randolph," he suddenly whispered, his blue eyes hungry for knowledge and darkened with anticipation. "You cannot tell a soul what is down here when we leave. I fear it is our only weapon against the forces that conspire against us."

They had not told Cyril where they were, not that it would do much good to him in his current state. The less people that knew about what they were up to, the better. Enemies were everywhere, unaccounted for and unrecognizable.

Randolph nodded, though he knew he would come to regret it.

"I also need you to walk in front of me," he spoke again

as they reached the final step. "If my theory proves right, you are the one to do this."

"Do what?" he asked, his mouth dry and his back soaked with sweat. "It is so bloody hot down here."

Dalton only smirked in response, gesturing as if to say *after you.*

Begrudgingly, Randolph stepped forward and into the chambers before them. His eyes took a moment to adjust to the darkness before the walls lined with candles lit unexpectedly. Before he had a moment to turn around and ask Dalton what in the name of King Cian was going on, a wall of fire blazed in front of them. He threw up a hand, the flames contained in a burning fury as they angrily pushed against his power.

The roaring of the flames pushed relentlessly. Randolph dug his boots into the cobblestones, fighting to keep upright. He had never seen such fire, felt such heat against his bones. Despite his greatest fears, he had never felt more whole. The fire danced against his power, twisting and turning as though it were a complement to his soul. Any hesitation he had before now made sense. His life flashed before him and played out within the flames.

He saw his sister, young and wearing the crown he had been born for. He saw his mother and father, not bogged down by the roles society made them play, but happy. He saw Dalton, seated at the right hand of King Cian as kindred spirits. He saw Charmaine, embracing her brother on the battlefield as if he had never drawn his final breath. He saw Elena holding his hand, embracing their friendship. He saw Lawton embracing Titan, the love so fierce in his eyes that Randolph could do nothing but silently sob at the joy that stood before him.

The fire was hope and glory. It was home.

Dalton's voice sounded behind him, as joyous as it was mad. All Randolph could hear was one name amongst the raging of the flames, one so old he imagined he was dreaming. It was the name that had been sung in the halls of his father, one of darkness and power, but one long forgotten to the stories of men. It was the name Dalton had refused to utter, in the fear that it would find them before he had a plan. Before he had a request.

Randolph knew why he had been included in Dalton's plans. It was not out of brotherly affection, but out of necessity.

Randolph was the King of Flames, and only he could command what Queen Ciara could not.

But these flames that fought against his tattooed hands were anything but legend, for they were as alive as the world was above them.

"Kai," Dalton yelled from behind. "I come to bargain for what the Queen of Fury could not."

The flames ceased instantly, leaving Randolph gasping for air at the sudden disconnect from his power's equalizer. He leaned over, his hands going to his knees to steady himself.

They both coughed against the smoke, so thick that nothing could be seen more than a foot before them. Seconds passed in silence, and Randolph feared that whatever had caused the flames was gone forever.

Randolph moved to open his mouth, to admit to Dalton that the power surge had shown him such joys when he heard chains rattle with movement. He instinctively moved to guard his king, though Dalton stepped in front of him and bowed. Without another glance upward, Randolph moved beside him and did the same.

The ground shook with raw power as whatever it was took another step toward them. Following Dalton's lead,

Randolph kept his eyes down on the floor in front of him.

It took all within him not to scream when three long claws scratched the floor within the length of his eyes, sparking the cobblestones impatiently. The white foot the claws were attached to was the largest Randolph had ever seen, the scales crusted in soot, but nonetheless blinding in the darkness. The creature breathed through its nose, then exhaled more smoke through its mouth.

Dalton's hands shook violently on his knee, though he did not dare to move beyond what he could not control. Randolph followed suit unintentionally.

"You may rise, Kings of Sarridolon."

Dalton and Randolph stood slowly, lifting their eyes at the same time to meet the dragon.

"Now, what is this of my dearest Queen of Fury?" Kai said, his amber eyes glistening with wisdom and humor.

"We wish to bargain for what she could not," Dalton repeated, his voice steady, despite the violent tremors that wracked his fingers.

The white dragon pondered this for a second before hissing, "And what shall I get out of this bargain? What could you possibly give me that my dearest Ciara Riagan could not?"

Dalton cleared his throat, his eyes flickering to the chains which bound the white dragon's neck and feet. "Your freedom in exchange for a favor."

Kai laughed, flames spurting from his nose sporadically. "And what would you have me do? Not even my dearest Riagan would bargain to set me free."

Bowing before the dragon once again, Dalton summoned the power of snow. Kai stepped back slowly, his chains barely rattling as they began to freeze. The dragon's eyes appeared stunned, speechless at the sight of the power which had not graced the world for one hundred years.

"It is quite simple, really," Dalton said, his dark hair a shadow of mystery and a tribute to his lineage. "I will merely have you burn down the world."

ACKNOWLEDGEMENTS

When I wrote the acknowledgements for TPOS, I was completely and utterly done. I didn't take my time, because how does one take their time when they just finish their first novel and their brain is a pile of mush? So I wrote about a sentence for everyone. I'm basically going to do that again. But it's good to acknowledge in the acknowledgements. You know?

First and foremost, thank you to my family for pushing TPOS on all of our extended family and neighbors. It is much appreciated. And for supporting me. Mom, I know you read about one book every decade, so I am honored that one of those books was my own.

To Will, thank you for always being so supportive and reading all the books I promise to you that are good. I would never lead you astray when it comes to a good book.

To Kieran and Feyre (my cats), thanks for sitting on my lap and being my emotional support while I wrote this. Your company is always welcome. Even though you're needy.

To Nicole Platania, thank you for alpha reading every scrap of a sentence I ever write. This book would have been thrown in the dumpster last summer if it was not without your encouragement.

To Chiara Gala, your soul is as beautiful as your writing. Thank you so much for meeting up with me in London and reminding me how important it is to write the book the way it was meant to be written.

To all of my other author friends—of which I am blessed to have many—thank you for your continued support of me and my characters. Namely Dalton and Randolph. I would be nobody without the following people supporting me: Nouha Jullienne, Imani Erriu, Christy R. Harrill, Carly H. Mannon, Isabel Strychacz, L.B. Benson, Katie Collupy, Jessica J. Ayala, Olivia Rose Darling, C.A. Farran, Max Francis, and Marissa Serrao. I love all of you, the stories you tell, and everything about you. Thank you for everything you do for me daily. To those who are not named, please know that I appreciate you and love you too.

To my "real-life" friends: Sabrina and Carly. Thanks for cheering me on in the flesh. I appreciate both of you.

To all of bookstagram, this series is truly a child born of your support. I never would have had the confidence to self-publish this story without it. I would like to thank Mic and Madi, specifically, for beta reading this story and giving me guidance when I saw no light.

And to you, readers of the TPOS series. Thank you for continuing the story of my many, many, many characters. They appreciate you. And I appreciate you.

See you in book three.

Live laugh love Dalton Saphirrus.

Stay warm,

L.B. Divine

ABOUT THE AUTHOR

L.B. Divine is a fantasy lover, cat mom, Outlander enthusiast, and has always dreamed about writing stories of the fantastical. When she's not writing, L.B. Divine can be found reading, petting her cats, running, and drinking an overpriced latte. L.B. Divine can be found on Instagram, Twitter, and TikTok at @lbdivineauthor.

www.ingramcontent.com/pod-product-compliance
Lightning Source LLC
Chambersburg PA
CBHW070605300726

48975CB00006B/1716